Homies, Lovers & Friends

A Brooklyn Love Story

5

D1566643

A NOVEL BY

JAHQUEL J.

A NOTE FROM THE AUTHOR:

This book took a while to complete. Truthfully, I was burned out and needed time to mentally prepare for this book. As I said, I wasn't going to do a part five, but I felt like I should update you guys on the couples. There won't be a spinoff because I think there's only so much I can say about Mello and Patsy's troubling marriage. In part five, I touched on Patsy getting the closure she needs to finally move on. This series was a bumpy ride and made me deal with some things that are near and dear to my heart. I always add a hundred percent into my books, so I pray you guys love this book. I do this for you all. When I'm down, I read your messages, inboxes, and comments. Y'all crazy as hell too, but I LOVE IT. I'm ending this book so I can give you guys some new works and finish some old ones. Please bear with me. I'm working as fast as I can. I got y'all!

So, this one is for you, Jah Gang!

Peace and love!

I present to you, the finale!

DEDICATION

To Jaya... Everything that I do is done with you in mind. I'm always going to strive to give you a better life than I had. So, this one's for you, Doodie.

I love you.

Kelsie

*I*t wasn't meant for me to live happily ever after with Miracle. I was only meant to struggle and face obstacle after obstacle with her. Who was I to believe that there would be a happily ever after for us, especially after all we've been through since she was conceived. I wanted to tear up all the papers sitting on my desk as I looked at the paper requesting my presence in court. Here I was, at work, trying to make a decent living, to be turned around and served with court papers. Why couldn't she just leave us alone? Miracle missed her nana dearly, still, she was still young and didn't understand that Marina didn't mean her well. Hell, it took me a while to realize that she didn't give a shit about Miracle, and it was all about Marcus. No matter how many chances I'd given her, she still turned around and spit in my face when she chose her son over her granddaughter.

"Why are you out here looking like you lost your best friend?" Kim walked out of her office and took a seat on the edge of my desk.

The tears were threatening to fall down my cheeks, still, I held them at bay. Kim didn't seem like the type that could console you while you were down. She seemed like she would give you this motivational speech that would help you, yet, you still would want to cry in the bathroom once she got done. She messed with her freshly manicured nails as she looked to me to tell her what was wrong with me. The last thing I wanted was to bring my issues to work and consume her work space with my mountain of issues.

"Nothing." I sniffled and shoved the papers into my purse.

Kim's eyebrow raised and she sighed before speaking. "What's going on with you, Kelsie?"

"Kim, it's really nothing. Tired of bothering everyone with my issues. What do you need me to do?"

She scrunched her face up and sucked her teeth. "You're dating my son. For Christ's sake, you're the mother of my new granddaughter. Your issues are just as much mine as my son's. Now, what's going on?"

I leaned back in the chair and rolled my eyes. "Marina is taking me to court for grandparents' rights."

"Is that even a thing? Because I might need to exercise my rights with Kenyetta's ass."

"Apparently so. Since Miracle has spent such a great amount of time with her, she can ask for visitation or even custody if they prove I'm an unfit mother."

"We know that's not the case, so she's not getting a damn thing. What do you think we have lawyers for? Milli pays that man's entire life, down to his children's private school."

"That's the thing. It's Milli's lawyer and I don't want to drag him into this bullshit, like I've dragged him into everything."

Kim stood up, straightened her skirt, and picked up her purse that set on the desk beside her. "This is your damn daughter we're talking about, Kelsie. If you don't want to accept the help to keep her in your home, then maybe I underestimated you as a mother," she told me as she slipped her purse onto her shoulder and headed to the door. "I have some business to handle for the rest of the day. Take messages," she added as she reached for the handle of the door.

Slamming my hand onto the desk, I leaned back further into the chair as tears slid down my cheeks. Kim was going to call Milli and put him on to what I had just told her. Soon as I stepped through the door of our apartment, he would be there waiting for an explanation. It was hard getting used to having to consult him when things happened with Miracle. Accepting help would have been easy, yet, I didn't want to have everything handled for me. I carried and had Miracle, so where did I fit into all of this? As a mother, I wanted to be the one to go and handle this without having to use Milli's resources.

The chiming of the alarm triggered when the front door was opened. I smiled when Patsy strolled in, pushing her stroller. We had made plans to have lunch together and with everything going on, it slipped my mind completely. She placed her Gucci diaper bag onto my desk. These days, Patsy was always looking like a damn snack. Between the smile she wore more often, the clothes she was always sporting, and her baby girl, who was healthy and so beautiful, there wasn't much she was frowning about. Everything was peachy in her life until it came to Mello, that's when the smile turned to a frown and she could give a damn about being all positive and happy go lucky.

"Where's Kim? She's the one who told me to bring Karmella with me." She looked straight to the back into Kim's open office door.

"She said she had something to handle. I don't mind princess joining us for lunch." I unstrapped Karmella and smothered her with kisses. "What are you feeding this child?"

"All this boob milk. These things hurt, and those white women walk around like it's the best thing ever."

"Pat, that's because it is. It's the healthiest thing for your baby. Miracle had too many health issues for me to even bring breastfeeding to the table. For the first few weeks of her life, I had to stare at her in an incubator with a feeding tube lodged in her nose. So, the last thing on my mind was breastfeeding."

"Yeah, I see all of that. This breast business isn't good for nobody. How am I supposed to let Walt brush up on these, when they hurt if I rub against the edge of her crib?"

"Maybe you should stop being so damn fresh." I giggled as I turned the lights down. The office manager wasn't there because Kim had cut her hours. Since she came back from having her baby, all she did was whine and complain about things that weren't her job duty. Kim had a talk with her and told her to come in part time so she could spend more time with her baby. Thankfully, that meant her ass came in on the days I was out in the field with Kim.

"Listen, this cookie hasn't been touched in a long while. Mello touched it long enough for me to have this little crumb snatcher." She caressed her baby's head then continued. "I just want to feel sexy and like a woman again. It's so hard to feel like a woman when you feel just like a mom," she vented.

"Preach to the choir. It took a while for me to feel normal after having Miracle. Mostly because, I didn't dress or do anything because my main concern was my daughter surviving. So yes, I feel you."

"These sweatpants are my lifeline right now," she continued and ran her hand through her hair. "Anyway, let's grab some food because I fed her in the car so we can eat peacefully."

I shutdown my computer and grabbed my things so we could go and catch up on our lives. Work had been my main focus lately, so I hadn't been catching up with my girls like I should have.

Walt

I leaned on the bar and ordered another drink as I held my cellphone to my ear. The voice on the other end of the line was my ex-wife, screaming about the amount of alimony I paid her. It was the afternoon, and instead of being in my office working over lunch with my assistant, I was in a damn bar, downing some bourbon in order to deal with this bullshit. Drinking wasn't my thing, yet, I needed something to help with the stress I had been dealing with lately. The bartender placed the glass of water in front of me, and I swallowed it down in one gulp. Caroline continued to complain that the alimony wasn't enough to afford the waterfront condo she wanted to live in with our children. My children deserved the world, and I would spend an endless amount of money to ensure that they lived in peace and benefited from the fruits of my labor.

"Who told you to move to a lakefront condominium? We have an entire home there. Why the sudden change, Carol?"

"Do you think I want to wake up in the bed I shared with my ex-husband every day? Walt, I'm nearly breaking, trying to manage everything without you here helping me. Instead, you decide to pick up and go back to New York after the divorce. What about the twins?"

"Knock the shit off, Carol. Nothing is breaking except the piggy bank you call your ex-husband. I refuse to pay for a condo, and apparently, the judge agrees with me. Our kids are homeschooled and we agreed to split time to avoid putting them through anymore court. Give up the condo and carry your ass back to the house." I ended the call and tossed my phone onto the bar counter.

Caroline was spoiled from the gate and I knew it. She grew up with a wealthy family and was given anything her heart desired. Brooklyn wasn't going to hand me anything except a gun or a basketball, which I sucked in. So, I applied to college and was accepted into Minnesota State College. It didn't matter that the winters there were more brutal than New York, or that I had never actually seen any black people there. My mind told me to pack my shit and get the hell out of Brooklyn. One night at a fraternity party, I happened to meet Caroline. She was there with a few friends trying to hit on some of the fraternity brothers. Right then and there, I should have turned the other way, yet, her blonde hair was like a magnet that made my crisp Jordans carry me across the room to her.

She played hard to get for a while. When I called, she wouldn't answer, or if I saw her on campus, she would act as if she was too busy to talk. Don't ask me what changed, but she came to my dorm and admitted that she had deep feelings for me; how she wanted to be with me, yet, was too scared to think what her parents would think of her dating a black man. I knew picking up and moving to a state like this that I would find some racism. All that mattered to me was getting a degree and getting the fuck on. With a beautiful angel sitting in my dorm crying her eyes out about how she had feelings for me, how could I just ignore it? Carol's parents didn't agree with our relationship. They figured it was just a college relationship and once we graduated, we would go our separate ways. Carol never finished college because school wasn't her thing. Still, she came to the school every chance she got. Lent me her BMW whenever I needed it to get around, and helped me pay for shit I needed.

She was my rider, and everyone knew she was my heart. Her heart was pure, and she never asked for anything in return. All she wanted was love, respect, and the pipe I delivered every night in my dorm room. Once I graduated, I was offered an internship at an agency. Being an unpaid intern that needed a place to live, food, and car wasn't the best thing in the world. Once again, Carol had her father purchase her a condo on the other side of town and moved me inside. It took three years before I landed the job and another two before I could bring my own clients on and close some deals. By then, Carol's parents had cut her off and kicked us out of her condo. Luckily for me, I had friends, and they allowed us to stay from couch to couch. Once I got my first check, I went and rented us a room for a week. Then, the next check I scouted for apartments and found one.

Carol stuck it out with a nigga and it meant a lot. When I started bringing in more money than I knew what to do with, I branched out on my own and upgraded our lifestyle. When she mentioned kids, she mentioned that she wanted to have two at one shot. Her figure meant the world to her, so she didn't want to ruin it with two pregnancies. In a tube, we conceived our twins and life took off after that. Long hours, constant bickering, and two children that cried daily, was enough to drive any two people crazy. When she cheated, I was hurt and cried a little. Then I thanked God because he had been pulling me to New York for the past few years. This was my out to head back to the concrete jungle, but did I want to take it? We built a life here, and now I was heading back to a life that I had abandoned in the end. Was it worth it?

It turned out to be more than worth it. I ran smack into my dreams as soon as I exited JFK airport. Things took off soon as the wheels of the plane hit the runway. Something was missing, besides my kids. A woman. Not just any woman—the woman. The one that was going to make me whole again. Show me that every woman wasn't self-absorbed and money hungry. Some days, I liked to believe that Carol stuck it out with me because she loved me. Then, I knew she didn't stick it out for love, but because she knew I would come through. Shorty saw the potential in me and decided to stick it out so she would no longer have to answer to her father's every wish, when it came to using his money.

Then, I had a sixteen-year-old daughter. I sent money every month to make sure she was well taken care of, and went to visit her on birthdays. Her mother didn't want me in her life at all, but I pushed myself into her life. On spring break, I fucked up and ended up sleeping with a woman. Well, when she showed up to my crib with a huge stomach, I knew I was in trouble. It didn't make sense to hide it because this woman wasn't the type to be hidden. Once I found out, I told Carol and she cried. At the end of the day, she still stuck it out with me until she wanted to be a fucking whore. Patsy didn't know anything about my oldest daughter, and I had been trying to figure out a way to tell her without her thinking I was keeping something from her.

"Man, your phone been ringing. You doing more than bourbon?" The bartender slid the phone across to me.

Sliding my finger across the screen, I placed the phone to my ear. "Hey, Walt, you want to do dinner tonight? Mello is taking our daughter, so I figured we could have some alone time." Patsy's angelic voice came through the other line.

"Whose phone are you calling me from?"

"Kelsie's. My phone died and I needed to know the answer before I told Mello he could take her."

"Why did you need to ask? Anytime I get to spend with you is a blessing to me. I'll come pick you up."

"You're so sweet. See you later tonight," she told me and ended the call.

Patsy was the type of woman that every nigga dreamed about, yet, only one got to live that dream. In Mello's case, he was able to live that dream for years before it came crashing down on him and their marriage. Luckily for me, I was able to get a glimpse of the dream girl that Patsy was. She was going through a divorce, and I knew we could never get as deep as I wanted. Shit, I still was dealing with a lot, and a nigga was divorced already. It was especially hard when Mello felt the need to pop over to her crib whenever he felt like it. A few times, I wanted to step to him and tell him that the shit wasn't cool and I didn't appreciate it. Patsy promised she would speak to him about it, and she did. You think that nigga listened? Nah. It was like he had a tracker whenever I stepped over the threshold of her townhouse.

After finishing another cup of water, I headed out the bar and back to my office. Between the deals I needed to secure for clients, I had no time to sit in a bar and be down about the bitch of an ex-wife that I was stuck with. In a few short weeks, the kids were going to come and stay with me for two full months. I couldn't wait to spend time with them and find out what was going on in their lives. It was lonely coming home to an empty house with no one there like you're used to. I was used to my son waiting for me to tell me about a game I had missed. Or my daughter telling me about her friends who were two faced. It didn't matter how much I despised Carol, nobody wanted to break up their family.

Milli

*T*he keys in the lock turned and then Kelsie's heels clacked on the wooden floors. I don't know how many times I told her ass to stop walking across these floors with those heels. Still, her ass decided to do it anyway and didn't bother to stop. In the end, I decided to pick my battles and not bring this up to her right now. My mama called me earlier and told me what happened with Kelsie and Marina. The shit pissed me off so bad that I had to keep myself from going to the office and dragging her out and tossing her into my whip. Her ass purposely stayed late at work, knowing there wasn't shit for her to do. When she came around the corner, she tossed her purse onto the chair and then plopped down on the love seat across from the armchair I was sitting in. With one hand, she snatched her heels off, sat up, and clasped her hands together as she stared into my eyes.

"Come on with the shit, Myshon. I'm not a fool and know your mother already been in your ear."

"Why the fuck didn't you call me?" I snarled.

"I'm handling it," was all she felt the need to tell me. She was handling it? How the fuck was she handling this without a lawyer? How the fuck was she going to handle this shit without the amount of money she needed?

"Kelsie, I would never put my hands on a woman, but you got me real close. Especially when it comes to Miracle."

"It wasn't Kim's place for her to tell you before I got the chance to."

"What the fuck you mean? Miracle is her granddaughter and you didn't think she would tell me? Yo, what the fuck is good with you?"

She stared at me for a bit longer before she broke down into tears. Removing myself from the armchair, I slid next to her on the couch and pulled her into my arms. "Every time something starts to look up, we go back twenty steps. Why is she trying to get my baby, Milli?" She continued to sob into my chest.

"Let me see the paper."

Pulling herself together, she walked to her bag and grabbed the paper. Before sitting down, she handed me the paper. My eyes scanned the document, and sure enough, Marina was trying to gain custody of Miracle.

"Why the fuck do they want to pull my leg?" It wasn't a question to anyone, but more of something I asked myself.

Marina was a nice lady. Full of bullshit, still a nice lady. She was so caught up in making her scumbag of a son a better father that she didn't realize what she was doing to Miracle. Marcus signed the papers, so she can't use him anymore. Her ass done went and googled anything and came up with this bullshit. I didn't get where I was today by letting old bitches pull my leg. She may have thought she was winning by pulling some stunt like this, yet, she didn't know the type of lawyer I had on retainer.

"Babe, you gotta stop hiding shit like this. What if you went to handle this alone and got Miracle taken away? We in this shit together, and you need to remember that."

"It's so hard, Milli. Soon as I saw the paper, my wheels were turning and I was trying to figure out how I was going to fix it."

"Stop trying to be Handy Mandy and start letting me know what the fuck is up. Go shower and get to bed, you look tired as fuck. I'll be back."

Her eyes followed my every move as I went to the hall and slid my boots onto my feet. It was winter, and the weather was brutal. Kelsie refused to move from the couch because she was silently asking me where I was going. She wanted answers and she wanted them now.

"Please," she begged.

"Kels, what the fuck I look like murking that nigga? The fact that you're begging for his life just pissed me off."

"Never pleading for his life." She slowly walked over to me. "I'm pleading for yours. Where would that leave you? I don't know the life you lived before me, and I don't want to know. I do want to know that the man I lay beside every night isn't keeping secrets from me."

"I'll see you when I get back," I told her and headed out the door. As I closed the door, she stared at me, still stuck in place.

In her mind, she just knew I was going to kill either Marcus or his mother. I just needed to get out the house and clear my mind. There was no destination in mind as I got behind the wheel of my whip and sped out of the parking garage. Tears fell down my cheeks as I thought about Miracle being taken away from my home. The shit was blurring my vision as I thought about having to have visitation with her. The shit fucked with me so bad that I wanted to reach behind the chair and grab my nine and head to his crib. Seeing the look on Kelsie's face was enough for me to stop. She didn't give a shit about Marcus, but she did care a lot about me. The last thing I wanted was to leave her out here raising Miracle alone again.

My wheels stopped in Hoboken, New Jersey. When I got out the car, I could see Manhattan right over the water. Walking into the building, I headed upstairs and knocked on the door. After waiting for a few minutes, I continued to bang on the door hard. The door was pulled open quickly.

"What the hell, Myshon? You know I have neighbors that complain about the sound of a pin drop," Larry complained as he welcomed me inside.

From his living room, you got the perfect view of the Freedom Tower. The condo was laced with expensive shit and looked as if it should be in one of those home and garden magazines. "I guess this is what you get when you're going through a divorce. Real low-key, Larry."

"Compared to what that bitch is staying in, this is low-key." He walked to the fridge and grabbed a bottle of chilled vodka and two glasses. "Who did you kill now, Myshon?" he nonchalantly asked as the sound of the liquor poured into the glasses.

"What? Why the fuck you asking me this?" The shit caught me off guard the way he asked and the context of the question.

He leaned on the counter and chuckled. "I know you, Thor, and Mello. Why else are you banging down my door at this time of the morning?"

"You know we left that life behind, Larry. My shorty's ex wants to take her to court over our daughter."

"The little girl you adopted?"

"Yeah."

"Well, he has no right. He signed those papers and they were submitted then filed. Case closed." He clapped his hands like he just solved the best mystery yet.

By the looks of those red bottoms, he had some blonde bombshell in his sheets he wanted to get back to. "It's not him, Einstein. It's his mother."

"Okay, now that's an issue. We can appear, hear what she's asking, and then come with our own terms. The ball is in your court since her son signed his rights over. Give her every other weekend or some foolishness like that."

"Nah, why the fuck should we bend to let her win?"

"Myshon, it's not about letting her win. It's about not dragging yourself and that child through court. Nothing is going to be solved tonight. Come by my office and I'll have my colleague look over the case. She specializes in court custody cases."

"What the fuck do I pay you for?"

"I'm a criminal lawyer. I can represent the case; yet, wouldn't you want someone who knows the ins and outs of shit like this?"

"Larry, your little friend better know what the fuck she talking about."

"Oh, I'm as good as it's going to get." A red-haired woman came out the bedroom with a silk robe tied around her thin waist.

"And you happened to be fucking her. Larry, you sure know how to pick them, huh?"

"It sounds like a classic family court case. Come to Larry's office tomorrow and we'll talk." She continued to talk business like she wasn't naked, or like I couldn't see her perky ass nipples clinging to the silk of the robe.

"I'll be there tomorrow." I turned and headed to the front door.

"You never miss a minute to handle business, huh? How the fuck did you know I wanted everyone to see who I'm banging?" Larry harshly whispered.

"Business came to me. You thought I was going to let it walk out the door without introducing myself?" She laughed, grabbed his vodka, and headed back to the bedroom.

Larry let me out the door and I turned and stared at him. "Go home, Larry. I've known you long enough to know that you like your woman on their back and pregnant. She's not going to lay down and she's not going to have kids for you."

"Good. I have enough with the three I have."

"I'll see you tomorrow," I told him and headed to the elevator.

I've met Larry's wife and she was a homemaker with a model face and body. Shopping, cooking, kids, and Larry were her life. It killed me how niggas were quick to give up their rocks for some side piece that wouldn't be there in a year. Mello was in the same boat with Pat. After doing all he did, he realized that she was who he needed to be with.

In his mind, he probably still thought that they would be together in the end. Patsy wanted nothing to do with his ass, and the sooner he realized, he might be better off. As I was about to hop in my whip, Thor's name flashed across my screen. Pressing the green icon, I placed the phone to my ear.

"What's good?"

"Shit. I called the crib and nobody answered, y'all good?"

Sighing, I leaned back onto the car. "I wish I could say we were."

"What happened now?"

After I explained to him all that went down, he said a quick prayer for us and then continued with what he was calling about. "I went to every damn store from my crib to damn Long Island… tell me you got some banana peppers in your crib."

"Michelle and those damn cravings again?"

"Hell yeah. She slapped the shit out of me to wake me up and get these shits. The supermarkets are closed and I'm tired as fuck."

"Damn. I know you can't wait for Titan to get here."

"Shit, if I could deliver his ass, he would be out right now. All she do is sleep, eat, and watch *Golden Girls*. That's my baby and she's carrying my baby, so I can't complain."

"That's why she got your ass looking for peppers at this time. Nah, I don't got that shit in my crib. Google twenty-four-hour spots."

"Ight, I'll holla at you tomorrow. Kiss Miracle and Kelsie for me, and tell her to keep her head up."

"You already know."

It took no time to navigate the highway and make it back home in one piece. I picked up Kelsie's heels that were tossed everywhere as I walked through our crib. She must have been upset and tossed them shits at the wall. In the morning, I planned to have someone come fix the dent she put into the wall. How could I fault her? Someone was trying to take the one person she had ever loved. Marina couldn't give Kelsie the space she needed to decide if she wanted her to take her daughter again, so her ass decided to hit her where it hurt. Well, I was gonna hit her old ass where it hurt, and if her son wanted some, he could get some too. Only difference, all I had was some hot lead for his ass.

After showering and making myself something to eat, I climbed into the bed beside Kelsie. For a minute, I just watched as she slept peacefully. Kelsie was everything to me, and I knew that the first time I slid between her legs. Instead of pushing her to the left after getting pussy, a nigga was trying to stick around and have breakfast. She was the one who pushed me to the door and was done with me after getting some bomb dick. It took a while for us to make it to this place. We lost a baby, argued, and said a lot of shit we didn't mean. If I had to go through all of that to get to this place, where do I sign up?

"Stop breathing on me," Kelsie groaned and turned onto her back. "Where did you go?" she questioned as she stared into my eyes.

"I stopped by my lawyer's house to make sure he can help us. He referred me to one of these bitches he fucking."

"So, the fate of my daughter is in the hands of some woman he's fucking?"

"Chill out, Kels. You acting like my lawyer some hood nigga. He knows a lot of people, and one of the women he knows and happens to be fucking is a lawyer that deals with shit like this."

"Myshon, all I know is that my daughter better stay under my roof."

"And that'll happen. Go back to sleep." I laid down and put my arm around her. "Tomorrow your ass gonna patch up that damn wall."

"I wish I would. Don't walk out the door and not explain shit to me ever again."

"Yeah, ight. Your ass gonna be down at the Salvation Army."

She giggled, turned toward me, and placed a kiss onto my lips, before laying on my chest. "You would never get rid of me, so please stop."

"Yeah, you right. Love you, bae."

"Love you too, Milli." We were both awake, yet, we continued to be quiet and let our thoughts consume us.

Patsy

*S*omething was different with Walt these days. He seemed as if he was distracted, and each time I saw him, he had this look that I couldn't explain. After we had dinner at his house the other night, I decided to give him a few days to himself. I had a list of issues of my own and I didn't need to add his issues to mine. If he had something he needed to sort out, he had all the time in the world to get it sorted. My main concern was my daughter, this divorce, and my sobriety. Mello felt that he could keep trying to put off signing the papers. At the end of the day, all I wanted to be was happy. Mello didn't do that for me anymore. Anytime I thought of us possibly having another chance at being together, the thought diminished when I thought of all the hurt and pain he caused over the last year.

The hurt and pain I felt when I listened, read, and thought about all the things he told Kenyetta, was unbearable. My chest tightened and it felt like I couldn't breathe in that moment. How could I begin to love him again after that? Some women decided to work on their marriage and that was fine for them. Except, this man had a child on me and took on the responsibility of raising another man's child. Not only did he do that, but he decided to stick the knife a little further when he fell in love with the bitch. How could I trust him to walk outside our home and not fall into some pussy? It was about trust with me, and if I couldn't trust my husband, then I couldn't be with him.

Karmella's whining deterred me from my morning cup of coffee.

She was lying down in her bassinet that I had sitting in the living room. Mello was coming over so we could talk about this whole divorce bullshit. He had the papers and was stalling, when all I wanted to do was put this behind me. My lawyer asked me daily what his moves were and what did he have planned. The best way to find out, was to find out what was going on with him. This needed to end so I could truly move on and do me. A lot of things stopped me from going further with Walt. Part of the reason was because I felt I needed to be single for a while. I had been with Mello for so long that I didn't know what it meant to be on my own. Moving into this townhouse and being alone after leaving Mello was one of the hardest things I've ever had to do. That alone, still wasn't a lot of time to be on my own and know if I liked being alone.

Walt was everything and I had strong feelings for him, still, I never wanted to move too fast with him. Both of our relationships ended with our significant others cheating on us. Trust was something we both needed to learn how to do again. My and Walt's relationship wasn't in the phase where we could accuse each other of doing something. It was light, fun, and not too deep. Yet, the closer we got and the more feelings we developed for each other, I knew those questions would rise from the both of us. From my side, I knew I had a lot of insecurities that I needed to sort out. Walt probably had a bunch of his own, so we needed to work on ourselves before trying to be whole for each other.

The doorbell sounded and I headed to the door to let Mello in. When I opened the door, he was standing there with food and drinks. I didn't plan on this being a long visit, but apparently, he thought we were going to be here all day chatting about this. All I needed to know was what was holding him up with signing the papers. According to him, he was trapped into being married and wasn't ready to be a married man. So, signing these papers should have been a cakewalk, not a procrastination fest.

"Hey, come in." I welcomed him inside.

Mello walked straight to the kitchen and placed the food on the counter. "Cold as hell out there. You didn't take my princess out in that shit, did you?"

"Yeah, I went to lunch with Kelsie the other day. You acting like I don't have a truck with heat."

"Don't matter. Why the fuck didn't you call me? I would have come and spent time with her while you went to have lunch."

Was this nigga serious? He was really in here trying to school me on being a mother. Last I checked, I was Mella's mother and I knew what was best for her. Before I even took her to lunch with me and Kelsie, we had been in the house for weeks. I needed—no, we needed some fresh air. Even if it was just for a few seconds, we needed the air and the outside communications. Mello came over and visited with Mella.

"Last I checked, I birthed this little girl. You're not about to tell me what the hell I can do with her. We were outside for less than two minutes each time we got out the car."

"Don't matter. She could have got sick, Pat."

"Karmello, don't do this right now. You came over to talk and see your daughter. Please, don't try me today."

He held his hands up as he looked around the kitchen for plates. "Where your plates at?"

"In the cabinet, next to the fridge. Keep your voice down before she starts hollering because she hears your voice."

He ignored me and started plating our food. It was as if he thought he ran this household again. Like he could waltz in here and demand that I do what he wanted with our child. Karmella was my child too. If we wanted to be honest, I did more to bring her into this world. All he did was give me some half ass dick, which helped in making her. I fought my demons for months to bring her safely into this world without him. All he did was bring more stress that made me want to turn to the bottle more and more. It was always something with Mello, and I was tired of it being all about him.

"Newsflash, this isn't the Karmello show," I blurted. He stopped putting chicken onto the plate and stared at me for a second.

"Yo, you be watching TV too much," he accused.

Yes, it sounded like something out of a cliché white movie. Yet, this was how I felt when it came to Mello. Once upon a time, I thought everything he did was amazing. He could brush his teeth and I would stare in amazement and question myself how I got so lucky. The more time we stayed separated, I realized that it was always about him and never about me. Did he even love me? Or was I just a convenience for him? Someone to tidy the sheets, make his food, and look good on his arm.

"I've put so much on the back burner for you and this marriage. I didn't pursue things that I've always wanted to do, for you. How do you repay me? You go cheat and have some kids on me." Tears were building up and I needed to keep them away. "All I want is for you to sign the damn papers. Let me be free and move on from the mess you've made of our marriage."

"Why the hell would I give up so easy? You acting like this is some high school relationship and you're asking me to lose your number. We're married and have a child. I'm not tossing shit away."

"Get the fuck out," I calmly stated.

"Huh?"

"Get out of my home. I thought we could have a conversation and come to terms. You're walking around like you didn't create this mess. You fucked up our lives, and now guess what? I have to pick up the pieces and continue to live. Just sign the damn papers. If you don't, don't come around neither of us."

I never wanted to tell Mello he couldn't be in Mella's life. Desperate times called for desperate measures. Maybe seeing that he couldn't just pop up and visit with his daughter whenever he wanted, would put some sense into his brain. What more did I have to do to convince him that I was over everything he's done to me. How many more tears could I cry or how much more screaming could I do? He needed to realize that we were done and there was no coming back from the betrayal that he did to me.

"You only want to end this marriage because of your little boyfriend. I'm the one to blame, but you're so quick to jump on another dick so fast."

Thrown off from his choice of words, I laughed. It was hilarious how this nigga could fuck, showboat, and provide another life for another woman, but I went and met someone months after I ended things in our marriage, and I was wrong.

"Walt has nothing to do with anything. Your problem is that you blame everyone for your fucked up mistakes. Stop worrying about the next man who isn't worried about you."

"Yeah, ight. My name probably in that nigga's mouth soon as he steps in this bitch."

"Walt doesn't give a fuck about you, Mello. All he's worried about is his kids, career, and me. We don't sit around and bash you, or even talk about you at all. He's the perfect distraction from all things you. When he's around, I never think about you."

"He better not be around my daughter," he threatened like I gave a shit.

Walt had been there when I was pregnant. It wasn't like I just met him when Karmella was born. The day she was born, he sent me up flowers, balloons, and my favorite food from the diner down the block. Of course, Mello made the whole shit about him and claimed it was disrespectful to him. How? He didn't ask to come up. He told me he respected that we just had our daughter and wanted to give us some space and respect.

"He actually taught me some things about heating her bottles and changing diapers. Karmella likes him and has fallen asleep on his chest a few times."

It was all a lie; still, I wanted to hurt the hell out of Mello. If he didn't want to sign the papers, then I was going to fuck with him until he couldn't take it anymore. By the time he signed those papers, he would be ready to strangle me right after signing them.

"Yo, let me get the fuck outta here before I put hands on you," he growled and headed toward the door.

"Your mother claimed your baby mother been calling her phone. Maybe you should be over there asking her some questions." I laughed as I held the door open and he stormed out. "Worried about me and I'm fine. Worry about yourself, Mello. What are you even doing with yourself?" I questioned, even though I didn't care or want the answer to it.

Before he could crack his mouth and speak, I slammed the door and walked into the kitchen. Only one thing came from his visit and that was the food he brought. After fixing myself a plate, I sat on the couch and surfed through the different channels before I settled on something. Karmella had soothed her own self from when I slammed the door and was sucking on her fist. I felt like she was trying to get her thumb in her mouth, but didn't know how to. Instead, she settled on her fist and that was alright with me. Just as I was about to place some food into my mouth, my phone started ringing. Snatching the phone, I slid my finger across the screen and held the phone to my ear.

"They're Braxton Hicks contractions. Calm down and relax, Michelle," I recited before even hearing what her new complaint was.

Michelle was due to give birth next month. Until she gave birth, I think she found satisfaction in getting on my nerves about every question. I don't know how many times she caused Thor to run every red light in Brooklyn to make it back to their condo. We were all waiting for her baby boy to show his face to the world, still, we needed to sleep a full night without Michelle ending up in the hospital for

Braxton Hicks.

"It sure doesn't feel like them. I know what they feel like and these are breaking my back, Pat," she moaned through the phone.

"Have you ever had a baby?"

"No."

"So every little pain you feel is going to feel like it's breaking your back. I remember when they first started with Mella, I was crawling around the floor looking for a phone. Mello came over and rushed me to the hospital only for them to tell me it was Braxton Hicks contractions."

"Can I just give birth already? I'm so miserable with all of this. I'm emotional, horny, and hungry all the time," she complained like she had done so many times.

"Remember you prayed for all of this. You got the man of your dreams, planning a wedding, and are about to have a baby. A little discomfort is worth all the doors that's opening for you."

"Why you gotta be positive Patty all the time? Let me have my moment, woman." She giggled and crunched on something.

"Because I know you've wanted everything that is happening for you. Be patient, and Titan will be here before we know it."

"From your mouth to God's ears. Anyway, what you doing?"

"Sitting here trying to watch TV. Mello's dumb ass just left."

"Uh oh. He didn't sign? What is he waiting on?"

I chuckled to myself before I replied, "A damn miracle. There's no way he's ever getting back with me after being all in love with Kenyetta.

That girl is so damn lost since he hasn't been seeing her."

"Hasn't been seeing her?"

"Yep, he has his mother or Milli go get the boys. He refuses to see her since he found out that Kenzel isn't his son."

"Humph. When you do dirt, it comes right back onto you. She's probably losing her mind."

"Girl, I don't give a damn about all of their drama. All I'm concerned about is my daughter and my well-being. Mello better go ahead with all the drama that follows his ass."

"He can't blame anyone except himself. What's going on with Walt?"

A smile crept upon my face because whenever Walt's name was mentioned, it made me so giddy. "We're cool. He brought me to his place the other night. It was a good time."

"Aww, that's cute. At least he gets your ass out the house."

"Yeah, but I think I'm going to break up with him." Immediately, Michelle started choking. "What?" she managed to choke out.

"I don't know, Chelle. He's a good man, funny, and has his head screwed on right. Still, I feel like I need to be on my own. There's no way I should be in another relationship already. I'm not even divorced and with another man."

"I can see where you're coming from. Don't break up with and push him away; continue to be friends with him, Pat. He's a good person and makes you happy."

"We'll probably say we'll be friends and then cut each other off. I

29

can't imagine him being cool with this."

"Give him some credit. He went through a divorce himself and may need the time just like you. I should have waited a while after Tasheem, but I'm glad I didn't. That doesn't happen for everybody, so do what you gotta do, babe."

"Yeah, I'm probably gonna talk to him about it tonight when he cal—"

"Pat, you better not do it over the phone. That's a face to face conversation."

"I just don't want to see him hurt, Michelle. Like, he did nothing to me, and I'm just telling him that I don't want to be with him. It's fucked up."

"No, you're doing something so you can possibly be better for him in the future. If he's any type of man, he'll understand your position."

"Uh huh, we'll see."

"Miracle is coming to spend the weekend with me. You heard about what Marina is doing?" she questioned.

"Kelsie told me over lunch. Why is she trying to put her through all of this? Just let her come to grips and decide if she wants to do visits."

"Marina only gives a damn about herself. Miracle probably misses her, but she wouldn't want to live with her grandmother."

"I thought she was only taking her for visitation?"

"There's something on the paper about custody or something. Only if she's able to prove that Kelsie is an unfit mother."

"Why is she dragging it though? I wanna punch her old ass in the face, for real."

"Girl, why does she drag everything. Milli wants to take Kelsie out of town and get her mind off everything."

"I pray that everything is handled and over with. Marina does know that when we win this, she won't ever see Miracle again, right?"

Michelle laughed into the phone. "Shorty has to know. Enough about that, these contractions are killing me."

"If your so-called contractions were killing you, you wouldn't be on the phone saying that. Get some rest and I'll talk to you later," I promised.

"Okay. Make sure you tell Walt in person, Patricia."

"Why you yelling my government like that?"

"I know you," she said and ended the call.

Left once again with my thoughts, I placed my food down because I didn't have much of an appetite. After thinking about what I needed to do, it hurt me to hurt Walt. The last thing I wanted was for him to think that it was him. It was me who needed to be single and worry about myself for once. It wouldn't hurt to have him around as a friend, because I did enjoy his company.

***

Kim called me and told me she wanted me to come over to her house. Of course she promised me that if I didn't bring her granddaughter, she wasn't opening the door. If it was one thing that Kim loved, it was being a grandmother. Between the boys, Miracle, and now Mella, she spoiled them crazy. Every other week I had a package coming to my door from her office. Mella had electric cars and things she couldn't even play with yet. When it came to the boys, she converted a bedroom upstairs for them. The way Mello tells it, she has them more than their mother these days.

"Let me get Glamma's baby girl." Kim rushed out the house as soon as we pulled into her driveway. She didn't wait for me to get out, she opened the back door and carefully got Mella out of her car seat.

"Well, dang. I guess I'm just her chauffeur," I laughed and closed the door behind me.

"You know you're my girl too. Mella gets all my loving first," she laughed and pecked me on the cheek. "How are you doing? You lost all of the baby weight quick." She examined me.

"Stressing will cause you to lose weight you never knew you needed to lose."

"What are you stressing about?"

I followed Kim into the living room where she took Mella's snowsuit off and kissed all over her face. "Your son won't sign the papers, Kim. I'm tired of going back and forth with him. It's been months since I handed them to him, and he hasn't done anything except make excuses."

"He thinks that you both are going to get back together. Of course, both me and Milli knows that's never going to happen. He still believes that you are going to make it work."

"Why does he believe that, Kim? I haven't told him or even showed him that it would happen. When it comes to our child, I'm cordial and we share some laughs. That doesn't mean that I'm willing to revisit my marriage with him."

"Baby cakes, that's something you have to ask him. I know you have your little boyfriend now, but make sure to handle this before getting too deep," she warned me.

If that wasn't another sign that I needed, I don't know what was. "I'm going to break up with him." I expected Kim to be surprised like Michelle was. Instead, she nodded her head and continued to cuddle my daughter. "Why aren't you surprised?"

"Because I already knew that's what needs to be done. Come on, you left your marriage and jumped right in with Walt. I don't doubt he's a nice man. I just know you need more than a few weeks of being alone. It's nothing wrong with being alone, Patsy."

I sighed because she was right. The word break up kept popping up, but we weren't together. Maybe it was because I knew that's what Walt wanted. He wasn't shy about saying he wanted me to be his woman. I had to stop being so scared and tell him that all we needed to be was friends right now. It wasn't because of Mello, Kim, or anybody, it was because of me and only me.

Mello

The sun came through the window and I turned over, giving the window my back. Lately, I've been feeling like fuck it. Everything I worked so hard for was failing. In the end, all I wanted was to be left alone. Patsy and Mella was my entire world. All I wanted was to be a family with them. The simplest thing seemed like the hardest thing to do. Each time I tried to speak to Patsy about the situation, she would block me out. She didn't want to hear anything that had to do with us getting back together. When I sat down and pictured us raising our daughter together, it was as if I could reach out and touch it. Instead, I was in this hotel room paying out the house to live here. Going back to our house hurt too bad.

My phone started ringing, so I reached out and grabbed it off the nightstand. When I saw Kenyetta's name flash across the screen, I hit decline and tossed it back onto the nightstand. She had been hitting my line and I kept ignoring her. The bitch lied to me and had fucked another nigga. If that wasn't enough, she had the nerve to go and get pregnant by him. Kenyetta had always been a good girl in my eyes. She did the right thing, listened to me, and made sure to keep our home together. All I saw when I thought of her was a mark ass bitch that couldn't keep her legs closed. Why she had to fuck up what we had going on? Why did she have to stroll into the Cheesecake Factory that day? If I could rewind back the hands of time, I wouldn't have moved

Patsy to Atlanta. It was something that she never wanted to do in the first place. Why did I push her to move there?

"Why did I have to have someone let me into your room?" I heard my mother's voice and leaned up in the bed.

She stepped over the clothes on the floor and set her Birkin on the bench at the end of the bed. "Ma, what you doing here? I said I would meet you at the office."

"I know what the hell you said. Imagine my surprise, when I walked into the office around twelve and you weren't there."

I quickly grabbed my phone and looked at the time. It was three in the afternoon. Shit, my mind had been everywhere and I wasn't paying attention to the time. She stood there with her arms folded and a disapproving glare on her face.

"I fucked up. Mama, I was tired and got in late last night," I tried to explain and she held her hand up.

"You created this damn mess, Karmello. It's like you and your brother swapped places. He's happy with his little family and you're in the damn club all night. What the fuck is going on and don't tell me you don't know." She raised her voice.

She didn't give me time to explain because she left the room. I grabbed my basketball shorts and followed her into the dining room. "Ma, I'm just chilling right now. My kids are taken care of and will always be. I… I just need time for myself."

"You don't need no damn time for yourself. What you need to do is pick up the pieces and rebuild your damn life. Do you think being in the club will change your life? All that's in there is girls looking for a come up. Isn't that how you ended up with a damn son?"

"Mama, I'm a grown man."

"Oh, you grown now? What about when you wanted me to speak to Patsy? Were you so grown then?"

There was no use in arguing with my moms. She was going to speak her mind and dared you to challenge her opinions. At the end of the day, if my kids were taken care of, I could do whatever the fuck I wanted when they weren't with me. At the end of the day, what I did with my life was my choice, not hers.

"Ma, I'm not going to get into it with you."

"Let me tell you something, Karmello. Your brother worked his ass off to get us where we are. He didn't do it the way I hoped he would, but he still put his work in. You need to quit partying at the club, where you know niggas are hateful. The same men shaking your hands and dapping you, are the same ones quick to pull the trigger and rob you for your jewels. Smarten the fuck up, asshole."

She went into the bedroom to grab her purse and stormed out the door. If dealing with a possible divorce, bitter baby mother, and kids wasn't enough, now, I had to make it right with my mama. All I wanted to see on my mama's face was a smile. She frowned for too many years providing for us. Me being the reason that she wasn't smiling wasn't right and I needed to fix things with us quick. Rushing into the hallway, I found my mother waiting for the elevator and went and put my arm around her shoulders and kissed the top of her head. Even with heels, she was still shorter than me.

"I'm sorry, Mama. You know shit been off the grid with me," I apologized to her.

She waved me off and tried to look away from me. "Mello, get off me. I'm tired of this destructive behavior you've been displaying. Sometimes I just wish you and Patsy could work things out. When she was in your life, you had your head on straight. Well, at least that's what it seemed like," she sighed and pressed the button.

"Come on, Mama. I'll order room service and we can have lunch."

She shook her head and stepped into the elevator. "When you get yourself together, then I'll come around. I refuse to stand around and watch this shit show."

I watched as the elevator door closed before walking back into my hotel suite. My moms never resisted coming to have lunch or spend time with me. Especially after I apologized to her. Seeing her so pissed hurt me, yet, she was asking something of me that I couldn't do. Why should I stop living my life? My wife didn't want to be with me, my son's mother was a lying bitch, and all of this was becoming too much for me. Why the fuck could they live their life without answering to anybody, but I had to answer to damn near everybody in my family? Shit wasn't right and I was tired of answering to everyone. This shit was life and I was grown the last time I had checked.

The front door chimed and broke me from my thought. Swaggering to the front door, I swung it open, expecting it to be my mother. Instead, it was a beautiful chocolate woman standing there with a clipboard.

"Good afternoon, Mr. Gibbens. My name is Choc Aarons, how are you?" She shifted the clipboard to the other hand and extended her hand.

"What's good? I'm fine."

"Perfect. How has your stay been?" she questioned and looked down at her clipboard. "Since you're in our private suites, instead of handling things downstairs at the desk, we come to you." She offered a bright smile with her pearly whites.

Holding the door wider, I signaled for her to come. The sound of her heels on the marble was the only sound in the suite. "So, I owe some bread, huh?"

"Pretty much," she giggled. "We know some of our clients like to pay cash, so we prefer to handle that in private. You've been here for a week, and you called and said to book you for three more?"

"Yeah."

"We do offer leasing of our suites. It'll come out cheaper than booking for days or even weeks."

"Oh word?"

"Yes. We have your information already, I can just go and complete everything for you, and bring the papers for you to sign," she offered.

"You get a commission for offering this, huh?" She was all too happy to do all of this for me. Yeah, leasing meant more business for the hotel, but that wasn't going into her pocket. So, I knew she had to make some kind of bank for offering that option.

"Kind of. It really does save you some money. If it's something you want, you can call my office and I'll handle it for you."

"Choc as in chocolate?"

"Yep. My mother named me that," she smiled. "Give me a call if you would like to lease the suite. I'm in my office until around 5."

"Nah, go ahead and do the paperwork. I'll be up here until later tonight, so knock on the door or slide the papers under the door."

"I'll be here until tonight too. The paperwork is a lot and I'll be here past 5. I'll have your papers up here soon." She walked to the door and then stopped. "Do you have a credit card?"

Walking over to my jeans tossed across the couch, I dug into my pockets and found my wallet. After picking through my wallet, I handed her my black card and she smiled. "I usually cringe when I hand this card over."

"No worries. I won't put any Louboutins on here," she sarcastically laughed.

"If only my wife said that."

"Should I add your wife to the lease as well? I would need her information." She turned around and got her pen and clipboard ready.

"Nah, we're separated, so this like my bachelor pad."

Laughing, she shook her head. "Perfect. There is three other units on this floor and they're all leasing as well. The tenant across from you is a football player, and the one down the hall is some rich mogul's son. They do tend to have parties, but they never get out of control."

"Sounds like you've been invited."

"Maybe to one." She winked and headed out the door.

Just seeing her ass sway from side to side had my dick hard. She had to be no more than around five-foot-three and with heels, she had to be around five-foot-five. I could tell from her small stature that she was petite. Her long black hair was pin straight and hanging down her back. The skirt she had on showed me how wide her hips were and how thick her thighs were.

"Have a nice day, Choc," I yelled back and she smiled.

"Ms. Aarons, will do," she giggled and closed the door behind her.

Shorty was a beautiful sight and she had a good ass job. With all the women I had in my life, I sure didn't need to add another woman. Not to mention, she worked where I was now going to live, so I couldn't shit where I laid my head. If she wanted, she could come up here and fuck my shit up if I fucked with her heart. I picked my phone up and dialed Kenyetta's number. Today I was going to spend the day with my seeds.

"Oh, you know how to return someone's phone call?" she answered already being a fucking smart ass.

"Get my son's dressed and pack them some clothes."

"Your mother is going to come pick them up? Because I'm tired of going through these people to give my kids to their father," she huffed into the phone.

"Kenyetta, long as I'm spending time with my boys, it shouldn't fucking matter to you."

"Well, I need to talk to you about some things. So, when do you think you're going to come over here and talk like adults?"

"I'll be over there in an hour. I'm keeping my sons for the rest of the week."

"Uh, just come over and we'll talk," she quickly rushed off the phone.

After laying around being lazy for an hour, I showered and got dressed. Kenyetta had me more curious than a virgin in a strip club. I didn't like the way she sounded when I told her I wanted the kids for the rest of the week. If she was going to try this bullshit where she was going to make shit hard, she better be prepared for me to get all in her ass. Shit was supposed to be so simple between us. She had everything she could ever dream of. I mean, in the end, all she wanted was me with her and the boys. That was something I couldn't guarantee when I had a wife at home waiting on me. She should have been satisfied because I spent more time with her than I did with Patsy. Now, I was going through a damn divorce because I neglected my wife for a bitch that couldn't keep her legs closed. Kenyetta was in Brooklyn, so I jumped into my whip and headed over the bridge to hear the bullshit she was about to lay on me.

"Yo, what's good with you?" Milli asked when I answered the phone.

"What you mean? Do I call you and get in your business?"

He sighed. I could tell he was getting upset with my question. "Nigga, I would appreciate the concern. Mama called me crying and talking about she saw pills on your night stand."

Shit. I meant to put that shit away from being out in the open. Then again, I didn't expect my moms to come busting in my shit like she was the police. "It ain't like that, she being extra. You know how

Mama can be."

"I do. And I know that Moms don't shed tears for no damn reason. What's the pills, Mello?"

"I got a few Xanax from my nigga last night. We were partying and I didn't get a chance to take them."

"Yo, what the fuck? Who the fuck you hanging with? Zombies?"

I laughed because this nigga was such a hypocrite. He was known for moving weight back then, and now he was so anti-drugs. "Nah, just to pop to get lit. Stop worrying about dumb shit, moms is dragging shit."

"If I find out that you're doing that shit, I'll put your head through the fucking wall," he threatened. "What the fuck is with you and Pat, man. She just got sober and now you are doing shit," he spoke more to himself than me.

"Nigga, I'm grown and if I wanna get lit, I can. You not about to treat me like a little ass kid." I ended the call because I was done having this conversation with him.

Milli complained that my mother put so much on him with raising me, then he took it upon himself to act like I'm his damn child. I had two damn kids, I'd be damn if that nigga was about to tell me he was going to beat my ass. Patsy's drinking was part of my fault and the other part was that it was in her DNA. She witnessed her mother drinking for years to solve her problems. I could take responsibility for part of it, yet, I wasn't going to take it for all of it. Milli accusing me of having a problem pissed me off because I didn't even take the damn pill and was getting shit for it. Everybody in my family was blowing mine and I needed to keep away from them for a little while.

I arrived at Kenyetta's condo and killed my engine. Parking across the street, I jogged across the street and rang her bell. She buzzed me in and I walked up the first flight to her floor. The door was already cracked open, so I walked inside. It was as if she didn't give a damn about decorating this condo for the kids. The shit still looked as if she just moved in, bare walls, no pictures, or furniture. Shit didn't even look lived in. Kenyetta was sitting on the couch with a glass of wine and watching a movie.

"The boys are taking a nap. I tried to keep them up, but they were getting so fussy," she explained. "Nice to finally see you." She stared at me.

"Hmph."

"You don't have to act so bothered by my presence, Mello. I did what I did and I can't change it, so why continue to be like that with me?"

"Because I didn't expect you to go and do no shit like that."

"Oh, so you can have a whole wife, and I couldn't do me?"

"I didn't go and have a kid and try to pass it as yours, did I?"

She sucked her teeth and took a sip of wine. "It didn't cross my mind that Kenzel wasn't yours. You don't think I would have took matters into my own hands and got him tested?"

"Yo, I asked you why he didn't look like KJ. You gave me excuses on how he looked like your grandfather, uncle, and every damn body except me, his father."

43

"I'm not going to argue about this anymore. Kenzel's real father wants to be in his life, and I want him to be."

The shit she just told me hit me like a ton of rocks. If I hit women, I would've slammed her head into the brick accent wall behind her. Fuck did she mean that Kenzel's father wanted to be a part of his life? Where the fuck was he all of this time when I was raising him?

"What the fuck?"

"Listen, I got him tested and he's the father. He just was released from prison and wants us to be a family. There's nothing happening here with us, and I have a chance to have a family."

"Every nigga wanna be a family when he gets out of prison, Kenyetta!" I yelled and she jumped. "Until your ass on the phone, crying and asking where he's at in the wee hours of the morning. This better be a fucking joke."

She set her wine glass down and stared at me. "This isn't something that I have come to terms with overnight. He's been coming to the city and spending time with us. He's flying us down to Atlanta to spend two weeks with him."

"Who the fuck is this nigga? And you had him around my sons and in my crib?"

"No, he booked a suite in the city for us. We had a great time and he loves the boys too."

Was God really playing a trick on me? This bitch couldn't be in my face telling me that she had another nigga around my seeds. This was the sneaky shit that I was talking about. And here she thought that the shit was cool and that I was going to agree like the shit was alright.

"If you ever bring another nigga around my sons, I'l—"

"Kenzel isn't your son, Mello. You can't tell me who I can bring around him. KJ wasn't around him. Remember the week that Kenzel stayed home because he was sick, and your mother picked up KJ so he wouldn't get sick too? That's when he flew in and spent time with us."

"Oh, he's not my seed, now? Where's all the money I spent for his care? The hospital bill when he was born? All the clothes, food, and shit he has needed since he came out that loose pussy?"

"Why are you being so petty? He's not your son and I know that it hurts. Still, he has a father and he wants to be very present in his life."

I stood up and shook my head. "So, I'm supposed to just forget him? Like I didn't raise him?"

"I don't expect you to forget him. He can still come with KJ, if his father is fine with it. Just like you have boundaries, we have the same," she added.

"Yo, this shit is wild funny to me. Does your new nigga know that you wanted to jump on my dick a few weeks ago? Weren't you texting me to come fill you up with cum? How you wanted to have my daughter? You a wack bitch on the real."

Her mouth dropped because she didn't think I was going to bring it up or remember it. "Why do you want to ruin what the fuck I have? I have a chance to be with someone and be happy."

"You wanna be happy now, huh? After you fucked my marriage up."

"I didn't fuck up anything. I'm tired of you and your family accusing me of doing things I haven't done. You decided to fuck me and make a child. Then, you fell in love with me. Yes, I could have stopped once I found out about your wife, but I didn't. I'm not the one who decided to go before God with vows, so I don't owe that bitch a damn thing."

"Watch your fucking mouth."

"This is why I'm moving on. You're free to take KJ for two weeks because me and Kenzel are going to Atlanta."

"You just leaving your son to run and play house with another nigga and his brother?"

She stood up and headed to the back, but turned around. "No, I'm leaving my son to spend time with his father, while I take my other son to do the same with his father. Stop trying to make me look like a crap mother because I'm far from one. Everything I do is for these boys." She pointed her finger and went to the boy's bedroom.

Ten minutes later, she was carrying KJ who was whining because she woke him out of his sleep. "Give me my son," I demanded.

She turned and rolled her eyes. "I love you, big boy. Mommy will see you soon, okay. Be good for Daddy, baby."

KJ allowed her to shower him with kisses then reached for me. "Hey, big man, you ready?"

He nodded his head and then laid on my shoulder. Kenyetta handed me his little book bag. "If you need anything, make sure to call me."

"You're the last bitch I'm going to call," I said and headed out the condo. I was going to take KJ back to the hotel to finish sleeping and sign those leasing papers.

Kenyetta

*M*ello was able to fuck with my heart, but when it came to me fucking with his, he couldn't take it. I sat back for years and allowed him to have his cake and eat it too. After I had KJ, I was tired and hormonal about being left alone with a newborn baby. Since I was born and raised in Atlanta, I knew people and one of those people happened to be my friend, Axe. We were in school from pre-k up until high school. When we finished high school, we both went to different colleges. While he went into the world of being a contractor and built his own business, I went the route of being a side chick. One night, my mother decided to give me a break. She took KJ and I went to a bar in midtown. How was I supposed to know that I was going to run into Axe? We kept it as friends at first.

He told me about how he ran a business and he was fighting in court over embezzling money. We continued our friendship for a while. I went to court with him and we hung out when Mello wasn't in town. He told me that my situation wasn't going to last and someone was going to get tired of being second, and it was going to be Mello or his wife. I was so sure that Mello was going to leave his wife and we would be happy with our son. That was until Mello promised to come down one weekend, and he ended up being in New York spending time with his wife. He wined and dined that woman and she was all too happy to broadcast it to social media. When I called him, he ignored me and never called me back. For the life of me, I couldn't understand how a man that claimed he hated his wife so much, could put up such a good front and ignore the woman he claimed he loved, the same woman that had given him his first son.

That night, I rushed over to Axe's house and was hit with the news that he was going to federal prison. He accepted a plea deal of three years. With good behavior, he could be out in a year. For the first time, we had sex all night and didn't think of the problems we would face in the morning. In the morning, I tipped out and went home and cried in the shower. My body shook from how hard I cried. If Mello knew I betrayed him, he wouldn't want anything to do with me. Axe reached out to me until he went to do his time. He sent his friends to check on me and give me money if I needed it, which I didn't. Life went on and we didn't reach out to each other at all. When I turned up pregnant, I never thought that Axe could be the father.

In my mind, I had been sleeping with Mello so much, that he had to be the father. When Kenzel was born, I didn't see any Axe in him. Mello constantly questioned why he looked so different than KJ when he was a baby. I told him he probably looked like the men in my family. Even then, I didn't think Kenzel wasn't Mello's son. Every sibling didn't look alike, so I wasn't stressing it. Eventually, Mello left it alone, until he brought the boys around his family. When they started asking questions, that's when he went to go get him tested behind my back. Part of me was relieved that the secret was out. I lied to Mello when he asked about Kenzel's real father. Part of me wanted him to make it work with me and our boys, so I told him that Kenzel's father wanted nothing to do with him. When that wasn't the truth because

Kenzel's father knew nothing about him. After many nights of crying myself to sleep, I reached out to Axe's best friend. He told me that he was home and gave me his new number.

Soon as I heard Axe's voice, it was like everything felt better. I explained to him everything that basically went down while we were out of touch. Then I broke down and told him about my son and how he wasn't Mello's son. He immediately requested that he gets tested and it turned out that he was Kenzel's father. That following week, he came to New York and wanted to meet his son. Kenzel was sick, so I had told Kim to take KJ so he wouldn't get sick. I bundled Kenzel up and met him in the city. He booked a suite at the Marriott and we spent the entire week together. Since Kenzel was sick, there wasn't much we could do, but it was nice to feel like I had a team member in all of this.

Since he left, Axe has been wanting me to move back to Atlanta with our son. I told him it wasn't easy because I had KJ and he needed his father as well. He understood my position and didn't make things harder by making me make that type of decision right away. Mello looked hurt by what I told him. He was the one who created this mess for us. All he had to do is choose who he wanted to be with. Instead, he thought he could have the both of us. In the end, he ruined his marriage and things with us ended up taking a turn for the worst. Some days, I missed my best friend. Laying up in the bed and talking about any and everything under the sun. More than anything, I missed us being together. Any chance of us getting back to that was ruined when he found out Kenzel wasn't his son.

The faint cries of Kenzel broke me from my trance. Getting up from the couch, I went into the boy's bedroom and picked him up. I changed his diaper and carried him back into the living room with me. Our flight was booked for later tonight. I couldn't wait to touch down back home and see my family. Being in New York for the past few months had been hell on earth. I didn't have any friends or family and everybody I did know was connected to Mello. For once, it was going to be nice to be around people that knew the real me. That didn't judge me because I slept and had babies with a married man. Well, my mother has always been judgmental when it came to my relationship with Mello, so I didn't expect for that to change when it came to her. If anything, she would say I told you so and keep it pushing.

Things were still new with me and Axe. It was like we were starting from square one since he was locked up and we let so much time go past. I couldn't lie and say that it didn't feel nice that we could start fresh and take things somewhere. Before, I was worried about Mello and couldn't afford to give Axe my all. Maybe this time around, we could take our relationship somewhere. I deserved to be loved and cherished by a man. For years, I sat back and allowed myself to be the other woman. It was time for someone to treat me like a queen and accept my kids as their own. Mello wouldn't like KJ being around Axe, but it was something he was going to have to deal with. Numerous times, I've asked him not to bring the boys around Patsy, and he ignored my wishes each time.

Since he was clearly allowed to do whatever he pleased, I was going to do the same. I pushed these boys out and went through the pain. I'd be damned if a nigga that had to lie to his wife to attend the births was going to dictate on how I was going to live my life. Mello had another thing coming if he thought things were going to be catered to how he liked them. Since he wanted to be disrespectful and send everyone else to get the kids, I was going to show him that I was no longer under his beck and call. He wasn't going to dismiss me and then deal with me when he felt like it. Patsy was drinking while pregnant with his child and she got more respect than I did. Kenzel wasn't his biological son, get the fuck over it. If I had to list all the shit I've had to put up with over the years, Mello would clearly lose. While Kenzel played on the floor with his wooden toys, I went to go pack our bags for our trip to Atlanta tonight.

Kelsie

*I*t seemed like all I did was eat, sleep, and work. I wanted to spend more time with Miracle, but time didn't allow me to. Milli told me to quit and although it sounded tempting, I couldn't allow him to finance my life. Since I've been a teen, working has been what I've done to get by. Milli didn't care about money and would continue to cash out on both me and Miracle. Since Miracle was his daughter, he was fine to do that. When it came to me, I wanted to be able to buy my own things and take care of myself. Plus, Kim was grooming me to be a real estate agent. All I had to do was go and take the test. It would be disrespectful of her time to just up and quit because her son could afford to take care of me. I don't think Milli thought of that when he tried to make me do things that he wanted. It would be amazing to be able to wake up and get Miracle ready for school, then be home once she returned. Life didn't work like that and just because Milli could make it happen, didn't mean that I should toss away a career. A career was something that I didn't have and it was something that I really wanted.

When I saw the way Kim walked around and commanded attention in meetings, it made me want to have the same thing. This woman took what her son gave her and was building an empire for her kids and grandchildren. Milli and Mello weren't hands on when it came to the company. They just tossed their money and told her to make something with it. They had no clue that she was about to buy an apartment building in the heart of Central Park. When they mentioned the price of the building, I choked on my coffee. Kim didn't break a sweat as she signed her name on the dotted line. In her words, she got the building for a steal. There were some things that needed to be updated in the building, but she was sure that it would be an investment that would continue to pay. She told me that it would be something that allowed her sons to officially step out of the street life.

All I wanted was to do the same for my daughter. When it was my time to go, what would I leave her? Unpaid bills? Everything that I was sacrificing was the for the greater good. Milli could leave her more than I could, and even though this wasn't a competition, it was more for my pride than anything else. Miracle needed to see me become something. I wanted her to be proud of me and be proud to say that I'm her mother. All she's used to seeing is me stress and breaking down in front of her. No mother wanted their child to see them struggling to raise them. I never wanted Miracle to think that it was her fault. She didn't ask to be born, so I wanted to make sure I gave her the best life that I could.

"I need to have a conference call with the boys about this building." Kim walked in the front from her office.

"I'll set it up for you."

She stared at the empty desk across from mine, then stared at mine. "Have someone come and put this desk into the middle of the floor. So, when someone comes in this is the first desk they're greeted with. Over there we can add a small sectional and coffee table."

"Why?" I questioned not bothering to stop replying to this email.

"Kelsie, I'm giving you a damn office. Why you got to make me say it out loud," she laughed and turned toward me. "You've come in here and put in more work than the girl that has been here."

"I'm honored. I appreciate that so much, Kim. Question, she's not going to like the fact that I'm in an office and she's been here first?"

"Well, maybe if she wasn't pregnant she could've shown me what she had. Instead, she went and got pregnant then comes in late. Your children should always come first, never be the reason for every excuse that falls out of your mouth."

Kim was always trying to preach and for the most part, she was always right. It was exciting that I would have my own office. "Thank you for the office. I really appreciate it."

"No problem. We have a meeting in two hours. I must sign some papers for the building and do a walk through. In the meantime, call some movers, who move things around and order some office furniture on the company's card," she instructed and stared down at her phone. "I have to take this, take messages for all my calls. Hey, baby," she told me then answered the phone.

I badly wanted to know who Kim's boo was. Whenever he called, she would rush into her office or walk away to handle their conversation. If it was one thing I could say, he had a permanent smile on her face. It was driving Milli crazy that he didn't know who this mysterious man was. He spent hours grilling me down and trying to get answers. Once he realized that I wasn't lying and I didn't know any information, he let me go and vented about his mama telling him everything. Getting Milli and Mello together was going to be tricky.

They both had different schedules and even then, they were going to grill me on why their mother needed to sit and have a meeting with them. Excusing myself from my desk, I went into the conference room and tidied up a bit. Then, I went back to my desk and called Mello on the phone. As excited I was to call movers and order furniture for my new office, I wanted to make sure these two stubborn boys showed up to this meeting.

"Mama, what happened?" he answered the phone.

"Umm, more than your mama just uses these phones, Karmello."

He chuckled. "Oh, what's up, Kelsie."

"Your mother needs you and your brother here tomorrow. She has to speak to you both about something."

"What she need to speak about?"

"If she wanted me to tell you, then she wouldn't be trying to schedule a meeting with you and your brother."

"Nah, I'm cool on being around Milli."

This was when I had to put on my sister-in-law hat. I didn't care about Mello and Milli's beef, but they weren't going to make my job difficult because they loved to throw their weight around.

"What happened?"

"He swears he's my father or some shit. Last I checked, I didn't come from this nigga's nut sack."

Milli cared about his brother a lot. He always wanted to make sure that Mello was alright. Even with the dumb decisions he had made lately, he still cared about his brother. It was easy for him to scream fuck you and be all team Patsy; instead, he decided to stop getting in the middle of their bullshit. He loved Patsy and he loved Mello, but he realized that he couldn't choose sides because then he would be the one to blame. Patsy would feel some way if he chooses to stick by Mello's side, and Mello felt a way when Milli was helping Patsy get through everything. Once Patsy was straight, he decided to leave all of that to me or Michelle. He checked on her and was always available to her, but he didn't want the drama coming from his brother.

"You know he just wants to look out for you."

"He got his own seed now. Shouldn't he be worried about her?" I could hear a kid crying in the background, so I assumed he had the boys.

"Mello, your brother cares about you. Stop being so shady all the time and accept some of his help. You think Milli wants to see his younger brother fail? He wants the best for you and your kids. Why do you doubt that so bad?"

"Kelsie, you just started fucking my brothe—"

"See, this isn't what we're about to do. I called you to come in because your mother asked. Bring yourself in because your mother wants both of you here. I'll try to remember not to bring up your little comment that you said, asshole." I ended the call and calmed down for a few before dialing Milli's number.

"Hey, baby, what's good?"

He already knew it was me calling him. If his mother called, it was always on her cellphone. When things were slow, I would call him and talk to pass time by. The comment that Mello said was still bothering

57

me. Why did he come at me hard, when all I was trying to do was help?

"Hey, babe. What are you doing?"

"Just woke up. I'm tired as fuck and can't shake this cold."

Milli was so stubborn and hated to go to the hospital. When it came to me or Miracle, he was pushing us out the door and forcing his to go to the doctors. Yet, with him, he was waiting it out and praying that it would pass.

"Babe, you need to just go to the doctors already."

"Hell nah, I can't take the chance of them keeping me. We got that mediation meeting with old guts next week." I laughed because he insisted on calling Marina 'old guts.'

"I doubt that'll keep you in the hospital, Myshon."

"Nah, can't chance the shit. You can get Miracle from the bus?"

Besides the task and meeting I had to go to with Kim, the day was going to be slow. Picking Miracle up from the bus wouldn't be too bad. We would get some time alone and be able to talk. It felt like forever since we had been able to do that.

"Yeah, I'll pick her up. We need some girl time anyway."

"She would like that. Feels like all you do is work, so y'all should do dinner or some shit. I wanted to take you away for the weekend, but I know you aren't going to get away from the office."

"Stop acting like I'm addicted to work. I just like making a living for myself. Guess what?" It had slipped my mind that quick, that Kim offered me my own office.

"What? You pregnant?"

Milli was dead set on making me get pregnant. Right now wasn't the right time, and we needed to get our relationship on the right track before taking on that reasonability. Right now, we were good, but one little fight and we would be at each other's throat. Was it so bad that I wanted to enjoy my man before bringing a baby into things?

"I told you about that, Myshon. You better stop trying to secretly get me pregnant."

"At some point, we need to have a conversation about this baby business. What about me? I want more kids."

"In the future, I want the same thing. Anyway, let me tell you the surprise."

"Ight, what happened?"

"Your mother offered me an office, babe. She really feels like I'm going to do great things for the company."

"That's what's up. I'm proud of you, babe."

"I really feel like I can make a career in this field. By the way, your mother wants you to come to the office tomorrow."

"Oh yeah? For what?"

"She wants you to meet her boyfriend." Lying was bad, but I didn't feel like arguing about why he had to come to the office. This was much easier than being vague on the details of why he had to come in for a visit with his mother. I kind of wished that I did the same thing with Mello, and I wouldn't have got that rude ass comment he felt the need to say.

"Word? I'm in there like swimwear. Need to know who this nigga is and what he wants with my mama."

"Uh huh, you can ask all of those questions tomorrow. So, I'll see you later on tonight, okay?"

"Okay. Love you, ma."

"Love you too, pa." he chuckled before we both ended the call. His ass was always calling me ma, so I started calling him pa. At first, he wanted me to stop, but then in the end, he stopped complaining and went along with it.

After ending the call with Milli, I decided to catch back up on the work I had on my desk. By the time I looked up, Kim was leaving her office with her purse on her shoulder.

"I'm going to sign the papers and do the walk through. Head home and get some rest, both of the boys will be in the office tomorrow and mad when they find out what I'm doing."

"Yeah, Mello isn't the happiest about it. And I may have lied to Milli about coming to the office."

"Whatever that will get them here. Elaine will be coming by for her check, so call and see what time she'll be here."

"Noted and noted."

"And as a surprise, I have some people coming in tomorrow to take some measurements of your new office."

"Really? Thank you so much, Kim. This means a whole lot to me."

"I know. Just continue to keep up the good work and don't slack off. We had that talk once before, so I know we won't be having it again, right?"

"No, we won't," I laughed thinking about the time she put me in my place about skipping out of work to get dick from Milli. Since we had that talk, it was as if something inside of me clicked. It made me think of myself first when it came to my relationship with Milli. He was going to be straight no matter what. He had money out the ass and could retire if he wanted. Me, I had to think of my pockets if we even decided to end things.

"Okay, see you tomorrow, pumpkin." She blew me an air kiss and headed out the door. Her Aston Martin was parked right out front, shining in this gloomy weather.

I called Elaine three times to ask what time she would be arriving. She told me she was ten minutes away, an hour ago. I understood that she had a child and traveling with a child was hard, but damn. If she didn't arrive sooner, I was going to have to leave her check in the mailbox outside of the office, or she was going to have to wait until tomorrow. After calling her and not getting a response again, I packed up my things, grabbed my keys, and headed out in Milli's car to get Miracle from the bus. Elaine was going to have to wait until tomorrow to get her damn check. If she ran into something, I was reasonable and would have arranged for Michelle to get Miracle. She didn't answer the phone when I called back and I had to leave the office, so she was going to have to travel her ass back home because tonight was mommy and daughter night with my princess.

"Hey, Mommy, I missed your face," Miracle said as I helped her into the car. "You smell so yummy." She caressed my face as I buckled her seatbelt.

"Why thank you, baby girl. You smell like paint."

"We painted in school, Mommy. I hate painting in school because those girls don't know how to keep it on their papers." She snapped her neck and rolled her little eyes.

"Oh really? Well then, you need to sit away from them, Toots."

"I tried, Mommy. Where's Daddy?"

"He's not feeling good, so I have him resting at home, okay?"

She nodded her head and stared out the window as I drove to our favorite pizza spot. "Can we bring him some soup home, Mommy?"

"We can do that, Toots."

It was bitter-sweet coming back to our old neighborhood. Bitter, because I had a memory on each one of these streets while going to catch the bus. Sweet, because I knew I was hopping back into this car and going to a nice condo in a safe neighborhood. After getting Miracle out, she danced on the sidewalk the best she could. We loved the pizza at this place and when I could afford it, we would order a whole pie for dinner. Sometimes, I would allow her to bring it for lunch to school.

"Yay! Frank's Pizza." She clapped her hands as we walked inside. This was one of the pizzerias that has been in this neighborhood way before Miracle and I were born. The owners passed it down from generation to generation.

"Kelsie! What you doing here? Heard you left the neighborhood," Frank Jr. called from behind the counter.

With all the robberies happening in all the stores in this area, Frank's never had that problem. I heard it was because Frank Sr. was connected with the mob. Last time someone tried to start trouble in his store, he made a call to his cousin in Jersey named Lorenzo. A few times, I've seen a fancy car or two parked in front of the shop.

"We moved, but there's no pizza like Frank's where we live."

"Nonsense, pizza is pizza," he laughed.

"Now, you know you don't believe one word that came out of your mouth."

He laughed and waved us over to a booth in the corner. "The usual for you and Magic," he smirked waiting for Miracle to correct him.

"It's Miracle, because I'm a Miracle," she corrected him.

"I know, I know," he chuckled and got right to work on making our pepperoni pizza with a large coke and apple juice on the side.

It felt nice to be out and about with my Toots. With working and school, we hadn't had time to just spend time with each other. Then, the whole court situation was in the back of mind all the time. Why couldn't Marina just leave well enough alone? Why couldn't she live with the fact that her son was scum and he signed his rights to his daughter over? As a mother, she had to see my hesitation when it came to allowing Miracle to go over there. Last time she was in her care, she pawned her off to Marcus and he nearly killed her giving her pineapples. So, who is to say that she won't have him around her?

"Baby, what's going on with you?" I questioned. Miracle was always ready for girl talk with me or Michelle. So, when she popped them lips and turned her full attention to me, I knew she was about to give more than an ear full.

"Mommy, can I be honest with you?"

"Of course."

"I don't want to live with Nana. I love Nana, but I don't want to live with her." She surprised the shit out of me when she said that.

Milli and I tried not to talk about it when she was around. It was time I stopped underestimating my own child and realize that she was growing up. The same things I used to be able to hide from her, she now understood and was afraid.

"Toot, where did you hear that from?"

"You and Daddy were arguing about it the other night. I love living with you and Daddy, Mommy."

I reached over and moved her curly hair out of her face. The look of fear on her face hurt my heart because this was something she shouldn't have to worry about. "Toot, Mommy and Daddy are going to do their best to prevent that from happening. You know Daddy doesn't take no for an answer, right?"

"He's stubborn, like you say," she giggled.

"Exactly. So know that you will always live with us, okay?"

She nodded her head and patted my hand. When she did that small gesture, the tears poured down my face. This little girl that almost didn't make it into this world was all mine. I had a part in raising her and instilling some of the compassion she carried in her heart. This little angel was all mine and I was happy that I got to share her with Milli. He was doing more than I could have asked for when it came to Miracle. She was finally witnessing what it was like for a father to care about their child.

"Yay pizza, Mr. Flunkie!" she yelled and purposely messed up his name.

"Flunkie? Okay, Mirror," he chuckled and set our pizza down. He tickled Miracle before going back behind the counter and taking more orders. Miracle and I dug into the pizza and enjoyed our little time together.

I struggled to carry Miracle, her book bag, and my purse upstairs to our condo. The doorman was nice enough to grab Miracle for me and help me upstairs. When we made it to the door, Milli heard me struggling with the keys and opened the door for me.

"Appreciate it, Trev." He nodded and took Miracle from the doorman. "Why you didn't call me, I would've came and helped you."

"It's fine. I know you're sick and being stubborn about going to the doctor."

"Yeah, whatever. Let me get her in pajamas and we'll chat," he told me and took Miracle into her bedroom.

Milli spared no expense when it came to turning one of the spare bedrooms into Miracle's Winter Wonderland. The whole entire room was white with sparkle snowflakes on the wall. Everything was what she wanted and Milli made sure of that. While he got her settled, I put his soup into a bowl and heated it up for him. Miracle wasn't trying to head home unless we stopped and got him soup from somebody's restaurant. Milli came out the room with her laundry and tossed it on the pile that was sitting near the laundry room.

"Why is that there?"

"I tried to do some laundry this morning. Shit is hard as fuck to do and I got tired," he admitted and I laughed.

"Humph, not as easy as you always make it seem. I'll start a load tonight and look over some of this homework that Miracle rushed in the car."

"What's this?"

"Soup. Your daughter didn't want to come home unless we got you some soup."

He smirked and smelled the soup. "That's really my baby, yo."

"She has you wrapped around her finger. Spoiled little ahh." We both broke out in laughter as he sat at the table. After reading through Miracle's homework, I put it back in her book bag and stared at this man; my man. Milli was so damn fine that my kitty jumped each time I laid my eyes on him.

"We gonna talk about this baby business?"

When he was dead set on something, he wouldn't leave it alone. If I didn't decide to have this conversation with him now, he was going to continue to harass me until I decided to. Since we lost our baby, I was scared to have another baby.

"Can we have it in the bedroom? I want to pull my clothes out for tomorrow and shower." He agreed and followed while slurping the soup into his mouth. "Can you not slurp? I know Kim didn't raise you like that."

"That's the beauty. I'm in my own damn crib and can do what the hell I want," he shot back like the smart ass he was.

"Whatever, Milli. Now, what do we need to discuss?" He watched as I walked in and out of our closet and grabbed clothing to match together.

"Why you don't want to give me a baby? This a dead ass question too. I wanna see where you coming from, babe. I'm trying to understand you."

Sighing, I leaned on the closet door and stared at him. "You really want to know?"

"Wouldn't be asking unless I wanted to know, ma."

I walked over to him and sat down next to him. Milli placed his bowl on the night table and pulled me onto his lap. "Pa, I'm so scared to bring another baby into this world. Maybe God was telling us something when I lost the baby."

He grabbed my face and stared right into my eyes. "That bastard took our chance at welcoming our child into this world. I believe in signs, and the signs I've been given was to keep you and Miracle close to me. Ma, I want a baby with you more than anything, this parent shit is me. I've never thought that I was the type to settle down and be a parent or have one chick on my arm. Coming home, and knowing that y'all here or on y'all way home warms my heart."

"I love what we have, but I don't want to mess that up. Miracle is older now, babe, she wasn't always this age and it took a lot of patience and sacrifices."

"You don't think I know that. Money ain't an issue, so what's your excuse? I'm not going no damn where and I don't care how much we argue about the shit. We in this shit for the long run, you heard?"

"What about my career? After I take the test, I'll be jumping right in and doing things with your mother. How does a baby fit into all of that?"

"How do millions of women do it every day? Kels, you making up hella excuses right now, but it's cool."

"Pa, don't be like that." I caressed his face.

By now, we both knew when we each needed our own space. The look in his eyes told me that he needed his own space right now, so I kissed him and went to soak in the tub. It was easy to make the decision to have a baby. Then, once you're pregnant, all those questions you should have taken into account before making the baby comes up. Milli deserved to be able to witness having a child from birth. I loved him so much that I was willing to take this leap and have a baby with him. Some of my excuses were valid, and then the others were bullshit and he knew it, that's why he called me out on it. After a long day, all I wanted was to lay back and soak in this tub, then jump into bed and snuggle with Milli.

Milli

Kelsie was so set on not driving to the office together this morning. She claimed that she had to go handle something and was going to be an hour late. I didn't know what the fuck she was up to, but I was going to let her rock and try not to question what the fuck she was up to. Bringing up this baby shit may not have been the right time with the court mediation with Marina coming up. Kelsie was probably stressed as fuck and this was bringing more stress to her, so I wasn't going to bring it up anymore. When she was ready to settle down and have another baby, then that's when we would have another child. Right now, Miracle was all we needed with her spoiled ass. We had to think about her and her feelings when trying to have another baby. Miracle had mentioned it once before, but it was only because her little friend's mother was pregnant. She came in questioning where babies came from and all that shit, so I shut it down and handed her a hundred-dollar bill. That still wasn't enough because she continued to question me all night, until I told her the whole stork story. The way she stared at me let me know that she didn't believe it.

When I walked in, I had to remember that Kelsie told me she would be getting her own office. Elaine's desk was right in the center of the room and some woman and man was measuring shit to the left of the room and talking amongst themselves. Elaine was too busy in her phone to realize that I had even walked through the door. When she finally looked up from her phone, she realized that I was standing in front of her. Usually, she would flip her hair or do some shit she thought would turn me on. Today, she nodded to the back where my mother's office was and powered her computer on. Shit, that meant I didn't have to speak, so I headed back to my mother's office. She was going through some papers when I tapped on her door. With her glasses on the bridge of her nose, she stared up at the door and a smile spread across her face.

"Hey, baby, you're here early," she smiled and came around the desk and hugged me. "Where's that woman of yours?"

"She told me she had to take care of something. What's with sour puss in the front?" I pointed out toward Elaine.

"Oh, she's mad because Kelsie is getting her own office," my mother explained and walked over to her door. "She better fix that damn face before she's standing outside on the unemployment line!" she yelled out the door and closed it behind her.

"Damn, Mama. That girl had been working here before Kelsie."

"Yeah, and that girl has never asked to know the business. She hasn't showed any interest in what we do here. If anything, she's ready to snatch her check on Friday and get the hell out of here. Kelsie came in and was curious. You can see the eagerness of learning real estate on her face. I see a lot of myself in that woman. Elaine is a good girl, just has her priorities wrong, and that's starting with that damn baby daddy of hers."

"That's her business though, Mama."

"It becomes my business when all her nigga's little girlfriends come to my place of business. I don't know how many times I've had to argue with them in front of the store. Baby, you don't know the half with this girl," she sighed.

"I see. Where's homeboy?"

"What?"

"Your little boyfriend," I replied and she smiled and waved someone in.

"I see someone got some act right into them," she smiled at Mello. He hugged my mother and sat down beside me. "Got your face trimmed and haircut, good."

"What's good, bro?" I tried to dap him and he ignored my hand. "Bet."

"Bet what? You gonna put hands on me, right?" He pumped his chest out like he was about to do something.

"You both better get it right or put that shit on mute. I refuse to have both of you in here fighting."

"Bitch, I just walked into this bitch and you wanna try me!" I heard Kelsie's voice and ran out the room.

She and Elaine were both in each other's faces arguing. Kelsie still had her purse on her arm with a cellphone in the other. "Call me a bitch one more time and I'll show you how this bitch gets down," Elaine threatened and Kelsie laughed.

"What the hell is going on?" My mother pushed through both me and Mello.

"I just finished setting up a time with the clients from last week.

The house in Long Island that's 1.5 million. They want to come in and put an offer on the house later today. This bitc—"

"You're better than this, Kels. Don't stoop to her level," My mother told Kelsie and you could tell she was counting down and trying to contain her anger.

"Sorry, Kim, but this girl walks up on me, in the middle of the conversation, and starts tossing around that because I'm fucking Milli that I got an office."

"Did the clients hear?"

"I'm pretty sure she did. She screamed excuse me into my ear before I hurried her off the line."

If looks could kill, Elaine would have been on the floor bleeding out of her mouth. "Elaine, I've been nice and understanding to all the bullshit you've brought through those doors. When it comes to the money that feeds my family, I don't play like that."

"Why does she get treated to a better position and an office? I've been here way before she has. Kim, I respect the shit out of you, but that shit isn't fair. Why? 'Cause she's fucking your son?"

"I'm tired of everyone tossing that shit out there. First Mello, now you. Everything I've done to get this job and keep it has nothing to do with Milli!" Kelsie screamed and stormed out of the office.

I ran out behind her and caught her just as she was about to jump into the car. "Ma, what you mean?"

"Babe, I'm tired of everybody feeling like because I jump on your dick most nights that I'm incapable of giving advice or even doing a damn job."

"That's what Mello said?"

"Yeah. I tried to give him some advice and he basically implied that because I'm fucking you that I can't give him advice. Something like that." She waved her hands and wiped her tears.

"Where you about to go?"

"I just need to cool down. Tell your mother I'm taking the rest of the day off," she told me and kissed me on the lips.

Once she was in the car and pulled off, I went back into the store where my mother was ripping Elaine a new one. "The only reason your ass isn't fired is because I give a shit about your baby and don't have time to train someone new. Try some shit like that again, and you'll be out before your shoes hit the threshold of this office, hear me?"

Elaine nodded her head and sat down at her desk. Mello and my mother went back into her office and I stood in front of Elaine. "What? You here to add on to what your mother said."

"Why you fucking with her?"

"Because I can do what the fuck I want. It ain't like I'm not telling the truth. Nobody can't tell me that she ain't get that job because she slobbing your knob."

"Mess with my girl again and I'll make sure your only source of income is from slobbing on knobs," I told her through gritted teeth.

One down and now onto the second one. My mother was laughing with Mello about cute little grandkid shit and I didn't give a shit as I interrupted. "Why the fuck you telling my girl that because she's fucking me, she can't give advice?"

"Language please," my mother said.

"Because she thinks she can tell me something. She need to calm down because she just jumped on your dick full time."

"Yo, who the fuck you think you're talking to? Nigga, I'll knock your fucking jaw the fuck off." I walked closer to him.

My mother jumped up and tried to jump in the middle of us. Mello took his shirt off like I gave a fuck about his little strip tease. "Nigga, I've been ready. You swear you bigger and better, nigga."

"I am bigger and better. Get the fuck outta here, little shrimp po' boy." I waved him off.

"Enough both of you. Stop before y'all say something you can't take back." My mother pushed me back into the corner of her desk.

"Nah, let him go, Ma. Let his little brother knock the shit out of him."

"Nigga, you a clown for real. What kind of nigga ignores his wife for the next bitch? Same bitch that turned around and cheated on your dumb ass. You gave up a damn diamond for a piece of glas—"

"Enough, Myshon."

"Nah, Mama, he need to fucking know. This nigga walking around all mad at the world, when he fucked his own life up. You fucked up your own shit and now you're paying for the shit. Can't even go home and climb into bed with your wife and daughter. Guess what the fuck I'm doing every night? Sliding into bed with my girl and my daughter every night, and you mad as fuck."

Mello rushed toward me and pushed my mother onto the floor. I saw red and punched the nigga right in his face. He stumbled back a few and I knocked the shit out of him. He fell to the floor and was out cold. I went and helped my mama off the floor. She had tears coming down her face as she looked at Mello onto the floor.

"Fucking knocking my mama on the damn floor. I'm sorry, Mama. He needs to know that he's the fuck up, not none of us."

"I didn't want you two arguing and fighting like this," she sobbed into my chest. "He's knocked out on the floor, Milli."

"He pushed you on the floor and came at me. What the fuck was I supposed to do?"

"I don't know, baby… I wish you boys would get along," she told me.

Kissing her on the forehead, I picked Mello up and leaned him in the chair. After splashing some water in his face, he woke up and stared around the room confused.

"Let me make one thing clear, knock my mother off her feet again and I'll put a bullet in your chest, heard?"

Mello didn't say anything and honestly, I didn't need him to say anything. His presence alone was pissing me off, so I had to leave before I punched his ass once more. I kissed my mother and headed out the office. Elaine's ass was doing her damn job when I got to the front room. I chuckled and left the office. Mello had me so pissed that I had to get up with my nigga, Thor. Dialing his number, I waited for him to answer.

"What's good, nigga?"

"I need to talk, where you at?"

"The restaurant. Come through," he told me.

"Say less," I replied and jumped into my whip and headed to the restaurant.

It took me no time to arrive at the restaurant. Maggie was leaving when I was walking in. Don't ask me how Thor got Maggie to get her shit together. All I knew was that the restaurant was booming and was the talk around the city. Thor was sitting at the bar when I walked in. I took a seat next to him and he poured some liquor into the empty glass.

"Sounded like you needed this, what's good?"

"I just had to lay my fucking brother out. Nigga came running at me and shoved my mama onto the floor."

"You lying? Fuck is going on with Mello?"

"Shit, I was about to ask your ass. He really be on a hate campaign since Patsy filed the divorce papers."

"Who can he blame for that though? He fucked around and lost his family because of his crazy ass decisions. Homie need to be worried about his seeds and not hating everybody else."

"That nigga never had to take responsibility for his shit. I bet he wished that I had some part in this shit so he could push the blame off on me." Thor poured some more liquor in my glass and I took it back to the head.

"What your moms had to say?"

"Nothing really. She was crying and shit. She's really trying hard to hold him accountable for his bullshit. I got my own life I'm trying to live and don't need to worry about my brother out there wilding in the streets."

"Kid need to realize that, although we're not in the streets anymore, niggas are still green at the fact that we're still getting money like we're hustling. Niggas won't hesitate to catch him slipping to get back at you."

Thor was always thinking two steps ahead. I left the game because it wasn't the same. I tried not to have enemies and leave shit on a good note. Still, there was niggas that wasn't happy that my name was still ringing bells and I was still raking in the dough. Mello was a prime target because they knew he was my brother and the shit would hurt. Mello needed to realize that the clubs wasn't somewhere he needed to be frequenting. If he wanted to work shit out with Patsy, he wasn't going to find the answers in the fucking club.

"Word, but what's going on with you and Michelle?" I was tired of speaking about Mello's ungrateful ass.

"Shit, we cooling and waiting on baby boy. I know I'm tired of waking up and making her all this weird shit she been craving."

"My god son should be coming soon, right? We all waiting on his stubborn ass," I laughed.

"You? Nigga, all I think about is my little shorty. I can't wait for him to enter this world for real."

"What y'all doing as far as the wedding?"

"Michelle wants something small. She doesn't want to plan a whole thing, but then changes her mind every other day. When she makes up her mind, I'll let you know." He chuckled and grabbed some nuts from the container. "How are you and Kels?"

"We good. That whole court shit is in the back of both of our minds. Other than that, we rocking."

"No babies yet?" he joked, not knowing I was dead serious about having a baby with Kelsie.

"Stop playing. She doesn't want to have none right now. All she keeps coming up with is hella excuses that can be fixed."

Thor shook his head. "Y'all didn't lose the baby too long ago. Why the rush, nigga?"

"To be real, seeing you and Mello be fathers has me wanting more kids. Miracle is my angel, but she needs siblings. Seeing Kelsie pregnant with my baby and us building a future together, got me excited. I've been thinking about putting the condo on the market and getting a crib out the city."

"Word? Your moms might kill you, you dropped bank on that condo."

"I know. With all the upgrades and shit, I can put it on the market for more money though."

"You spoke to Kelsie about it?"

"Nah. I think I'm just going to do it."

Thor patted my shoulder as he walked around the bar. "See, y'all gotta stop doing that shit. Mil, you know you're my nigga, but tell her about it. Matter fact, don't tell her, ask her what she thinks. When you moved her into the condo, you made that both of y'all home. How you think she gonna feel uprooting to a new crib without having a say? She's not Miracle, she's an adult and your woman, feel me?"

As I was soaking in what Thor was telling me, I realized that it wasn't right. How could I be mad at her for not being honest and telling me shit, when I was about to do the same thing? For the past few weeks, I had been looking through some listings my moms had. The condo life was better when I was single. The more I thought about me having to carry Miracle from the parking garage because the walk was too far to our front door made me want to move even more. When she wanted to go out and play, we had to take the same walk to the whip and she was tired by the time we arrived at the park. A backyard with a pool and space for her to play was good for us. Right now, I had a decent size closet, but with all Kelsie's shit, I didn't know how much I can say that it was decently sized. She had taken over my entire side and was working on the spare bedroom. Soon, we would need more space and I'd rather it happens now, rather than later.

"You right. I can't even be mad because you're absolutely right."

"Talk to shorty and be real with her. What's the worst that can happen?"

Once I downed my drink, I nodded my head in agreement. The most she could say was that she wasn't ready to move yet. It wasn't like we were running out of space in this exact moment. All I wanted to do was make it easier on Miracle at the end of the day. Making her life easier was number one on my list.

"Yeah, I'm gonna holla at her tonight about it. We got into something small last night about the baby situation. I wanna smooth shit over with her."

"Never go to bed upset, bruh. I never believed that shit until getting Michelle. I never want to sleep next to her mad as shit. Fix it and find a common ground. Y'all not going to agree on everything."

"You right." I looked down at my phone and sighed. Sonya's ass had just called me and then hung up. I knew she wanted me to call back so we could strike up a conversation. Little did she know, I slid my finger across the screen and blocked her number. Kelsie wasn't about to go upside my head for seeing her number in my phone.

"I know I'm right. Nigga, I'm a genius." Thor chuckled and fixed himself another drink. "Some chick booked a dinner for her birthday tonight, so I'm gonna be working late."

"You really happy running this shit?"

"On the real? Yeah, this shit is peaceful and I don't have to look over my shoulder. I'm making money for my family the legit way."

"What about the guns? What we doing with those? Niggas been hitting us up and we've been ignoring them. Yung also been questioning shit."

"Yung need to calm his ass down. I'm not in a rush to re-up on guns right now. With my seed on the way, I don't have time to be out there."

"You know I'm not going to make no moves until you're ready. Take your time and get your family and household in order."

We dapped and continued to drink like he wasn't running a business. A few people came in for lunch and the staff seated them. In between kicking back with Thor, he took a few calls and ordered some more shit for the restaurant.

"You know what I've been thinking?" He broke our silence.

"What?"

"This shit right here is good. I'm bringing in good money and everybody chatting about it. When I first started looking for places, we ran into this nice ass place in the city. Big ass place, we should go half and make that shit the upscale jawn to this one. Make it a little strip joint."

"Word? You wanna open a strip club? I'm down all the way, where I toss my money at?"

"Nah, seriously. Some nigga gave me the idea the other day. Him and his lady was sitting at the bar having dinner. When she went to the bathroom, he was talking my ear off about the food and about how he wished the strip joint he frequented in Jersey had food and drinks like this. Niggas would pay money to see a good piece of ass."

He was onto something and thinking back to when I was single, I used to make it rain in the strip club. The stale ass chicken wings they served wasn't the best, but then again, I was there for the chicks so who was I to complain? If they had some bomb ass food and drinks that weren't watered down, I sure as hell would have been in that shit like I lived there.

"About these women of ours…." My voice trailed off and Thor choked on his drinks.

"I know right off the back, Kelsie not going to be with the shits. Michelle, might think of the business side before she thinks of the chicks."

"If you wanna make this a real thing, let's get to work on doing

81

what we gotta do. You know my money always good, so let's get this bread together." We both dapped hands and took a shot back to celebrate a new business venture.

Thor was like my brother, nah, he was my brother. So, if he thought something was a good move for us, then I was going to trust it and rock out with it. In the end, all I was trying to do was build my money up. It wasn't just me anymore, I had a family to provide for and I'd be damned if I let them down. When I told Kelsie, I was done with games and I wanted to be with her, I promised to take care of her mentally, physically, and financially. Kelsie didn't want nor need me to take care of her financially, but I took that upon myself. She spent so much time struggling to make ends meet for both her and Miracle. Now it was someone else's turn to look out for her and give her what she wanted.

"For sure." Thor dapped me and I got up.

"Let me head to the crib. I wasn't even supposed to be out this long, but that Jack Daniels helped with this cold."

"Wait, I got some soup Maggie made. Shit mad good and spicy," he told me and went to the back. He came back ten minutes later with a to go bag. "I added some hot wings in there for Kelsie."

"Always coming through. Kiss Chelle for me and we'll get up soon," I told him and headed out the restaurant. Once I jumped in my whip, I headed home to take some medicine, smash down this food, and sleep for the rest of the day.

***

"Babe, what the?" I heard Kelsie squeal as she violently shook me. "Why do you have sauce all over the bed, your clothes, and face?"

When I opened my eyes, it was bright as fuck. I remembered closing the shades and making sure the lights were off. Glancing at the clock on my side table, I realized it was nine at night. The brightness that was burning my eyes weren't the opened curtains, it was all these damn lights Kelsie had on.

"Shit, that soup and chicken had a nigga gone. I didn't even know I fell asleep with the shit in my arms," I chuckled and leaned up on the bed.

"Good thing your mother picked up Miracle tonight. What happened today with you and Mello?"

"Knocked that nigga out. Tried to run up on me and got put on his ass…. I don't even feel like speaking on that nigga."

Kelsie nodded her head and put her purse down. "I miss my cousin," she blurted.

"Go see her. You acting like she's dead or something."

She sighed and wiped her tears. "I feel like I'm holding everything in and I'm at my breaking point. Michelle is pregnant and doesn't need to hear my drama," she continued to whine.

"How many times have you come through for your cousin? You don't think she wouldn't want to be there for you? Y'all more like sisters than cousins, so knock that shit off."

Wiping her tears, she stared at me and nodded her head in

agreement. "I just feel so bad tossing all my shit onto her."

"Then tell me, what's up?"

She turned around and sat Indian style on the bed facing me. "Us. I don't want to be in this relationship and I'm holding you back."

"How you feel like I'm holding you back?"

She stared down at her hands and then looked up into my eyes. "You want a baby. Why wait on me when you can have a baby with anybody."

"I don't want to have a baby with anybody. Let me ask you this; you don't want to have another baby?"

"I want to have another baby. Milli, I'm scared of having another baby with you. It's something about our relationship that I love, but it also scares the hell out of me. What happens if things go wrong and we have a baby on the way?"

"Things can go wrong now and we have a child already. All that shit you speaking on is fear, and with fear, you're never going to do anything. I'm not rushing you, so take your time, ma. I'm happy to just come home and know you and Miracle is right here with me."

"You're right, pa. It's just something I need to work on, but enough about me. What did you do today besides be violent?" She giggled.

"Stopped by and chopped it up with Thor for a bit. We chatted about some business and shit we want to do."

"Ohh, what business?"

"We want to open a strip club." Soon as the words left my mouth, she screwed her face up and rolled her eyes. "Hear me out, we gonna serve the food he does at the restaurant. So, it'll be a lounge too."

"So, if I wanted to come with the girls, I can come and not see sweaty hoes shaking their asses?"

"Yeah, it'll be a private area for the fellas."

"Hmph. I don't know, Milli. You being around all that pussy and calling it work. That's like your dream job."

"You trust me?"

"You know I do."

"Then you know I'm all about stacking that money for us. I'm not thinking about those chicks on the pole. They making a living for their family too."

"Well, I needed money but my ass didn't jump on a pole."

"You not them, and they're not you."

I laughed because she still had this stank look on her face. She wasn't feeling this idea, but she knew to let me rock. Those chicks couldn't do shit for me and I wasn't thinking about them. Right now was as good of a time to ask her about moving.

"You're right about that."

"What you think of putting the condo on the market and getting a house?"

"I like the condo, what's wrong with it?"

"Ma, I know how hard it is to get Miracle to the door. This shit is good for me and you, but her walking all the way from the parking garage is hard on her sometimes. Just last night, you had the doorman carry her to the door."

She sighed and agreed silently. "You're right. I just don't want you to give up your things because of Miracle's disability."

"It's no sweat for me. I want to make sure she's comfortable and doesn't have to struggle. We need more space anyway."

"How? This place is big enough for both me, you, and Miracle."

"So, you want to stay?"

"That's not what I'm saying."

"What you saying then?"

"Babe, I'm going with whatever you think is best for our family. If you think moving is smart for us, then I'm not going to argue. We're a team and I trust anything you do is for the best."

"Come here." I waved her over to me and she crawled over to me. "I love the shit out of you, ight?"

"I know that now." She stared up into my eyes as she stroked my cheeks. "You know I love you too, ight?" she mocked me.

"Yo, I'm 'bout to whip your ass, keep mocking me," I threatened and tickled her.

She giggled and then sat up. "Change these shits because you have food everywhere." She prepared herself to get up and I pulled her back down.

"Nah, you love me, so you gonna lay in this with me."

"Eww, Myshon, I'm not about to lay in buffalo sauce with you. I bet Thor sent those for me, didn't he?"

"Nah."

"You're such a liar." She slapped me and then rushed off the bed, giggling. "Clean this mess up or I'm sleeping in my baby's room."

"Shit, I'll join you," I yelled back and chased her ass out the room.

Thor

*M*aggie's ass ended up being late back to the restaurant. She knew we had booked a birthday dinner and she left my ass to handle this shit with our staff. Thankfully, I knew a little something about the damn business or I would have been screwed. The dinner went off good and the girl even asked about renting the whole place out for her best friend's birthday dinner there. Apparently, her friend was a big deal that needed to rent the entire place out. Shit, I didn't care because that meant more money in my pockets. Knowing I had a seed and a soon to be wife, I needed all the money I could get. After making sure the staff knew what to do, I went and sat in the back office and caught my breath. I didn't give enough credit to Maggie because she ran this shit and never complained. Once in a blue moon, I came in and helped her when I didn't have shit to do. With Michelle's mood swings, I was dipping out the house more often. One minute, she was horny and wanted to fuck me, then the next she was crying about some shit that had nothing to do with us.

Maggie plopped down onto the couch in front of the desk and scrolled through her phone. She sighed and then set her phone down onto the side table. I watched her and didn't bother to ask what was wrong. Right now, we were in a simple place where she didn't ask about my business and I didn't ask about hers. After all the shit she put me through, she was lucky to even have a paying job to take care of her son. When she sighed even louder, I knew she wanted me to ask her what was the matter.

"You good?"

"Why do men feel the need to play games? If I like you and you like me, why can't it be that simple?"

"Women play games too. You told him that you like him?"

She rolled her eyes and started scrolling her phone again. "No, but he knows I'm feeling him and hasn't even made a move. Why are we still in this weird friend zone?"

"You want him to pick up on signs and you're the one playing games. Tell that nigga how you feel and boss the fuck up."

"It's easier for men. Women aren't like that and I'm not going to tell him and get my feelings hurt, nope."

"You just said the nigga liked you."

"He acts like he does... what if I'm just looking too far into things?" I wanted to tell Maggie to focus on her son and stop worrying about niggas. But since I didn't feel like having to bark on her tonight, I figured I'd shut my mouth and be happy that she wasn't worrying about me and my girl anymore.

"You're a big girl and you'll figure it out," I told her and stood up. "I'm about to head home, I won't be in tomorrow because I have some shit to do."

"Cool. I know what to do. Have a good night," she called as I walked out of the office. "Wait, how's Michelle and the baby?"

"They're good. Any day now, we're on his time."

"We're always on their time. Tell her I asked about her," she smiled and I nodded my head.

Maggie had it in her head that she and Michelle were friends. Michelle didn't dislike Maggie, she just couldn't see herself hanging around her. Especially since she felt the need to try and fuck our relationship over. My baby went from that soft spoken, non-confrontational person, to this woman who spoke her mind and didn't give a shit how you felt about it. Maybe it was the baby, but it was more her if you asked me. After handing the staff all a hundred-dollar tip for coming through, I headed out and straight home. It was nice living not too far from the restaurant. I checked my watch and knew Michelle was still up. We were at the point in our pregnancy where she was always uncomfortable and could never get comfortable. Her sleeping pattern was fucked up so that meant mine was fucked up too.

Parking the car, I headed upstairs and unlocked the door. The lights were off and the TV's flashing from the bedroom could be seen into the dark living room. Kicking my boots off, I made my way into our bedroom to find Michelle crying. Shorty was crying like she lost a brother or some shit. Rushing over to her, I sat down and held her in my arms as she continued to cry.

"Babe, what's the matter?"

She sniffled, then broke down again in tears. "Wh…why did it have to end?" she continued to sob into my chest.

"End? What ended?"

"Dorothy just had to get married and now all the girls are split up," she wailed loudly.

Was she serious? She was in here crying over the damn Golden Girls. I didn't want to say the wrong thing because she would swing on me and call me insensitive. This pregnancy shit was confusing as fuck and I was winging it each day. A day she didn't break down or throw something at me was a good day.

"Babe, you know this show like twenty years old, right?"

"It doesn't matter, Shannon! She had to go get married and leave them. She left her own mother and went with Blanche's uncle," she cried out again.

"Ight, stop crying and upsetting my baby. This is crazy."

Her body jerked away from me and she looked at me in disbelief. Like I had just cursed at her and slapped her around. "Get your ass in the living room. Since you think I'm so damn crazy, sleep in the living room away from my crazy ass!" she screamed and tossed pillows at me.

"Yo, what the fuck, Michelle? I came home and all I wanna do is lay up with my fiancée and rub your belly and feel my son."

"Shannon, I will leave and go to Patsy or Kelsie's house. Leave!" she threatened and tossed her bottle of water at my head.

"Can't win for losing with this, man!" I barked and punched the wall.

The baby was probably making her crazy. Not even probably, I knew the baby was making her crazy. The doctor warned me that her hormones will be crazy and it would scare me at times. When he told me, I didn't take him seriously. I just thought that she would shed a few tears and that would be the end of it. Michelle was going through some demon hormones because she was putting a nigga through it. At the end of the day, all I wanted was my son and Michelle to get through delivery happy and healthy.

I took a quick shower and went into the living room. After watching the late-night show for a bit, I grabbed a pillow and blanket out of the hall closet and got comfortable on the couch. I might as well turn the living room into my bedroom. All I did was get yelled at and tossed out here, while Michelle laid all in the bed comfortable. Let me stop, knowing my girl was comfortable while carrying our child made this much easier. This was something I always wanted. To have a woman who loved me and saw past all the money and shit that I could do for her. To have a child with that same woman and give her my last name. Michelle came into my life when she was broken. One would see a woman with all the issues she had and run the other way. She made me want to dig deeper and get to know the real her. What did she like, what did she dislike? Tasheem had her mind so warped that she wasn't thinking for herself anymore.

Watching my baby break out of that shell Tasheem put her in was like watching a butterfly burst from a cocoon, or whatever that shit is called. Getting to know her mother and step-pops and seeing where she came from also put the missing pieces of Michelle together. It was all a part of God's plan because now, we were welcoming our baby very soon. I would be lying if I said I didn't miss my mother every day. When I get down about it, I just thank God for the many blessings he keeps putting in my life. The Lord knows I tried to help my mother. There was no limit to the amount of money I would spend to keep her clean. Every day, I blamed myself because I should have stayed instead of running to handle business. If I didn't go, she would have probably been alive right now. Asking Michelle to babysit her was too much. She had just been released from the hospital from a scare with the baby. All I pray is that my mother is finally at peace up there. It wasn't too long before I closed my eyes and got as comfortable as I could so I could be knocked the fuck out on this couch.

The cable box read four in the morning when I heard sniffling from the baby's bedroom. Wiping my eyes, I got up from the couch and stretched before walking. You know when you just wake up and walk how everything be cracking? My damn feet, knees, and legs were all fucking cracking. When I got to the baby's room, Michelle was in the middle of the floor with a bunch of our son's clothes surrounding her. Tears were pouring down her eyes and she was tossing clothes like a mad woman. Yo, she had to be one of the worst pregnant women I've ever experienced. Patsy was so calm and cool when she was pregnant. Besides being emotional with the shit with Mello, she was laid back and wasn't going through this shit like Michelle.

Getting down on the floor with her, I stared at her and didn't say anything. I mean, what can I say? It seemed like everything I said these days was wrong. Just a few hours ago, she hit me, tossed pillows, and cursed me out for being insensitive over the Golden Girls. She wiped her eyes and then studied the shirt she was holding in her hands.

"I… I can't do this, Shannon," she sobbed and wiped her tears with the shirt.

Touching her hand, I rubbed it. "Can't do what, baby?"

"Be a mother. I don't want to give birth and have this baby. I'm going to fail him as a mother, I'm too weak," she continued to cry.

Pulling her over to me, I was low-key cautious. Last thing I wanted her to do was swing on me. "You're not weak, babe. Why you saying that about yourself?"

"Shannon, how am I going to be a mother to him? He'll run over me, I allowed Tasheem to run over me. What's so different with my son?"

"Because he has a father that'll spank that ass. Not to mention, you're not the same person you were a year ago, babe. Michelle, you've changed so much… look where the fuck I'm sleeping?"

She laughed and wiped her tears from her eyes. "I can't control it. It's like fire burning inside of me and then it comes out as tears and frustration. I'm really trying." She hugged me around the neck and I kissed her cheek.

"Aye, listen to me. Don't you ever say you're a weak woman. I would never put a ring on your finger if you were. You're so much stronger than you give yourself credit for. Stop with all that, we moving forward not backwards."

"I'm sorry," she apologized like she had done something to me.

"Stop apologizing. You know what your problem is? This house. I'm calling Pat and Kelsie and they're going to take you out before the baby comes."

"I do miss my girls," she sighed.

"They miss you too, so you're going to hang out with them later today."

She put her face into my chest and agreed. We sat on the floor and folded all the clothes up and I put them away as Michelle watched. She was so giddy after damn near throwing a whole tantrum. Me putting the clothes away, turned into me moving a dresser and changing table, then fixing some other shit. Michelle was acting like this was the afternoon and not early in the morning. Still, I did it because it put a smile on her face and I didn't want her crying anymore.

"Can I go back to sleep?" I questioned and she nodded her head. She reached her hands up and I helped her up from the floor. "What would you do if I wasn't here to lift you up?"

"Crawl to the bedroom and then get into the bed," she replied and waddled back to the bedroom. As I was walking past the bedroom, she grabbed my hand and pulled me into the bedroom. "I want you to lay with me," she whined.

Climbing into our king size, plush bed felt like baby angels were caressing my joints. Michelle got comfortable and I palmed her stomach like I always did before we fell asleep. Feeling how tight her stomach is, was amazing. It really felt like a basketball. I could only imagine how uncomfortable it was to try and sleep with that on your stomach. When I heard her snoring, I bent down and kissed her stomach and then wrapped my arms around her and fell asleep.

Michelle

*P*regnancy wasn't what I thought it would be. Women on the commercials or shows made it seem like it was such a beautiful thing. Don't get me wrong, it was something beautiful. Still, there was so many things that your body went through that wasn't beautiful. My stomach was stretched to the size of a watermelon and I had more stretch marks than I had when I started. My emotions were never one emotion. Instead, I was happy, sad, and mad within minutes of each other. Sleeping was unbearable and if I wanted a good night's sleep, I usually had to sleep with my back up against the headboard. Then the contractions that I felt were no joke. Everybody, including my doctor, kept telling me that it wasn't anything compared to the real thing. One thing I did feel bad for was the way I acted toward Thor. When I was feeling emotions or pain from sleeping, when I stared at him sleeping peacefully, it just made me upset. He was the one who did this to me and here he was getting a beautiful night's sleep.

The fun part was doing the nursery with Thor and being able to buy all of his clothes. He was fully prepared and all we were waiting for him. My hospital bag was packed, the suite for the hospital was booked, and both Thor and I just couldn't wait for this to be over. Holding my son in my arms would be something I would remember for the rest of my life. The one thing we hadn't done was move into our townhouse. I knew this place was entirely too small and had way too many stairs for me to bring the baby home to. This condo was holding me here and I couldn't figure out why. Maybe because it was the first time I truly felt like it was home. Would the new place feel like home to me? Prolonging the move was irritating Thor, so I knew we needed to move quick.

Being nine months pregnant and due any day, I really needed to have things together in that place. Titan's room was crowded with all the things we bought for him. My mother and stepfather were back and forth from the place they were renting here in the city. They were coming in this week to finally stay until the baby was born. When my mother left to head back to Florida, I promised her that I would be in the new place. I also promised that I would stop being difficult with Thor. I lied twice because the things I promised I would and wouldn't do, I haven't and have done.

"Babe, I'm about to head out. Kelsie and Patsy are coming to pick you up, alright?" Thor bent down and kissed me. He looked from my face to the computer screen. "Why you looking up more shit? Where we going to put it?"

"Why are you picking on me? This stroller is super cute."

"Yeah, but where we going to put it, Michelle? Babe, you need to stop and allow us to move into the new place. It's no way we're going to be moved in before he comes, but at least we've started."

"The only thing that excites me about moving is being close to Patsy."

Thor kissed me once more and then headed to the door. "We're moving into the new crib and I don't want to hear shit. You got me paying a mortgage on a place that we're not even living in," he replied and headed out the door.

I guess I needed someone to tell me what to do. If it was up to me, we would have still been in this condo with a baby in tow. Change was coming and just because I didn't move, didn't mean that things would stay the same. A baby, husband, and a new house were a lot of changes that I had prayed for. Now that they were happening and happening so soon, I was scared. Would I be an amazing mother and wife? Could I take care of a home much bigger than this, have a career, and manage to be a good mother along with being a wife? These were all things that kept me up at night. My career was important to me, but with a child and a husband, my career was pushed to the bottom of the list. I worked so hard to have a career when Tasheem ruined it for me. The one thing I didn't want to do was give it up and become a stay at home mom.

It was no secret that Thor wanted his wife to stay home with his kid. Working and being a mother was a no for him, and he had no problem telling me that. When he thought about his wife and kid, he thought of his wife being home and having dinner ready for him. It wasn't like I didn't know that Thor was traditional and wanted me barefoot and pregnant. The more time we've been together, I thought that it would change. Maybe he would see that I was a career woman and that I could be both. Dinner wouldn't be hot and fresh from the stove, but Uber eats would be one minute away with a hot meal.

"Why you sitting here with the door opened?" Kelsie came into the house and came to kiss me. She rubbed my stomach for a few and then pushed it to see if Titan kicked back. When he did, she got excited and kissed my stomach.

"I was supposed to lock it behind Thor. He had literally just left, you didn't see him?"

"No, I took a cab over here. Patsy said she'll drive, so I'll have her drive me home when we're done. What's going on with you, darling?"

"Pregnant and uncomfortable."

"I can't relate. With Miracle, she was born early so I never got to that stage of pregnancy. It'll be over soon, you look like you're about to deliver soon." She pushed a box and came around the kitchen counter.

"Don't start." I knew where she was going soon as she kicked the box.

"You told us you didn't want a baby shower and we allowed that. Instead, we bought you a whole bunch of stuff for the baby, but why is it all in the living room and kitchen? When are you going to move?"

"You must have seen Thor because he just told me we're moving and he doesn't care what I think."

"Good. Why are you holding onto this condo? It was nice when it was just you and him, but with a baby, it's going to be too small for you guys."

"Why are all of you on my case today? We're going to move, so enough," I snapped.

"Pregnancy has made you an evil little something," she giggled. "We're moving too. Milli thinks we need to move so it's easier on Miracle."

"Easier?"

"Yeah, the walk from the car garage to our front door."

"I never even thought of her. It is super long and I can see her getting tired from that walk. This is a good move for the both of you."

"I'm excited and scare—"

"When a bad bitch walks through, she shuts it down," Patsy sang as she walked into the condo with a fur coat on, Birkin on her arm, and a pair of six-inch heels.

"Why are you so dressed up and happy?" I questioned. Last we spoke, she was stressing over her and Walt's situation.

"Girl, God woke me and my baby up this morning. I got money in the bank, roof over my head, and keys to a new G wagon, so I'm blessed!" she yelled and went into the fridge and grabbed a water bottle.

"Walt gave you some dick last night?" Kelsie questioned.

"Hell no, I just sat down and realized I need to stop stressing about things I can't control. Mello will sign that paper when he's ready and Walt and I's relationship will happen when it does."

"So, you don't want to be divorced from Mello now?" Kelsie and I both asked at the same time.

"Yeah, but what is me rushing and pushing him to sign going to do? It's going to stress me out and it has. Not to mention, the longer he waits the more leverage I have on my end. What's going on with you two? Feels like I haven't kicked it with the girls in a while."

"We haven't," Kelsie replied. "Michelle's pregnant, you're a mommy, and I'm always working."

"Ain't that the truth. Mello came and picked Mella up this morning with KJ. I asked him about Kenzel and he shrugged me off. Guess something must have happened."

"Kenyetta probably being extra petty. She knows it'll hurt him," I responded.

"Probably… What's going on with you, Kels? Y'all went to court or what?" Patsy clapped her hands together.

"This week for mediation. If we can't agree on nothing, then we'll go to court."

"Old bitter bitch," she rolled her eyes. "What's going on with you and Milli? Feels like I haven't seen him in a while. Well, I saw his work, not him."

"His work?" I asked confused.

"Mello got a huge cookie on the side of his eye. Asked him what happened and he told me Milli snuck him… Milli got up in that ass and that made my day too."

"Damn, when will they get it together."

"Mello needs to learn how to stop blaming everybody for his shit," Kelsie blurted. "Anyway, I'm thinking about taking my birth control out."

"When did you get one in?" Patsy asked.

"After I miscarried, I got one in place so that it would never happen. Milli thinks when he doesn't pull out that I'm gonna get pregnant. He's been wanting a baby and I've been ignoring him about it. We finally had a talk and I feel better about it."

"You don't need to feel better about it. You need to be ready and willing to have a baby with him. Remember, he wants this baby, but we have to carry and do all the pain for this child," Patsy told Kelsie.

"I want another baby. I'm scared to have another one because of Miracle. What if the baby doesn't have any problems, what am I going to tell Miracle? She'll probably feel sad."

She leaned on the counter and sighed. "You tell Miracle that she's a blessing. A special gem that we all were blessed with. You can't stop and let Miracle scare you from having a life. She's so happy that you and Milli are together and are her parents. You don't give her enough credit, Kels." She nodded her head at me.

"I lied and told Milli it was because of us. I'm scared that if I have another disabled child, he'll blame me like Marcus did." She wiped a tear. "I know he wouldn't do that because he took Miracle in and doesn't give a damn about her disability. It's something in my mind that makes me believe that."

"Marcus made that fear real for you. Milli is nothing like Marcus and will love this baby. He doesn't care if something is wrong. You need to stop thinking like that." Patsy hugged her.

She took a deep breath. "I think I'm going to take my birth control out."

"Yay, another baby. You going to tell Milli?"

"Michelle, do you want me to sleep on your couch? He would be hurt if I told him that I got on birth control and never told him."

"Y'all weren't together when you did it though," Patsy pointed out.

"I still didn't tell him. When he would say, he wasn't pulling out tonight, I would laugh and act like I could get pregnant. It's best for me not to mention anything to him and just get it removed quickly."

"You think lying is better?" Patsy narrowed her eyes at Kelsie. "Y'all whole relationship was based around both of you keeping things from one another. You think that's smart?"

"Yes. It's something small, Pat. You acting like I'm lying about a whole big thing." Kelsie started to get irritated.

"Whatever, your life." Patsy sat beside me. "What's going on with you, mama?" She looked to me to update her on everything.

"Pregnant."

"That's her answer to everything," Kelsie laughed.

I guess she could laugh now that the heat wasn't on her. Although she and Milli promised to stop keeping things from each other, it was in Kelsie's blood. She was so used to handling things on her own. She didn't know what it was like to make decisions with someone else. Even though it was her body and she was free to do whatever she wanted, she still should have a conversation with Milli. They weren't just playing cat and mouse games anymore. They were house hunting and raising a child together. It wasn't just her and Miracle anymore, it was her, Milli, and Miracle now.

"Well, I went over and tried to borrow sugar and realized that the townhouse is still empty," Patsy joked. "What's going on with that?"

"We're moving, leave me alone," I laughed. "Y'all are too nosey."

"When? Because this baby isn't going to wait until you're moved in."

Patsy reached and rubbed my stomach.

"I know. It'll get done, even if we have to bring the baby to this house for the first few months."

"It's not going to take no damn months to move y'all in. Thor got too much and know too many people. Anyway, what we doing because I'm hot with this damn fur on?"

"I need to go shower and get dressed, so take it off until we get going," I told her and went into my bedroom to find something to wear.

One of those contractions ripped through my back and I leaned onto the bed. I didn't know which were the Braxton Hicks or the real thing. I guess it wasn't the real thing because I didn't go pee and my son fall out into the toilet. Slowly, I made it into the closet and found something comfortable. These hoes weren't about to catch me out in jeans and heels. A comfy pair of sweats would do just fine with a T-shirt.

Mello

$\mathcal{M}$ella's ass wouldn't stop shitting, so we couldn't make it out the crib. Patsy told me to come get her and spend some time with her. When I arrived, Patsy was dressed like she was about to become a hustler's wife all over again. She even hugged me and kissed Mella before shoving me out the door with her car seat. It was early as fuck in the morning, so I headed back to my crib and we fell back to sleep. Now, here it was the afternoon, and I couldn't get out the door because she kept shitting all her diapers and KJ didn't want to hold her diaper bag. How the fuck did women do this shit with two or three kids? Right now, I was over here struggling and we hadn't made it down the hallway to the elevator. Mella's diaper was lighting up the hallway with that stank ass smell, and all she was doing was blowing spit bubbles and laughing.

"You think it's funny, huh? Why you giving Daddy so much work?" I asked her and looked back at KJ. He was right behind me, but the diaper bag was back at my door. "KJ, go and get your sister's bag now," I added some authority into my voice.

He blankly stared at me and ran to the elevator to push the button. "Dada, I pushed the button!" he yelled like I was going to be excited for his hard-headed ass.

"Now go pick up your sister's bag or I'm going to beat your little ass."

Again, he stared at me blankly and leaned against the wall as if he was waiting for me. Sitting Mella's car seat down, I walked back down the hall and grabbed the bag. The elevator opened and KJ was about to sprint inside of it.

"Wait one second little one, where are you going?" I heard a familiar voice. Seconds later, Choc stepped out the elevator. "Are these escapee's yours?" she giggled as I walked back down the hall.

"You don't even want to know the half." I chuckled.

"It's funny I run into you because I was coming to bring you the papers. I know I was supposed to bring them that day, but I had to head out to my second job."

"Nah, don't worry about it. What's the verdict?"

"Everything is done and went through perfect. Welcome to Waldorf's Apartments." She held her hand out and shook mine.

"Thank ya, Thank ya. I hope that brought you a nice little commission."

"It did. So, I guess I should thank you as well. Uh… do you need help?" She looked down at Mella and then KJ going through the diaper bag I was holding in my hand.

"Nah, I got it."

The way she was smiling and staring at me had me wanting to ask her out. Then, I thought of all the shit I was going through. I didn't need to drag another woman through this. It wasn't fair to her. Not to mention, a woman should be the last thing I was thinking about. Still, asking her out was on the tip of my tongue.

"Well, enjoy your new condo. Make sure to watch these little ones. Would hate to see them hitch hiking next time I run into them," she joked and pressed the button to the elevator.

"I would hope you would bring them back to me."

"Of course." She winked and stepped into the elevator. The moment I planned to take was gone and here I was in the hall with a daughter with shit on her and a son who was in desperate need of a damn nap.

Instead of continuing with the day, I turned around and carried all the stuff back to the apartment. It was supposed to snow anyway, so where the fuck did I think I was going with two kids? Soon as we got into the apartment, I changed Mella's diaper and placed her in the bouncy shit that Patsy sent me with. Once she was out the way, I went and got KJ down for a nap. He fought me for a minute until he laid there with his sippy cup staring at the ceiling. By the time I made it back into the living room, Mella was sucking on her fingers on her way to sleep too. Seeing both kids going to sleep at the same time was better than sex.

Just as I was about to make me a quick sandwich, my phone started ringing. It was a FaceTime from Kenyetta. Answering, I stared blankly into the camera; probably looking exactly like KJ was staring at me.

"Where's my son? I want to speak to him," she immediately demanded. Shorty didn't even ask if I was straight or even greeted me.

"He's sleep."

"Okay? I still want to speak to him so put him on the phone," she continued like she was the ruler of what the fuck I did.

"If you know what I had to go through to put h—"

"To be honest, I really don't give a shit. This is what I do all day everyday with two kids. So, I really could careless, Karmello!" she yelled through the phone. Mella jumped and then started crying. "Oh, Patsy got you babysitting your daughter too."

"I'm her fucking father, I'm not babysitting shit. He's sleep and unless you come knock on this door, I'm not going to wake him."

"I swear I should have just brought him with me." She rolled her eyes.

"Babe, you good?" I heard in the background and she smiled.

"I'm fine, babe. Give me a second, he spilled juice all over himself." She knew the shit was pissing me off because she kept smiling.

Hearing her with another nigga didn't bother me. Kenyetta wasn't Patsy, so I didn't give a shit about what nigga she was fucking. Listening to her tell another nigga to take care of my son pissed me off. I've been there since he came out and this was how I was repaid. How was I supposed to just act like he didn't exist? How did fathers walk away from their seeds like it wasn't nothing?

"I'll have him call you when he wakes up," I told her.

With a smile on her face, she twirled her hair around her fingers. "You good? You're not looking too good right now."

"Nah, I'm fine... how about you? I heard being a hoe takes a toll on you." Her face dropped and the FaceTime ended.

You ever have one of those laughs that you have to bend over and grab your knee? Well, my ass was bent over and grabbing my knee because the shit had me weak. She thought she was making me upset when I didn't give a fuck about Kenyetta. She could have ten dicks in her at one time and the shit wouldn't bother me the least. All it was about was my son and making sure she was doing her part when it came to him. Anything else was irrelevant to me. I grabbed the papers that Choc handed me and found her office number. I dialed down to her number and waited for her to answer.

"Choc Aarons, how may I help you?"

"It's Karmello. How you doing?"

"Considering that I just saw you, I guess I'm doing fine. Did I not explain something to you?"

"No, I'm actually real confused. Can I get a second of your time?"

She sighed. "Sure, do you mind if I bring my lunch? I literally just got it delivered and I haven't eaten all day."

"You good."

"Be there in a few minutes."

A smile crept across my face as I got Mella back to sleep. I put her in the bassinet that I had for her. KJ was knocked out cold while holding onto his little cup for dear life. While I was brushing my teeth, there was a knock at the door. As I quickly spit the toothpaste out my mouth, I rushed over to the door. Choc was standing there with a salad, bottle of water, and purse in her hand.

"You were dead ass about your lunch?"

"Yes, I'm starving and it's super busy down there. Valentine's weekend is coming, so everyone is booking like crazy."

"Oh yeah, I forgot about Valentine's Day."

"Me too. Ain't no romance in my life, so why would I remember... I think the whole thing is dumb anyway. It was a massacre."

"Word. Come into the kitchen." I waved her over to where I was attempting to make a sandwich.

"Why didn't you just order one? Room service still comes up here even though you're leasing."

"Oh word? Thought all that shit ended when you started leasing."

"Uh, no. The amount you're paying for this place, they should come up here and feed it to you," she joked. "Now, what aren't you understanding?"

I smirked as I smeared mayo on my sandwich. "Y'all clean the pools in the main area?"

"Are you serious? You didn't have a question," she laughed as she tossed a lettuce across the counter.

"So, maid services come with it too? 'Cause I'm gonna need one after you."

"You just made me bring my entire lunch up here for that dumb question. What do you want, big head?"

"Word? I haven't heard someone call me big head since I was a kid."

"I'm a throwback type of chick." She smirked and chewed her salad slowly.

"Nah, I wanted to talk to you. You obviously don't got a man, or he's not doing a good job of keeping romance in your life."

"And you're better?"

"Shit, I might be."

"I highly doubt that. You have two kids and their mother isn't nowhere to be found. In fact, you told me you were separated."

"Mothers."

"Great. I always attract the niggas with a bunch of kids and baby mamas." She slapped the table then continued to eat her salad.

"What's wrong with a nigga with kids? I see you didn't get up and leave, so what that say about you?"

"Oh, I'm going to continue to eat my lunch. You dragged me up here under false pretenses, so I'm going to finish this food."

"Why you judging me though? I feel real judged."

"I am... why you have so many baby mothers?"

"First off, I got two. One is my wife, so she's not just a baby mother. The second is a baby mama, so I won't deny that."

"At least you spend time with your kids. That's more than I can say about some of these men." She rolled her eyes. "Make these kids and then want to spit in the mother's faces by running off."

"The women are to blame too. They know half these niggas ain't shit and get involved."

"So, they're to blame because they choose to see the good in niggas? We know some of y'all ain't shit, but choose to believe that y'all just need some guidance or a good woman."

"You can't change a man if he already showed you who he was the first time."

"Maybe that has some truth to it."

"You know it does. That's why your ass stopped chomping down on that lettuce like that."

She tossed another lettuce and laughed. "Oh, shut the heck up."

"Let me take you out. Me and you, no kids; I promise."

She debated with herself for a few before she finally looked up at me and smiled. "I might be asking for trouble saying yes. I guess we can go for a drink or something."

"You doing it right now."

"What?" she asked completely confused.

"Figuring out how you can get to know me and change me if that's necessary."

She closed her container and then leaned further onto the counter. "How do you know that I don't want a nigga with money?"

"Because a chick that just wanted money wouldn't say that. Trust, I've been with chicks that just want the green. You got a good job too, you don't need my money."

"I wouldn't say my job is great," she sighed. "The title is misleading. All I do is try to get long term guest to lease. The higher ups sit behind their desk and send me to do their job. Meanwhile, I get paid for how many people I can get to lease their rooms or suites."

"Shit, I couldn't tell. You came with these heels and looking like you own the place."

"Presentation is everything, huh? Bet you thought I drove some foreign car and live in a condo right here in the city."

"You don't?"

"Boy, please. Now that you've wasted enough of my time… I need to get back to work." She stood up, straightened her clothes, and then tossed the container into the trash.

"When can I take you out?"

"Tomorrow night. You can meet me downstairs after my shift."

"Bet. See you tomorrow." I walked her to the front door.

She stepped out the door and turned around. "And don't you ever lie to get my upstairs. You're too cute to have to lie to get a woman to your room," she winked and walked down to the elevator.

"So, you think I'm cute, huh?"

Choc pressed the elevator button and smirked before she spoke. "I didn't say all of that."

"Nah, you just said that."

"I'll see you tomorrow, Mr. Gibbens," she told me before she stepped onto the elevator.

Quietly closing the door, I went and sat on the couch. I dialed Patsy's number because she didn't tell me when she wanted me to bring Mella back to her. I would be a fool to think that she would be spending the night with me. Patsy was overbearing with our daughter, as she should be. Mella was only a couple months and she needed her mother more than she needed me.

"What's up, Mello? I'm still out with the girls," she explained soon as she answered the phone.

"You wanted me to keep Mella for the night? I don't mind and I have plenty of breast milk you sent."

The line went quiet.

"Mello, I really want you to be there for Mella, but I'm not pre—"

"You good, Pat. I'm not tripping on that. She's still young and you don't feel comfortable with her being with me overnight."

"It's not that I don't feel comfortable. I trust that you'll take care of her. She's just still my baby," she laughed.

"Alright, helicopter mom… want me to bring her to you tonight?"

"I can stop by and pick her up. I'll be in the city to drop Kelsie off anyway, so I can just stop by and get her."

"Bet."

We ended the call and I decided to bring KJ to my moms tomorrow. She had been wanting to take him to the toy store like she promised weeks ago. KJ couldn't listen to anything else, but when his nana spoke he damn sure listened and straightened up his act. Kenyetta's petty ass still had me boiling like she could make me jealous. If she wanted to fuck that nigga, then she was free to do that. Playing both sides with a little boy I've grown to love was fucked up. Kenzel wasn't a pawn and it wasn't right that she was acting like he was. Shorty really had me fooled with the way she was acting. All along, I thought she was goodie-goodie and she was really fucking another nigga and hiding her pettiness. All I could pray was that this new nigga really wanted to be a father and didn't just want to fuck Kenyetta.

I don't know when I fell asleep, but all I heard was knocking on the door. The kids were still asleep and I was shocked as shit. Picking myself up from the couch, I went to the door and opened it. Patsy walked in still looking like she was about to go meet with her trap king husband once she left here. Maybe she did this on purpose, she wanted me to drool or some shit. 'Cause a nigga's tongue was on the damn floor. She set her bag on the coffee table and turned to look around my new place.

"This is nice. How long you've been staying here?"

"A few weeks. Can't bring myself to stay at the crib anymore... I gotta put it on the market." I stuffed my hands in my jeans pocket and leaned on the wall near the kitchen.

"I wish you would stop and put it on the market. Why are you paying to stay here when you can stay at your mother's house?"

"This is my new crib. I'm leasing it now. What I look like still staying at my mama's crib."

She rolled her eyes and walked over to the kitchen. "Leasing? Why? That makes no sense when you can buy a place and build equity. You're paying out the ass to stay here."

Shrugging my shoulders, she turned on her heels and looked my way. "Doesn't matter. I didn't feel like looking for places and this place was perfect."

"Your brother is about to move. Why not buy his place, you know what it looks like? Plus, it's big enough for you and the kids."

"Fuck outta here. What I look like living in his shit?" The shit had me so mad that I contemplated on tossing her ass out my condo. Why would she even think I would move into Milli's old shit? "Fuck I look like getting a hand me down condo?"

"Wow, you really hate your brother. Nobody else would have looked at it the way you did. We're not handing down sneakers or clothes, it's a condo you can buy from your brother."

"Don't matter. I don't want to buy his fucking condo, Pat."

"Does this have to do with what went down between you two?" She walked closer to me and stared up into my eyes. It was as if she was searching my eyes for something and when she didn't find it, she backed up some.

"He sucker punched me… Fuck that nigga, he always felt like he was better than me."

"He's your brother, Mello. Milli has always wanted better for you than himself. Remember when he tried to send you to college? You fought him and argued that all he wanted was to be the only nigga running things in the streets. Milli has always done for you and wanted better for you. Why do you fight that?"

"He only wanted me to go to college so he could continue to ball out. Fuck that shit, I got in the streets and made money just like him. Look at the life we live, Pat. What would I be doing if I went to college?"

"Maybe playing ball, or running a business the legit way. Your brother has always wanted better for you and you've always rebelled against him, and even I know that. How many times have I had to lay in bed and listen to you complain about him… Mello, you hate your brother and for some reason, I can't understand why. He saved my life, your daughter's life, and you hate him with a passion." She touched my chest and then walked to the back.

While everyone loved to think that my mother babied me, she did. Still, when it came to things she always went to Milli. She never came to me to handle anything. When something was wrong, my mother was always calling, or going to Milli about what she needed. When I asked her to let me handle something, she looked at me with a smile and patted my cheek and told me not to worry myself. I'm a man too and just as capable of handling business like my brother. Even when I married Patsy, bought a home, and was handling business, she still saw me as a little ass boy. Milli was in the club, fucking bitches, and making dumb ass decisions, but I was still considered the little boy.

"She's been sleep the whole time? Baby got drool on her little lips," Patsy laughed and laid her down on the couch and started putting her snowsuit on.

"Yeah, I actually fell asleep myself. You woke me up when you knocked on the door. KJ still sleep?"

"He was just waking up when I walked in the room. He's still a little dazed, so he'll be running out here soon."

Tomorrow I had a therapy session with Patsy's therapist. I didn't think I was the type of person who would benefit from therapy, but I was. Talking with her made me feel like she wasn't judging me. She was genuinely listening to me and offering me helpful tips. My mind was on getting my wife back, but if I couldn't, then it would be nice to have a friendship with her. More than anything, I wanted her to trust me again. Look at me with those same brown eyes that trusted my every move. Although she was cordial, I could tell she didn't trust me as far as she could throw me.

"I got a therapy session in the morning… You want to come with me?"

She placed Mella's arm through the snowsuit and then started to button it up. "For what?" she questioned, not bothering to look my way.

"Because I want you there."

Patsy laughed to herself and stood up before she picked Mella up and placed her into the car seat. "I don't think there's a need for therapy. We're on our way to divorce soon as you sign the papers. Me sitting in on your session is going to do nothing for me."

"It's not supposed to do something for you alone. It'll do something for us."

"Mello, please just stop before you hurt yourself. It's bad enough that you want to use my same therapist, but I refuse to go to therapy with you."

"I'll sign the papers if you go with me." It was my last attempt to make it better. I prayed that after our session, she wouldn't feel the need for me to sign it anymore.

"Tempting, but I'm not going. Sign those papers because you want to, not because you're trying to bribe me. It's not like I'm getting married anytime soon anyway." She grabbed the carrier, diaper bag, and purse and headed out the door.

"Pat, I've been begging you for months. Babe, forgive me, I've learned that I fucked up."

"Have you, Mello? You haven't learned your lesson at all. Learning your lesson isn't sitting in therapy and thinking that's pleasing me. Go because you need to fix yourself, not because you think that'll bring you closer to fixing our marriage."

There was nothing left for me to say because she hurried down the hall. Soon as she got on the elevator, I closed the door. Sure enough, KJ was coming out the bedroom crying. He was probably hungry and got scared from being in the room by himself.

"Aye, stop crying, man…. You want some food?"

He nodded his head at me and extended his hands for me to pick him up. I picked him up and went into the kitchen to make him some food.

***

"Sorry for running late. I had to drop my son off to my mom's crib this morning," I apologized as I rushed into the office.

She was sitting behind her desk and looked up from her computer. "It's fine. Take a seat and I'll be right over. Do you need water, coffee, or tea?"

"Nah, I'm straight. Had me some orange juice before I left my mom's crib."

"Noted." She smiled and continued typing something up before she walked over to her seat. Slowly, she sat down and crossed her legs then set her notepad in front of it. "So, what's new with you?"

"Patsy let me take our daughter by myself yesterday. Had her the whole entire day."

"Exciting. How did that feel?"

"Made me feel like I was gaining her trust back. Since Mella has been born, she hasn't let me take her out the crib unless my mother was with me, or she was going with me."

"You have to understand. That's how mothers are with their babies. It has nothing to do with her lack of trust for you as a husband. I think Patsy knows you're a good father, it has nothing to do with that."

"In that moment, it made me feel like we were going somewhere. She was being nice to me and shit, and didn't have this sour look on her face."

"Have you signed your divorce papers yet?"

"Nah."

"Why not?"

"Because I don't feel like it. Why everybody rushing me?"

"I'm not rushing you. Do you feel like everyone's rushing you?"

"Yeah. Everybody always questioning me about it. Do I get a chance to process that my marriage might be over?"

"Might?"

"Yeah."

"Do you feel like there is hope for you and Patricia's marriage?"

"I do."

"Why do you feel like that?"

I grabbed a pillow from beside me and messed with the fringes on it. "This pillow ugly as fuck."

"Karmello?"

"Because we grew up together. All my first, I've done with her. I mean, not losing my virginity because I was getting pussy before her."

"You love Patricia?"

"More than myself."

"So, why did you ignore her? What inside you caused you to lose focus on your marriage and sought out another source?"

"Man, why do men do half the shit we do?"

"I'm not asking men. I'm asking you."

"How many times am I going to repeat this shit to you and Patsy?"

"Until you start to feel, Karmello. You don't realize that you just say things and don't feel them. The only time you've felt was when your wife served those same papers right in this office."

"You don't think I feel? I'm feeling the shit every time I walk into my empty condo. Each time Patsy sends me a video and I'm smiling while watching my daughter on my phone, instead of being there in person."

"So how did your wife feel? Explain the level of hurt she felt?"

"I hurt her bad. She was really hurt behind the bullshit that I did."

She jotted something down and then stared at me. Before I never felt that she judged me, but today that changed. "Can I just be honest with you?"

"That's why I pay you."

"Your wife was crying out for you. She needed you more than

she needed to breathe. Patsy watched her mother drink and destroy both of their lives. That woman never had a childhood because her father enabled her mother. The little bit of childhood she had was the few months or month her mother was cleaned. So, for this woman to turn to the one thing that single handedly destroyed her childhood and took her mother, she must be low and desperate for help."

Listening to her break down how Patsy felt put things in perspective for me. When I thought of how hurt she was, I never thought of the alcohol part of her hurt. All I thought about was the lonely nights and all the times I skipped out on her because I didn't feel like arguing with her.

"Damn."

"Deep, huh? Now just sit and think on that for a few, then I'll ask the question again." She sat back further and picked up her coffee mug.

While I was dipping around and loving on Kenyetta, my wife was sitting home waiting on me. I was telling Kenyetta shit about my wife that should have never been mentioned. All for what? Because she wanted to spend time with me. All I complained about was how Patsy nagged me. She nagged me because she gave a fuck about me and wanted to make sure I was always good. The small shit she did for me made me realize that I was the fucked up one. All she asked was for her husband to come home and sleep next to her at night. And if I couldn't make it home, she wanted me to call to make sure I was straight. She wasn't asking me to stop running the streets or choose her or the streets. Somewhere, things changed and I can admit that it was me. When we met, shit was fun and carefree. Once we got married, I can admit that real life happened and I wasn't ready for it.

Instead of partying and chilling on the block with my niggas, I was forced to spend time with my wife. Doing stupid shit like shopping for cribs or furniture. When my niggas called to come out, Patsy pouted and never wanted me to go out. Eventually, I felt like I was suffocating. That was around the time I ended up meeting Kenyetta. Hearing my wife go down voicemails and messages that I've sent Kenyetta probably broke her spirits down more.

"I did love Kenyetta. Now that I'm caught, I can't deny it or say that I didn't love her."

"Did. What changed?"

"The bitch lied and betrayed my fucking trust. She fucked another nigga and then tried to pin his baby on me. I would say that qualifies for hate."

"So, what happened to your wife happened to you?"

"That's exactly what happened to me."

"Channel what you felt when you found out Kenzel wasn't your son. How did that make you feel?"

The tears were burning my eyes. I hated showing emotion when it came to this topic. I've never been hurt so bad in my life. Reading those results in the car made me feel like someone ran me over then pissed all over me. I felt disrespected, disregarded, and less than. The woman I held higher than my wife, the same woman I ruined my marriage over, lied to me. Not only did she lie to me, she had sex with another man, unprotected and had me taking care of the baby. I held this little boy when he came out the womb. Handed him my last name and had no problem signing the birth certificate.

"Go ahead. Let it out."

My tears flooded down my face as I leaned back and stared at the ceiling. Just going back to that day that changed my entire life hurt like a bitch. Then thinking of the petty shit that Kenyetta was doing with Kenzel, hurt me even further.

"If Pat felt half of how I feel about what Kenyetta did to me, I understand." I sniffled and grabbed the tissue she offered me.

"It's easy to say you hurt someone. It's another thing to feel what they've felt. You may never feel what your wife felt during that time, but just that you feel a small piece means you can start on repairing your relationship."

"You do think there's hope for our marriage?"

"No. Karmello, when I say repairing your relationship, I mean before you were married. Before you took the steps to make her your girlfriend then wife, you were friends, correct?"

"Yeah."

"You need to take a step back and take your marriage out the equation. Fixing your relationship is more important than trying to fix your marriage. People end up in marriages every day and have shitty relationships with each other. She needs to trust you as a friend before you both can take steps into fixing your marriage. Don't go into this thinking you'll get your wife back, because the reality is that, that may never happen. Go into this trying to get your friend back."

When I thought about it, I never put it like the therapist did. All I was thinking about was trying to put my marriage back together. How could I do that when Patsy couldn't stand me as a person? We needed to get back to that place where we would laugh about anything and wanted to spend time together. Back to the times, when she would call me when anything exciting happened to her. The time before I took her virginity and we ended up getting into a deep love, then marriage. In all honesty, I did miss my friend and I would do anything to get her back.

"You're right. I gotta get that out my mind and focus on what's important."

"Schedule your next appointment with my secretary. Remember what we spoke about today, Karmello. It's hard, but nothing easy is worth doing."

Before leaving the office, I stopped by the bathroom to make sure my face was straight. Fucking therapist made me cry and that wasn't what I planned on doing. I needed to stop worrying about my marriage and start working on my friendship with Patsy. If I couldn't have her as my wife, even though that would be hard, I would rather have her as a friend.

Choc

"We know you all have been working hard on building our leasing division up. We've decided that we're going to bring in a qualified team to handle this department. Don't worry, you'll all still be able to sign guest up for leasing agreements." When the words left my supervisor, I felt like I had been punched in the throat.

"What does that mean for us? You promised us that we can take over the leasing division if we got guest to lease. I've been getting guest to lease with us for four months."

"I said we would possibly open it up for you guys. You're not out of a job, Choc. The owners think it's best if we bring some people who are more qualified."

Grabbing my purse, I stood up and stormed out. They were barely paying us enough as is, then they wanted to bring more people to take jobs that we earned. I was so tired of this job, but I needed this job more than I needed air. Moving from Delaware to New York was a big decision, but I had a whole plan in my head. Since my adoptive mother had died, I felt the urge to find my birth mother and she lived in New York City. Well, the last place listed on my adoption papers said she was. We had an open adoption, but she never reached out or tried to have a relationship with me. It was just me and my mother before she passed away from a car accident. A drunk driver crashed into her at red light and totaled the car with her inside of it. I've never felt hurt like I felt having to be the only person there to bury my mother.

She was white and adopted a chocolate baby. When she held me in her arms for the first time, she knew that we were supposed to be together. So, she named me Choc. Her parents didn't agree with her adopting, then adopting a black baby was worse. My mother called off her engagement at the time and signed those papers. There wasn't a thing I needed growing up with her. She treated me like her own and raised me without a man. Of course, some men came and went, but that never took away from the love and the way she raised me. When she passed, I felt like I lost a part of me. Now, it was just me in the world and I had no other family. Since her parents never approved, I never met them and even if I did, I would refuse to meet them.

Soon as I walked into the lobby, Karmello was sitting there on his phone. When he noticed me, he waved me over and I took a seat on the chair across from him. I was silent as he was finishing up his phone call. He sounded like he was getting heated by each second of the phone call. Once he was done, he stood up and shoved his phone into his pocket.

"You ready?" I nodded my head and we both walked alongside each other out of the hotel. It didn't take a rocket scientist to figure that we both had bad days today. Even though mine was considered a bad minute. My day had been going pretty good until my supervisor came into the office with this bullshit.

"What bar do you want to head to? I know a cool one two blocks down so we don't have to drive."

"It's cold as fuck out here. You think I'm 'bout to walk down these blocks."

Laughing, I shook my head because he had on a cashmere sweater with no coat. So, of course he was going to be cold. "Stop trying to be too cool and put on a coat. A cold don't care how cool you are."

"I drive, so I don't like all that bulky shit on me. I'm in and out of my destinations," he clarified.

"It's two blocks down. When we're done, I can walk back to the hotel and get my car."

"Bet," he said as he held the passenger's door open for me. His Lexus truck was real nice and had that new car smell. It resembled a spaceship with all the navigation and buttons that was up front.

"Karmello, this is really nice," I complimented.

"Just call me, Mello. You remind me of my wife each time you call me that," he chuckled and pulled off.

His driving could be better because the nigga pulled out and didn't look right or left. Then, he was doing fifty miles per hour with a thirty speed limit. I didn't know what he did, but for my sake, I prayed it wasn't drugs. Because a chick didn't have time to be getting pulled over by the police. Like promised, the bar wasn't too far and we found a parking spot right out front. Getting out the car, I hopped down and walked to the door and pulled it open for Mello.

"Damn, this really some little stuffy place," he examined the place. It was a small place that seated a few people. During the day, it was business men trying to grab a drink before heading back to their demanding offices. At night, it transformed into a mini club that ended up in front of the club because there were so many people. The owner was some white man that owned this property since the sixties. He had told me his story on how many developers wanted to buy him out because his bar was an eyesore. Some even offered to him to renovate it into something nicer. Each time, he refused because he wanted to stay true to his business.

"Yeah, but it's nice and the drinks aren't watered down. I think this is the only place in the city that you can still get buzzed off a Long Island Iced Tea."

"Shit, I haven't had one of those in a good while. Last one I had tasted like damn juice."

"You, my friend, will get to witness a real Long Island Iced Tea." I patted his shoulder as we slid into the booth in front.

"Their food isn't too good. I usually get fries and eat those between drinks so I don't get buzzed too quickly."

"You sound like a damn pro or some shit," Mello joked as I waved the bartender over. Once she took our order, we both stared at each other and wondered what to say next.

"Did you have a bad day? I noticed from your conversation."

"Yeah, I don't feel like talking about it."

That was fair. He was entitled to feel how he felt and not want to talk to me about it. "Look, I'm not trying to get in your business. We're both here having drinks and we can probably help each other with our problems."

"I just had a full morning of telling someone my problems and then the chick made me cry."

"You cry? Nooo," I sarcastically laughed.

"Shut up… I'm just going through shit with my wife. She filed divorce papers and I don't want to sign them. So, I've been going through therapy trying to fix myself and my marriage."

"Why does she want a divorce? It's not every day that a woman just files for divorce unless it's some shit."

I could tell from his face that he didn't want to reveal why his wife filed for divorce. It must have been some deep shit because, when the bartender brought our drinks over, he ordered another one.

"I did some shit that I'm not proud of."

"What was it?"

"I cheated on my wife with another chick and had two kids with her." He paused, then he continued to tell me everything that happened. At one point, it looked as if he was about to break down and cry right here in the bar. Still, he held it all together.

"Damn. You really fucked that woman over," I blurted.

There was no need to sugar coat shit and try to make him feel better. He cheated on his wife and she damn near lost her life and the life she was carrying. He was acting like he was the one who was cheated on when he found out that his side chick had fucked another dude.

"You don't have to say all that."

"But I do. Your karma was that little boy not being yours. Serves you right." I sipped my drink and took some fries from the plate.

"Damn, you asked me and I told you, now you're ganging up on me."

"It's not ganging up on you, Mello. You're not a little boy and I'm picking on you. As a grown man, you know what you did was fucked up. Have you apologized?"

"Yeah."

"No, have you really apologized and showed that you were truly sorry for your actions? Sorry doesn't change things, but it can make things a little better. I mean, at least she knows you're sorry and you care to show her that you're very sorry for what you've done."

"The thing is, she's not feeling it. Before she was acting shitty to me and didn't even want to talk to me. Now, she's cool with me being around our daughter, but I can tell, when I look her in the eyes, that she doesn't care anymore. The love she held for me is gone, but I keep trying to see past that."

"How long are you going to ignore it?"

"It's easier to ignore than to deal with the shit, honestly." I watched as he rubbed the rim of his glass.

"A lot of things are easy to ignore. I would love to ignore all my bills and act like they don't exist, but in the end, who ends up fucked over? Me."

"You don't understand, we've been down since we were young. These past few months we've been living apart have been different. On one half, I love having my own space, no one to answer to and being able to kickback without having to worry about my wife nagging. Then, on the other hand, I miss laughing, chilling, and being with her."

"Sounds like you shouldn't be asking me out on a date. You're still in love with your wife."

I didn't need to get involved with someone who was still in love with their wife. Getting my feelings caught up into someone, only to get my heart broken, wasn't in my plan. Mello was cool and I could see myself hanging out with him, but after hearing his past, I felt like I couldn't trust him. If he did this to a woman he described to be the perfect woman and held him down, what would he do to a woman he just met?

"The only reason that I asked you out was because I like you. You were funny, smart, and looked to have something going for yourself. All I'm trying to do is put the shit behind me with my wife. Today, I realized that I need to stop trying to fight for my marriage and fight for the friendship we had."

"Smart. I'm all down for being friends. I don't have too many here, well none at all."

"Where you from? You all in my business and I didn't get to ask where you're from."

"Delaware. I was born here in the city, but was given up for adoption in Delaware," I explained, not caring that I revealed too much of myself. In fact, I was an open book and didn't care about people knowing about me. Maybe the more people that knew could point me to where my mother was.

"Oh yeah. The city dragged you back here?"

"You can say that. My adoptive mother passed away, so I came down to the city to possibly reconnect with my birth mother. It's lonely not having family or friends, so I'm hoping we can build a bond or something."

"Now, I have to be your damn friend. You all lonely and shit," Mello joked.

"Oh be quiet… It feels like nothing goes right for me since I moved to this city. I moved down here and found this job at the hotel. After they announced that they're going to start a leasing department, I was on top of it. I just knew I would become a part of it because I bring the most leasing guests. Today, my supervisor announced that they're bringing in more experienced people. "

"That's fucked up."

"Exactly. I've been working there and busting my ass only to be told that they'd rather hire other people to do what I've been doing. It's whatever, I have an interview tomorrow for a night position at another place."

"When the fuck you gonna sleep?"

"They'll be cutting my hours, so I'll go home and sleep until later. The night shift says it doesn't start 'til around twelve, so I'll get enough sleep."

"When you gonna chill with me?"

"You can come to my place, or I come hang with you before I leave from work."

"Nah, I don't want you coming to my crib…. You might fall asleep at my crib," Mello laughed and pushed his drink away.

"You wanna keep being shady, huh?"

He laughed and stared at me. "On the real, you're beautiful… why you don't have a man?"

"Because I don't have time for the games niggas play. I don't even think I should be sitting here with you because you seem to play the most games."

"How you figure?"

"Umm, did you not just tell me about all that has been going on with your life. You, sir, play the most games."

"You about to judge me from my past?"

"It's very much still your present. You're still going through the things you've told me about."

"You right, can't even argue."

We stayed at the bar for a few more hours and talked. It was easy talking to him because he was just as flawed as I was, if not more. He didn't judge and he really sat and listened instead of giving half his attention. What made me smile and like him more was when he silenced his phone so I could continue talking. It showed me that he wanted to hear what I was saying and that he was putting me first in this exact moment. When we were done, he paid for all our drinks and food and drove me back to my car. It felt more like two friends getting together than a date and that was fine with me. Mello had far too much going on for me to become a romantic part of his life. I'd rather be a shoulder to lean on and an ear to listen to his problems. As I got into my car and started my engine, I smiled because I had met a friend. Yeah, he had a lot of shit with him, but he was someone I could smile, laugh, and talk to. It was lonely having to handle things by yourself and have conversations with the owner of a rundown bar. Only time would tell what would go on with me and Mello.

Kelsie

he day had finally come and I was shaking out my boots as we walked into the courthouse. Although we weren't going before a judge, just both of our lawyers; I was scared. Miracle was my world and I didn't feel like I should be forced into sharing her with a woman I didn't want to. Marina loved Miracle and I didn't doubt that for a second. Still, the question I had trouble with was who did she love more; her son or Miracle. All of her actions pointed to Marcus and then Miracle was left to fend for herself. Some of the things that she had done wasn't right and could have killed my child. She probably felt sad because she went from having Miracle almost every weekend to never seeing her anymore.

We entered a room with a long table. Marina was already sitting there with Marcus's girlfriend. She had the baby in the stroller in the back of them. I heard that their baby was having a lot of health issues and was always in the hospital. I never would wish that on any mother, so I sympathized with what she was going through as a mother. We all wanted our children to be healthy and outlive us, but sometimes, God had other plans for us that we couldn't question. She was tending to the baby with her back turned while Marina spoke with her lawyer. My and Milli's lawyer was with us already and went right to the other lawyer, while we sat down across from Marina and Marcus's girlfriend.

"Hi, Kelsie, you can speak to me," Marina had the nerve to crack her mouth. We wouldn't have been in this situation if it wasn't for her.

"How you doing, Marina?" Milli spoke for me. I didn't want to say a thing to her. Just sitting across from her was hurting my stomach.

Marina didn't bother to speak back to Milli. "He asked how you're doing? You're upset because you're sitting across from a man that actually takes care of his child?"

"If you're referring to my fiancé, he's not here to defend himself and I am. He's there day and night for our daughter."

"Yeah, that daughter. What about the daughter he walked out on when she was a preemie in NICU? Now he wants to be a father, but wasn't trying to claim his first daughter."

"It doesn't matter who went wrong. We're here for that little girl and none of this matters," his little fiancée felt the need to clarify.

"I don't want to pop your bubble or even insinuate that I keep tabs on that bastard, but you might want to do a sniff test when he comes into the house. Heard you're not the only person he's been fucking."

"Chill, ma, we don't need to show our colors. Clearly, they're mad because they had to take the train into the city and we arrived via car service," Milli laughed as he pointed out the MetroCard that was sitting on the table next to her phone.

His little chick was about to say something slick until our lawyer cleared his throat. "Okay, this is meditation and we're going to try and work things out before going before a judge. If we work things out and everyone agrees, we'll get it in writing and we won't have to waste time and court fees going before the judge… everyone understands."

We all shook our head and understood. It took long enough to get this damn hearing, I didn't want to drag this shit on any longer. Marina was the main one to blame for why it took so long to sit at this damn table in the first place. Then, she didn't think to come alone, she wanted to bring Marcus's fiancée, like her word mattered.

"Can I request something?" I spoke up and poured some water into my glass.

"Yes?" my lawyer asked.

"She has no relevance to this, so I would like to request that she steps out the room." If looks could kill, I would have been dead. Marina and his little fiancée gave me the nastiest looks.

"I'm her son's fiancée, so I have every reason to be here. I'm going to be in this little girl's life."

"I think the fuck not," Milli blurted.

"Since your son signed over his rights, he no longer has any rights here. If the mother of the child request that you leave the room, you must leave the room."

She gathered her things loudly, while ranting to herself under her breath. Marina patted her shoulder and she strolled out the room while pushing her stroller. I smiled and waved as she slammed the door, being extra.

"Okay, now that we handled that. Let's start this so we can get out in time for lunch," Marina's lawyer stated and took a seat. "My client has been in the child's life since she was a child and it's only right that she maintains some kind of visitation or custody with the child. Now, since we're getting right to the point, we're asking for every other weekend, two holidays, and one overnight weekday."

"What the hell? She's her grandmother, not her parent. I refuse to give her that!" I yelled and stood up.

Milli pulled me down, back into my seat. My blood was boiling, that she thought she could even ask for what she had asked for. Two holidays? Miracle belonged with the family that cared about her on holidays. Being that Marina never spent a holiday away from Marcus, that meant that my daughter would have to be around him.

"I've been there for that child since she was born. Diapers, bottles, or anything that you needed, I was there and provided for you. Weekends you needed a break, I came and picked her up and took her to school that following Monday morning. Doctor's appointment, physical therapy, and anything else I stepped in and helped. Where was your mother, Kelsie?"

"Why does my mother even matter? You've helped because you felt bad because your son refused to acknowledge that she was born and his daughter. Let's bring up how your son ignored his own daughter each time you brought him around. Or about the time that he fed her pineapples and knew she was allergic."

"What about your cousin's abusive husband shooting my granddaughter?"

"Marina, you know she had nothing to do with that. He broke into her apartment and tried to kill her, and Miracle was shot. Social Services ruled that it was no foul play on my part, so she can't use that in court if she wanted to."

Marina just thought she was going to end the case bringing up that Miracle was shot. After Miracle was shot, Social Services had to do an investigation. Once the cops provided information proving that Tasheem broke in, and Miracle was in a safe environment, they did the routine home check and cleared me. I had all the papers and the reports waiting for Marina's ass.

"If you would like to see the reports we can provide those for you," our lawyer spoke. After going back and forth with Milli's regular lawyer's little fuck buddy, we decided to go with him. She wanted too much money and she had a nasty attitude.

Marina's lawyer reached for the papers and our lawyer passed it right on over to him. "Look, we get you have a relationship with Miracle. I know she won't forget you overnight and I'm willing to allow her to see you. I'm thinking three supervised visits a week and if things go well, we'll agree to unsupervised weekends later down the line. That's only if she doesn't bring that fuck boy around our child," Milli proposed what we had agreed on previously to this meditation.

"Supervised visits? I have never harmed that little girl."

"Maybe not intentionally, but we have a hospital bill and records from when you left her in your son's care," Larry added. "I think what they are asking is fair. We can go to court and fight this and she could get nothing. Technically, her son signed his rights over and wanted nothing to do with the child."

"Marcus didn't understand what he was doing at the time. She sent him to get the paper signed and this fool attacked my son."

"I attacked your son after he signed the papers. Ask him what left his mouth before taking his side. How the fuck do you claim to love your granddaughter so much, but always taking the side of the man that despises his own flesh and blood." Milli stared across the table waiting for a reply.

Marina didn't have any answer just by looking at her face. "The time they're offering is fine with me. I don't agree with the supervised visits. And how am I supposed to spend time with my son if I can't have Miracle around him?"

"You need to choose between your son and spending time with your granddaughter. As far as supervised, we're adamant about keeping it supervised," Larry told her.

"Who would supervise the visits?" her lawyer questioned.

"She can come to our home and do all the visits. I also don't mind doing dinner with her once a week with all three of us. I will do whatever I have to do to ensure my daughter is safe."

"Is everybody in agreement?" Larry questioned.

We all shook our heads and both of our lawyers wrote things down in their little books. "We'll meet next week to type this agreement and have everyone sign. Next month, the visits can start." Larry smiled, closed his briefcase, and shook Milli's hand.

I was so relieved that we didn't have to go to court. If I had to put up with Marina three times a week, then that was the price to pay to keep my child under our roof. We walked out into the hallway past Marcus's fiancée who was on the phone smacking her lips. As I walked past the stroller, I noticed that their daughter had a cleft palate.

"Kelsie, can I speak to you?" Marina called behind me.

I let Milli know that it was alright and turned around. Milli looked as if he didn't want to leave, but he respected my wishes and walked a few feet away and spoke to Larry. Marina's heels clacked on the floor as she made her way over to me. If talking to her wasn't enough in the meditation meeting, now she wanted to have a conversation with me, when all I wanted to do was go home and have something to eat.

"You know good and darn well that I love Miracle like she's my own daughter. I've cared for her better than you half the time."

"Marina, I'm trying really hard to respect you. You're making it so hard and I'm trying so hard. I've always taken care of my daughter very well, better than myself. You've been a great grandmother, I give you that. But, I don't know what you've been drinking or smoking because your judgment is terrible when it comes to my daughter."

"I made one mistake. My job was on the line and I had to do what was important at the moment. Marcus made a mistake that he's deeply sorry for."

"A mistake that could have cost me my daughter. I don't trust him and want nothing to do with him. My daughter isn't to be around him and today I made sure of it."

"The only reason I'm not fighting this is because I don't have the money to keep going to court. I only pray that you start to trust me with Miracle again and we're able to have that relationship we once had."

"I don't think we'll ever have that relationship again. As far as trusting you back with Miracle, I think only time will tell, Marina. For that little girl's sake, I pray that your son is in her life more than he was with Miracle."

Turning on my heels, I turned around and went over to Milli. We finished talking with Larry and left the courthouse. Milli wanted to get as far away from the courthouse as possible. He held the door open for me and allowed me to climb into the truck first.

"Are you happy with what we came up with, babe?" he questioned.

"I am. I'm happy we didn't have to deal with going to court or anything like that. Marina pulled me to the side and claimed that she loved Miracle more than me. Bitch, please, you love the thought that you can try and raise her better than you raised your terrible son."

"She got some nerve thinking that bitch was gonna sit up in the room. Why she even worried about what the fuck is going on with Miracle when she's engaged to Marcus bitch ass."

"First, I heard that he was cheating on her anyway. That's Marcus's behavior, when shit gets too tough, he breaks away. That's probably why she's leeching onto Marina. It's exactly what I did when Marcus first ended things."

"Ain't our problem anymore, baby. We let her see Miracle and keep it going for the courts. We don't need no issues and we got everything we basically wanted." Milli grabbed my face and kissed me on the lips.

"We did. Now, when are we going house hunting?"

"Shit, I was going to ask my moms to take us tomorrow... You don't work and I don't have shit to do."

"I have an appointment with the dentist in the morning. Do it in the afternoon," I lied to him.

"Bet. We can go in the afternoon. I'll probably sleep in while you take care of your grill and shit. Make sure you ask him why it smells so bad in the morning, ight?"

"Myshon, I know damn well you're not talking about someone's mouth. Boy, your mouth stank soon as your head hits the pillow at night."

"You flexing right now… stop wearing the bonnet shit on your head too. I roll over and be ready to fuck, then I look at you looking like Mama Bear from the Bernstein Bears."

I punched him in the arm and moved away from him while fake pouting. "That's why you're not going to get none for a long time either."

"If I want some, I'mma get some. You know you can't tell me no," he whispered in my ear and it made me super wet.

Milli knew that I couldn't resist him. Even when we weren't together and he would do small things, I couldn't stop from having sex with him. When it came to Myshon Gibbens, he knew I couldn't resist him at all. He was like a drug and I needed him in my life. I'm glad that we got over that part of our relationship when we had to fake our feelings for each other. It felt good telling him that I loved or missed him. That playing hard to get shit was annoying and sent mixed signals. It took forever before we could come together and truly be happy.

"Ugh, I can't stand you," I giggled and kissed him on the lips.

"Yeah, that's why you thinking about how you gonna fuck the shit outta me when we step through the door."

"Nope, I'm on my period," I lied once again. My GYN had warned me not to have sex before coming to take the birth control out. It was going to be hard to resist, which is why I decided that I was going to get into work so Milli couldn't tempt me. "Plus, I have some things do at work."

"Damn, I thought we could spend the day together. My moms took off and she's with Miracle, so I thought me and you could spend some time together."

"Babe, we can spend tomorrow together. Once I'm done with my appointment, we can go house hunting then do dinner, okay?"

"Ight, I'll just ride with you over there and pick you up later when you're done," he told me, then told the cab driver the same thing.

As we rode to Kim's office, I leaned my head on the window and thanked God that I had a man that loved and wanted to spend time with me. This made my decision to remove my birth control that much easier. Milli deserved to have a kid of his own and experience the things that couples experienced when pregnant. I've never experienced having a full pregnancy or having a man rub my feet or stomach. It would be a new experience for the both of us.

***

Last night, I got in after midnight with Milli. I didn't realize that I had so much work that needed to be done. Truthfully, I was looking over the houses that Kim pulled for us. She had some great houses, but I ended up replacing some with others. When it was time to wake up, Milli had to drag me from the bed because I was so tired. Once I remembered what I had to do this morning, my ass shot up and I got the hell out the door and to this appointment. It was empty besides another woman who seemed to be too engrossed in her phone.

Butterflies were swarming around my stomach as I realized what I was about to do in a few minutes. It was nice to think of it and tell myself I was ready, another thing, when I was moments from going to take the birth control out and becoming open to getting pregnant anytime me and Milli had sex. I whipped my phone out so fast that I nearly dropped it onto the floor. Dialing Michelle's number, I waited for her to answer.

"You know I'm sleeping, right?"

"All you do is sleep... You need to stop holding that baby in and let him come out," I joked with her. Michelle was having the longest pregnancy ever.

"I wish. It's so uncomfortable to sleep. What's up?"

I sighed and leaned back into the chair. "I'm at my doctor's office."

"Oh, you were serious?"

"Uh duh. You and Pat didn't take me serious, did you?"

"Nope. Kels, you change your mind about stuff every other day. We just wanted to be sure that you were serious before we got excited."

"I'm very serious. Now, I'm second guessing if I'm going to do. Taking my birth control out is a huge deal, Michelle. Milli adopted Miracle and he's a good father to her, but what would he do with a new baby?"

"How about letting him find out?" Michelle's voice echoed through the doctor's office. My ear pressed the speaker button. The woman and the nurses looked unbothered, so I decided to leave it on speaker. My ear was getting hot from the phone anyway.

"Michelle, you act like this is a small decision. If things don't go right, then I'll have two children to raise."

"You keep forgetting that you'll have two children to raise with their father. If you and Milli didn't work out, he would still be there for you and the kids. Stop overthinking things and just allow it to happen."

"I'll talk to you later," I said and ended the call. Michelle wasn't understanding me and was pissing me off.

I sat waiting for someone to call me with my legs crossed. "Your friend is right," the woman said and stood up.

She walked over to me and sat in the seat right across from me. "I know I had my phone on speaker, but it wasn't your business."

"Child, you had the phone blaring and thought I wasn't going to add my two cents? You got a man that adopted a child that isn't his I assume, right?"

"Yeah."

"So, why do you think he would bail on a child that is biologically his? He's raising your daughter that's not related to him… I heard you just tell that to whoever that was."

"It's none of your business, though."

This woman had some nerve, ear hustling, then thought she was about to tell me about myself. "In the end, you're going to end up alone with two babies. You know why? Because he's going to get tired of you underestimating him. And the reason you'll be alone with two children won't be because he got tired, it'll be because you'll think that's what's best for the kids. Stop overthinking a good thing and just live, sweetheart," she told me.

"Tammy, you come on back," the nurse called the woman and she stood up.

"If you'll excuse me, while you're taking yours out, I'm going to get mine put in," she laughed and headed to the back.

I smiled because if I heard this from a complete stranger, then I must have been truly overthinking things with me and Milli. He would never do anything to intentionally hurt me or Miracle, so I had to trust that he would do the same thing with our child, if we had one. I loved Milli and I wanted to make him a father because this was what he really wanted. All he spoke about was getting me pregnant, and I couldn't lie and say I wasn't having slight baby fever with both Michelle and Patsy. Sometimes you had to take a risk and this was what I was doing.

The process was quick and easy. I was warned not to have sex for two days, but that was something small. I had bought myself time by telling Milli that I was on my period. I drove to meet Kim and Milli at a house in Long Island. I was late as hell, but I was pushing almost eighty on the highway. Milli had called me a bunch of times and told me to hurry my ass on. House shopping was exciting, so I knew he was anxious to look at the house. When I finally arrived, he and Kim was waiting outside their cars for me.

"Sorry. My appointment ran late. This is the house?"

"Yeah, I meant to ask you what were you looking for in a house?" Kim stepped forward.

"I want a house with character. These new houses look too much alike and I want ours to stand out." I beamed with pride. When I thought of our house, I thought of having the most unique and beautiful house on the block. What fun was having a house that looked like the next-door neighbor's house.

"Mama, my bad. She been watching too much of those shows. We don't want no shit with Annabelle running around," Milli told his mother.

"Why did I sign up to this in the first place. Both of you are going to drive me insane with your wants and needs. This is a new build and it's finished so all you have to do is move in and bring your toothbrush," Kim told us as we walked up the driveway.

Milli was already complaining about it not having a front gate. "Babe, you can put that in."

"No the hell I can't if this shit is over budget. Mama, how much this?"

"Two point five million. It's in a beautiful neighborhood and I know what you can afford so be quiet," she told him and opened the door.

Soon as you walked in, there was a beautiful spiral staircase. It was gorgeous with a huge chandelier hanging from the ceiling. The house just had this smell of being new. When we walked down the hall, we passed a formal living and dining room. Then, there was a huge office that Milli claimed for his own. Once we got to the kitchen, I knew I would be in here all the time. The island was massive and I could see me and Miracle doing homework while I'm cooking. Never did I imagine having a kitchen like this in my life. Milli was all in the fridge and testing the water pressure like he knew what the hell he was doing.

"This kitchen big as fuck. Mama, you can come over and cook us dinner three times a week," Milli joked and Kim rolled her eyes.

"I'm not coming over here to cook and then have to clean this big shit." She walked down the hall and showed us some guest-bedrooms. One of the bedrooms was perfect for Miracle. She didn't have to climb the stairs to get to her bedroom.

"I don't know how I feel about having her on the main floor and we're upstairs," I voiced my concern. We've never lived in a house before and Miracle might be scared being on the main floor alone.

"You didn't think I was not going to have my grandbaby's back, huh?" Kim walked down the hall and opened the door. "This was one of the main reasons I wanted to show you this house first. There's an elevator for her."

"Shit, that's why this shit cost so much. Our whole point was to make it easier on Miracle, so I'm feeling that this house has an elevator." Milli nodded his head in approval of the elevator.

We all piled into the elevator and took it to the second floor. We opened the door and it led right to the balcony that overlooked the foyer and gave you a good glimpse into how beautiful the chandelier really is.

"Down this hall, there are three bedrooms and four baths. Each bedroom has their own bathroom, and then there is a hall bath. This way, is the master suite." Kim opened the double doors with two hands and we were led into a huge bedroom with a king size bed, chaise lounge, and sitting area near a fireplace. The TV was hanging over the fireplace and at first, I thought it was a painting until Kim pressed the

remote and showed us that the TV came with the house.

We saw the three-car garage, backyard with a resort style pool, and the guest house out back. It was big, but beautiful and I could see us growing into this house. We walked back into the kitchen and I noticed Milli continued to click his phone. Curiosity got the best of me and I wanted to know who was calling him so much? He looked up from clicking his phone and his eyes met mine.

"What do you guy's think? I found a few more houses, but none of them have elevators. Of course, you can put that in."

"I personally love the house. Everything is done and we wouldn't have to do anything except move in. The guesthouse is amazing for when you come over or my mother finally visits." Kim's face told another story when I mentioned my mother. "What do you think, babe?"

"Milli? What is so damn important on your phone?" Kim demanded to know.

Milli looked up and tried to act like he was paying attention the whole time. "I like the house. It's big enough for when we have more kids. Shit is fire as fuck, I want to put an offer in."

"Kelsie? Are you sold or do you want to look for more options?" Kim checked with me first.

"The elevator sold me, but there is nothing that I hate about this house. If Milli feels like we should make an offer, I'm down." I clapped my hands excited.

"Let's clarify this thing first. When signing papers and doing all the paperwork, this house will be in both of your names. Kelsie, I know you were cool with letting Myshon take over the house, but as a woman, I can't allow you to do that."

I was trying to hold back my tears, but they wouldn't allow me to be great. My tears fell down my cheeks as I looked at Kim. This woman had taken me under her wing and never steered me wrong. If anything, she made me look at things different. For her to not only look out for her son, but look out for me too, it meant the world to me. Other mothers wouldn't have even considered putting their son's girlfriend's name on anything. Her, she was cut from a different cloth and didn't see it that way.

"Kels, don't get all weak on me," she laughed and hugged me. "You love my son and I know that. I don't think neither of you would ever do anything to hurt each other, especially with Miracle in the picture. I've never seen Milli this happy in my life, so I know you're doing something right."

"Yeah in the bedroom," Milli added and we turned toward him.

"Really, Myshon?" Kim laughed.

"I'm playing… I love all three of the ladies in my life. At least Mama likes you, 'cause if she didn't, you would get that Kenyetta treatment," Milli poked fun.

"Don't mention that hoe in this house. Don't need to taint this house with her name." Kim got upset and then went to gather her papers.

"Mama, I'm sorry," Milli apologized.

"When are you and your brother going to fix it?"

Milli didn't want to answer, but seeing that his mother was tapping her toes waiting for his answer, he decided to answer. "I'm around, Mama. If Mello wants to talk to me he knows where to find me. That man has an issue with me. I ain't did shit except be there for him."

"I hate seeing my baby boy like that."

"He's not a baby boy anymore, Mama. Stop treating him like one. That's why he running around here pouting and throwing tantrums when shit don't go his way."

"I'm tired of having you both fighting and arguing with each other. Sunday, you all come to my house because we're going to fix this," she demanded as she walked out of the house.

Milli stood there shocked that she left without finishing their conversation. Me, on the other hand, was curious as to why we all had to be there. I didn't want to see Mello and Milli arguing and fighting. Mello wasn't my favorite person right now, so I didn't want to see his ass at all.

"See how she storms off? She never wants to hear the truth about her precious Mello. Nigga dug himself into the hole he's been in."

"Your mother has to see it for herself, babe. You have one brother and you both need to fix this. I'm not saying it's your fault, but be the bigger brother and reach out to him."

"Be the bigger brother? I'm always the bigger something when it comes to my moms and Mello. How about she starts putting him in his place when he's wrong? I didn't have a childhood because my mother was too busy treating me like her nigga instead of her son. I was making adult decisions at thirteen years old!" his voice roared through the empty house.

Grabbing his hand, I stared into his eyes. "You need to talk to your mother about it. Give her the raw just like you gave me."

His phone started buzzing again and he looked at the screen. "Babe, let me go handle this, ight? Call me when you get home, okay?"

"Who the fuck is blowing your phone up like that anyway, Myshon?" I got enraged and placed my hand on my hips.

Here we were having a whole conversation and he just ups and wants to leave when he gets yet another call on his phone. He turned around and looked at me sideways like I'm the one tripping. "Don't start this shit, ma. You know I'm not doing nothing."

"So, tell me where you're going?"

"I'll tell you later," he told me before leaving out the door.

Kim was still outside when I walked out the house. She was on her phone and waved for me to go ahead so she can lock up the house. My first instinct was to follow his ass and see where he was going, but I decided to head home. Whenever he decided to come into the house, he would tell me what was so urgent that he had to rush out the house and jump into his car. He better hope he's not doing no sneaky shit because Milli knew I would be done with him. You don't get many chances with me, and I wasn't going to go through bullshit and we were about to buy a house.

Patsy

*B*eing the big punk that I was, I never had the conversation with Walt. We weren't together, so why did I have to 'break up' with him? It didn't make sense complicating things and adding strain on our relationship. We liked to hang around each other because it was easy. There was no expectations or arguments. We've been through that with our ex's and we didn't want to do that with each other. The more I thought about it, the more I realized that Walt might not be my forever person. He was fine for right now, but who knew where or who I would end up with? We both were enjoying each other and weren't thinking of a relationship. Well, I wasn't thinking of a relationship. I didn't know what Walt was thinking because we never spoke about it.

Mella was spending time with Kim for the weekend. I fought her about it, but she told me that I needed to get out the house and reminded me that she raised two boys by herself. I finally allowed her to take Mella. The only reason I gave up and didn't fight her on it was because she was three months and it was time I started letting her go with Mello and Kim for a night or two. I provided them with enough breast milk and if my daughter needed it, then I would drive in the middle of the night to Kim's house and bring it to her. My father invited me and Walt over to his house to have dinner and drinks with his little boy toy. My father was trying hard to mend our relationship and try to bring us closer. Especially since the baby was coming, and he wanted me to be there every step of the way.

I spoke to my father at least once a week and he came by my house occasionally. Now, when it came to Erick, I couldn't stand that man at all. All he did was throw shade and act like he was better than me. My father always wanted me to come and spend time with him, but I turned it down. As long as he was living there, I wasn't going to spend more time than I needed to there. My father promised me that he would behave and really wanted me to come over. He claimed this would be their last time to entertain before the baby came. Plus, he had done a ton of renovations to the house and he was dying for me to see it.

Outside, you gonna come out today or tomorrow? Walt sent me a message and I cracked a smile, grabbed my purse, and headed out the door.

Walt was leaning on his car with his head down in his phone. I walked down the stairs and stood in front of him. He pushed his phone into his pocket and smiled when he looked down at me. Walt looked good enough to eat when he was dressed down. I mostly saw him when he was done with work, or if he came to my house to have breakfast before going to work. Walt was dressed down in a Ralph Lauren sweater, dark distressed jeans, and a pair of Polo boots with the buckle across them.

"How do you manage to look finer and finer each time I see you?" he questioned and I shrugged my shoulders.

"Black don't crack, baby," I giggled and gave him the hug he was waiting on.

Walt walked me around the car and opened my door for me. I slid inside and reached over and opened his door. As a kid, I remember watching Bronx Tale and seeing that part always made me do that. When I was married to Mello, whenever he opened my car door, I would reach over and open his for him.

"What's been going on with you?" Walt asked when he got into the car.

"Besides tending to Mella's every need, nothing much. Her grandmother basically kidnapped her," I giggled.

"You need some time for yourself. I've been asking you out and you been ducking my calls, what's up with that?"

How was I supposed to explain that I didn't want to get too close? That I didn't want to get my feelings too involved too soon? "I just been laying low and trying to spend time with my daughter."

"I get that, but damn, you gotta cut me off like that?"

"Oh, please. I did not cut you off. Just because I didn't answer a phone call or two doesn't mean that I cut you off. Being a new mother is very time consuming." It was an excuse and he knew it was an excuse.

"Thought you got back with your ex…. Had me worried for a second."

"Walt, don't play me like that. Even if I did by some strange chance get with Mello, I wouldn't throw our friendship out the window."

"Friendship? That's what we're doing?" he inquired like he didn't know.

"We've never discussed being more than friends. What's so wrong with being friends?"

He laughed to himself and continued to drive for a few before he replied. "I got friend zoned real quick."

"Knock it off, Walt."

"What do I need to knock off? You giving me mixed signals, Patsy. One minute we're flirting, sexting, and making plans to fuck, then the next minute, you wanna throw friendship into the equations; I'm fucking confused." He raised his voice.

"I'm not ready to jump into a relationship, Walt. You said no expectations and that's where we left it. If all those things led you on, then I'm sorry, but I don't want to get into a relationship right away."

"So when were you going to tell me that?"

"I didn't think that I needed to. You went through the same thing that I did, so I thought you understood and I didn't need to explain."

"It's alright... why you getting all mad and shit. We're cool," he tried to convince me. Maybe it was the tone of his voice or his choice of words. Either way, I wasn't convinced that he was cool with what I had just said.

Over the past few months, we did get cool. So cool, that it felt like we were in a relationship at one point. The moment I knew I needed to back off was when I had the talk with Michelle. Here I was, ranting and raving about breaking up with someone I wasn't even in a relationship with. Yeah, I ignored a few of his calls or made excuses as to why I couldn't hang out with him. For once, I needed to be alone and do things I've never done for myself. Go on vacation with my girls because I wanted, party to the wee hours of the morning, or just do nothing at all because I didn't have to answer to anyone.

"Which house your pops live in?" he broke our silence that was present during most of our ride. If he wanted to convince me that he was so cool, he wouldn't have been so quiet during the ride over here.

"That house on the corner," I pointed.

He pulled into the driveway and killed the engine. I didn't want to go into that house and have this awkward tension between us. "Look, let's have a nice dinner and enjoy our self."

"I brought your pops a bottle of wine." He reached into the back and showed me the bottle of wine wrapped up in tissue paper.

"He'll like that." I smiled and got out of the car.

Soon as we got to the front door, I rang the doorbell and waited for my father to answer the door. Instead, Erick's extra ass swung the door open and smiled. "Welcome to our home. You guys are late, but it's alright," he made a point to mention.

"Wasn't ever given a time. My father just said for dinner and he usually serves his dinner around this time," I replied and walked past him. "This is my friend, Walt." I tossed their introduction over my shoulder.

Walking into the house I was raised in, wasn't the same. It was like Erick took every opportunity he could to wipe my mother's presence clean from this house. He succeeded because I couldn't find any pictures of my mother anywhere. Hell, I couldn't even find a picture of myself either.

"Patricia, I'm glad you could make it." My father hugged me. My eyes hurt from this loud ass silk shirt he was wearing.

"I said I would come," I replied and accepted his embrace. "Where's all of me and Mom's pictures?" I looked around the living room, once again. It was as if I was wishing that a picture or two would pop up or something.

"I'll explain later… Who is your friend?" He eyed Walt.

"Dad, this is my friend Walt. Walt, this is my father."

"Fred, how are you doing?" my father introduced himself to Walt.

"Fred?" I blurted and tried to hold back my laugh.

"Yes, I like to go by my middle name now," he explained. "Enough about that, we have some Chinese in the dining room, come." He waved us into the dining room.

The round table that I had remembered growing up was gone. The picture of me when I graduated elementary school was no longer on the wall. He erased everything about me or my mother out of this home. The dining table was a long wooden table with metal chairs seated around it. I guess Erick was going for a modern or contemporary design. Erick came out the kitchen with two bottles of the wine. He set them on the table, then slipped his ass into the seat that was at the head of the table. My father went and started plating the food and took a seat on the other side of the table.

"So, where did all of my mama's pictures go?" At this point, I didn't give a damn about my pictures. It was more about why he decided to toss my mother's pictures away like she never existed.

"Patricia, that's a conversation that we'll have alone… We have a guest," my father said and then raised the wine bottle and poured wine into Walt's glass.

"Everything is changed, Dad. You're acting like you didn't toss everything I've known and got rid of it."

"Listen, getting this table was not easy. We overpaid for it, but it was so worth it," Erick whispered to Walt who didn't even look bothered.

"I'm doing my best to live my life. I can't let the passing of your mother stop me from living. She's been gone for years, Pat. It's about time that I've lived my life," he told me. "Now, can we please just have a nice dinner?"

"Fine." I sat down and took a sip of water.

"If you want some grape juice, we have some in the fridge," Erick felt the need to tell me.

"I'm fine with my water," I replied and started messing with my food.

Erick took a sip of wine and then sat it down. The room was so quiet that you could hear a pin drop. Nobody said anything and I guess my father was trying to find the right words to say. He knew I was pissed about the pictures and the remodel of the house. If he just remodeled the house, but kept some pictures up, I wouldn't be too mad. Except, there were no pictures of me or my mother. How could he just toss our pictures to the side like we didn't matter?

"How's little Mella?" Erick asked about Karmella. I wanted to tell him that she was fine and not to waste flapping his dick suckers asking about her.

"She's fine. Getting bigger by the day."

"So, still no issues from…." He allowed his words to trail off.

What pissed me off about Erick was that he felt the need to ask that right here and now. What if I never told Walt about my drinking? My father never saw the shady shit that Erick did. Every time I got smart or decided to say something back to him, he wanted me to shut down and be quiet. Yet, Erick could say smart shit and my father never put him in his place. He'll just sugar coat something and tell him to behave. The shit irritated me and made me realize why I stayed away from my father's house. He came over to my house occasionally and we spoke once a week, still, he had never mentioned anything about redoing the house to this extreme. This was more than what he mentioned. He completely wiped any memory of me and my mother out of this house.

"Oh, you're asking if she has any issues from me drinking while pregnant? None at all, she's very healthy," I sarcastically replied.

"I'm missing my little sweet pea… Where is she?" my father added.

"Kim's watching her for the weekend. She felt I needed a break."

"You work?" Erick blurted.

Walt squeezed my leg and I tried not to respond to his pettiness, yet, he knew what he was asking for when he asked that question. "Being a mother is a full-time job. So, yes, I work."

"I mean, do you work a nine to five, where you would actually need a break from your child? Doesn't seem like you need a break to me."

"Erick, why the fuck are you wearing that loud ass pink hair? Did I come up in here and ask why you're wearing that terrible ass wig?"

"Patricia."

"No, this nigga always walks around and thinks he can say anything he wants about my life. Stop talking about my life while y'all being butt buddies, Dad!" I yelled.

"Yo… I think I'm full," Walt choked on his food and pushed his plate away. "Can I use your bathroom?"

"Sure, it's down the hall. We converted an old hall closet into a half bathroom," Erick gloated.

Once Walt left the room, my father leaned across the table and stared me in the eyes. "Why do you insist on being difficult each time you come around us?"

"Me? Difficult? How? Every time I come over here it's with good intentions. Last time I came, he said my daughter didn't look like Mello. How come you keep dismissing his shade and disrespect, but you want to amplify mine. He must suck a good dick at night," I countered.

He thought I didn't bring Mella around because she was still young and it was cold. No, I didn't bring her around because his boyfriend was disrespectful. Why bring my daughter around someone who I clearly disliked?

"Erick is straightforward, Patricia. It might be hard to deal with because you're not used to someone like that."

"Oh, I'm very used to someone like that. My friends and real family tell me the real when I need it. I don't need someone I barely even know to try and tell me shit."

"Who? The man who cheated on your family?" Erick laughed. "Sweetie, I do this for a career, so I see right through you."

"And, baby, I do this for a career and could school you." He looked confused by my statement.

"What is that, hun?" he asked stumped by my statement.

"Slaying. It's obvious you don't have any real friends, because they couldn't have told you that what you're wearing is hot," I told him and stood up. "Where's my mother's pictures?"

"Patrici—"

"I know my name dammit… Where are the pictures?"

"In the basement. I hope you can sit down and finish dinner once you lay eyes on the pictures," he added.

"I wouldn't sit down to have dinner with y'all if my ass was on fire and this flamboyant nigga was the only one with water."

Walt was standing by the door. I guess he knew shit was going to go down soon as he went to the bathroom and didn't bother to sit back down. I rushed down to the basement and looked around until I located a box with pictures, awards, and different things from my bedroom. I guess he finally allowed him to turn my bedroom into his office or yoga studio. What pissed me off wasn't that my father moved on or was gay. If this was what he wanted to do with his life, then it was fine with me. I felt that he should move on and live after my mother died. Even after I left the house, it was time for him to live. Now that he was doing that, I wanted to be happy for him; except, he went and got someone that was so hell bent on hating me for no reason. The first time I met Erick, he had a smart mouth and tossed the whole palm tree my way with his shade.

My mother was a terrible mom and I was the first to admit that. I should slam these pictures onto the floor and continue to stomp on them until I felt better. What I learned to accept was that she failed herself and the world failed her. She wasn't lucky enough to have a brother-in-law who cared about her, or a mother-in-law that was real with her all the time. All she had was a daughter that was too young to do anything and a husband that was too weak to do anything. No, I couldn't tell my daughter that I've ever learned how to ride a bike from my mom, or she had the bird and the bees talk with me. But, I could tell her the real about my relationship with my mother so she could appreciate ours.

I carried the whole box upstairs and Walt helped me. My father sat at the table with his hands folded pleading with me with his eyes to just sit down. Erick, on the other hand, had moved his frail ass to the couch in the kitchen and was watching me leave with satisfaction all over his face.

"Dad, if you really want to talk, come to my place. It's decorated better than this place anyway." And with that, I walked out the door that Walt held open the door.

"She wishes her house looked like this one. Babe, you need to put that one right into her place… The new baby will not be disrespectful like her," he called behind me.

Walt wouldn't let me go back even if I wanted. He stood guard of the door and nodded for me to get into the car, that was the only reason I didn't run in there and snatch that terrible wig off, and slap the hell out of him. Instead, I got into the car and allowed Walt to put the box into the trunk. When he got into the car, there was silence until he fumbled with his keys and started the car.

"What the hell was that? I've seen dysfunction, but damn," he commented.

"It's never like that when it's me and my father. We've had our issues and I believe we still have issues, but we're always good together. Once he met that bitch, he started changing and letting him speak more on my life. I'm a grown ass woman, so he's not about to sit there and speak to me anyway."

"Damn, calm down. You are screaming at me like I've done something to you." Walt raised his voice a bit. It pissed me off because Mello would have never done that. He would allow me to vent and it didn't matter how loud I got, he would allow me to say what I wanted. Walt, acted like I was blaming him.

"You know what, can you just drop me back home? I had a long night and all I want to do is just shower and sleep."

"No problem." He was all too happy to follow that command. Walt was acting like he had a problem with me. If I cared, I would have asked him what his issue was. Except, I didn't care at this moment and I knew what his issue was. He was pissed about us being just friends, and it was clear from the tone of his voice and attitude toward me.

It took him no time to whip through the streets, highway, and lights to get me home. When we pulled in front of my house, I touched his arm and stopped him from getting out the car.

"I'm good. I can carry it into the house. Talk to you later?"

"Yeah," he replied.

I stared at him for a second longer before I descended from the car, grabbed the box, and struggled up the stairs with the box. When I got inside, I waved him off and closed the door behind me. Flicking a light on, I walked over to my couch and plopped down. Every time something was going good in my life, something had to go and ruin it. Here I was, excited that I had finally figured out my and Walt's relationship and here he goes and gets upset by it. Then, I go to my dad's house, thinking we'll have a nice dinner and talk about his and Erick's baby. I get ambushed by his new décor and smart mouth bottom. Right now, I could use Mella and her sweet baby smell to make me feel better. At this moment, all I wanted to do was grab a bottle of wine and finish the entire bottle.

***

"Pat, I've been calling you all morning," Michelle waddled into my house. I wasn't alarmed because both she and Kelsie had keys to my townhouse.

"What happened?" I leaned up in the bed as she was breathing hard.

"I think I'm in labor… Water fell between my legs and I walked over here."

I sprung up from the bed and handed her my house phone. "Call Thor and let him know… I'm going to change into something," I told her as I got my naked ass up from the bed.

"Baby, these aren't no Braxton Hicks," she whined into the phone. "Huh, what? I can't hear you, you're breaking up." She walked around my room trying to get service. "His phone is breaking up," she told me.

"Don't worry. I'll call him back; do you need to change?"

"No, I Googled what I should do and took a bath like they suggested. These are real, Patsy. You weren't lying."

I was balancing on one leg and trying to pull my leggings on my other leg. Michelle kept rubbing her stomach as she sat on my bed. "Okay, good… Breathe in and out," I instructed.

"The baby's room isn't even done in the new house. We have boxes everywhere." She started to panic.

"If your ass wouldn't have been so stubborn, you would have been moved in already. That's beside the point, we need to get you to the hospital." I pulled on my leggings, slipped my feet into a pair of flip flops, and grabbed my sweater off a hanger in my closet.

I helped her onto the couch in the living room, then grabbed my phone, and dialed Thor's number. His line went to voicemail, and he called back right away. "Thor, Michelle is in labor. You need to come to my house now so we can go to the hospital."

"Labor? What the fuck? She called me talking about some nigga named Braxton tried to kick it to her. Got me out here ready to fuck somebody up," he vented.

"Braxton Hicks, Thor." I tried hard to keep my laughter in. One thing about Thor, he didn't play games, but another thing was, he didn't play about Michelle. She was his queen and everything revolved around her. It was admirable and made you want a man to feel the same way that Thor felt for Michelle.

"I'm like twenty minutes away from your crib. Leave the front door open," he instructed and then we ended our call.

Michelle was sitting on the couch and rubbing her stomach and breathing. I sat beside her and joined in on rubbing her stomach. "Scared?"

"Super scared. This isn't a pet or something. I'm about to birth a human being that I'm going to be responsible for."

"It's not too bad," I smiled. "When I had Mella, I knew I would never fail her as long as I was breathing. Just smelling, holding, and loving on her was enough payment for my whole entire life. If I can do this as a single mother, you can do this with a man that loves and adores you."

Michelle offered me a weak smile. I could tell she took in everything I said, but she wouldn't truly understand what I meant until she held her son in her arms. "The Lord knows I prayed for these things that's happening in my life. I can't help but to feel overwhelmed by all of it, and a small part of me doesn't want things to change."

"Babe, change is good. You're going to have a new home, healthy baby, and a husband who loves you to death. Not to mention, your career is going to pick right back up soon as you drop him."

"Raquan told me that I always have a job with him. The only thing, he had to go back to the West Coast for a bit, and said I would need to frequently fly there and work on location for weeks at a time. That's not something I can do with a newborn baby. Not to mention, Thor wouldn't go for that." She started to panic again.

"Calm down… How about working for yourself, Chelle. You're a stylist and you've worked in plenty of shops. Why don't you open your own shop up? I've been thinking about getting out the house and working."

"There's too much with that though. I would have to take a bunch of loans and hire staff, it would be too much. Working, you? What you wanna do?"

"Uhh, I do know things about business. It's something to think about." I winked at her. "Oh, and you don't need to worry about money. I have some money put up and your future husband opened a whole restaurant for a hoe that did him wrong, so I'm confident that he'll front the money for your salon."

Michelle giggled and leaned back on the couch and grabbed her hip. "Whew! These things are intense," she whispered while trying to get through a contraction.

The front door opened and Thor walked through. "It's time to deliver my boy!" he yelled and clapped his hands together. "I already called and they're getting your suite together," he told Michelle and came over to the couch.

"Thor, what are you about to do?" I questioned.

"Picking my woman up. You think I'm gonna make her walk all them damn stairs you got?" he told me as he grabbed Michelle and picked her up with ease. "You ready to deliver my little man, baby?"

Michelle smiled and nodded her head. "Yes, I want him out." She kissed him on the cheek.

I shut down all the lights and locked up right behind him. Thor put Michelle into his truck and held the door open for me to climb into the back. Once he got in, we headed to the hospital to have baby Titan.

Milli

"*D*amn, keep doing it like that, ma," I moaned as Kelsie rode the shit out my dick. She finally stopped fronting and let me hit this shit.

After she called herself screaming at me at the crib we went to see, I had to explain to her that I wasn't cheating on her. Every time that I had to run out and couldn't explain, didn't mean I was going to meet up with another bitch. Once she realized that shit, she would stop making herself crazy. I know we went through shit in the past and I was out there wilding and wanting to hurt her, but damn, she had to give me some credit. My dick didn't even get hard for other bitches anymore. My only concerns were Miracle and Kelsie. Whenever I made moves, it was them who I thought of, not other bitches.

"Babe, your phone," Kelsie moaned as she continued to squeeze those pussy muscles. I didn't want to grab my phone because I was concentrating on busting this nut.

There were loud bangs at the door and we both knew who it was. Miracle was up for the morning and she was about to be a little cock blocker. It was as if she knew when to cock block.

"Mommy, I want something to eat before school," she called through the door. "Daddy, you in there too?"

"Toots, we're coming, okay? Go watch cartoons until we're done," Kelsie called out trying hard not to moan the words out, while I was ramming my shit into her while she remained on top.

"Shit too good," I continued until we both came. It wasn't our usual fuck session, but we had to get this quickie in before Miracle circled back to this door.

My phone rang for the second time, so I grabbed it and placed the phone to my ear. "Yo." Kelsie was pulling her robe on and staring at me intensely. That night I came home, I never told her why I had to rush out. I just told her to trust that I wasn't out here wilding with another bitch.

"Milli, I really need you right now. Moon locked me out the house because he swears I'm fucking somebody else," Kendel cried on the other end of the line.

"Yo, this the second time I had to bail your ass out," I told her.

"Please, you're all I have to call. My mother isn't going to help me."

Sighing, I agreed to come help her. "Text me where you're at," I told her and ended the call.

Kelsie was leaning on the door on her phone. When she ended the call, she walked over to me and kissed me on the cheek. "Michelle is having the baby... I'm going to drop Miracle off and I'll be up there for the day."

"Word. I'm gonna swing by once I handle this."

"Can you tell me what you need to handle?"

"It was my sister."

"Sister?"

"My pops has a daughter and when I went to visit him, he told me to keep an eye on her. Shorty didn't want nothing to do with me, but she's been calling me to help her out. That's where I dipped off to the other day."

"Was that so hard?" She smiled.

"Nah, just didn't want to involve you in all of my shit. I see you smile more than I've ever seen you smile."

"Doesn't mean I will stop smiling. This isn't real if you don't let me help you with your issues, baby. Remember that, okay?" With that, she got up from the bed and smiled before heading to the living room, where our demanding daughter was waiting. "Oh, babe. I'm going to take the jeep; the Benz is in the shop being serviced," she told me and I nodded.

Kelsie needed her own car. It wasn't because I didn't want her driving my whips, it was because she deserved her own car. When one of the cars were being serviced, she had to switch cars, and I knew she hated doing that. I mean, that's nothing to complain about because some people have to take the cab or bus if their car is being serviced. But, in this case, she hated doing it because she always got used to driving one car, then she had to learn the buttons of the next car.

I showered and tossed on a pair of joggers, hoodie, and a leather jacket. While I was shoving my feet into my boots, Miracle ran over and hugged my legs like she did every morning.

"Daddy, can I have four hundred dollars?" she asked and Kelsie choked on her coffee.

"Miracle! Enough out of you this morning, missy," Kelsie scolded her and she held her head down.

"Why do you need four hundred dollars, toots?"

If my little girl wanted a thousand dollars, I was going to hand that rack with no problems. Picking Miracle up, I carried her over to the island and sat her down between me and her mother. Kelsie had a stern expression across her face as she looked to Miracle, who refused to give her eye contact.

"I want to buy myself a little brother or sister. The kids on YouTube said they bought their little brother for that much."

This generation of kids would rather watch children play on YouTube than play with their own toys. Miracle spent hours zoned out on that damn app. "Baby, you can't buy a human baby," Kelsie told her.

"Speak for yourself. I know some crackheads that'll sell me a ba—"

"Myshon, please," she cut me off before I could finish my statement.

This parenting shit was hard because I didn't have a filter. Each day that passed, I realized that you had to have a strong filter being around kids. They would repeat everything, and since Miracle went to school and was telling her teacher the Knicks ain't shit, Kelsie was stricter on me not cursing or saying things in front of her.

"Ight, my bad… I'll see you two ladies later. Love y'all." I kissed both on their forehead and headed out the door.

Back to this Kendel situation. It was nice finding out that I had a sister and I wanted to make sure she was straight, but damn. Shorty was messing with this nigga from Maryland. He was running shit there and was making his way to New York. It wasn't my concern because I didn't deal with that shit anymore. Here she was, fucking with this nigga and of course, he was filling her closet with designer clothes and pockets with money, so of course she was going to gravitate to him like flies on shit.

The nigga was treating her like shit and she continued to fuck with him. The other day, he made her get out his whip on the Brooklyn Bridge. She lucky I got there in time because her ass would have been in the back of the cop car. When I told her that she needed to leave this nigga alone, she told me that I was just her ride and didn't need to tell her what to do with her life. Once I heard that, I dropped her ass off and figured I'd stop answering my jack for her. Low and behold, she calls me from a different number and needs my help again. At eighteen, she needs to take her ass to school or something, not chasing behind some nigga that's not even her age. Why did I get stuck with hard headed ass siblings? Both Kendel and Mello were being stupid and dragging me into their shit. I still hadn't heard from my brother and I didn't plan on it. Mello wasn't going to reach out because he felt he was right and not to mention, he was too stubborn.

It took me less than thirty minutes to arrive at Kendel's crib in Harlem. She lived in one of those nice newly built condominium buildings. She came out of the lobby and got into my car. She had dried up tears on her face, her make-up was all smeared, and her hair was all over the place. It was safe to say, shorty had a fucked-up night.

"What happened now, Kendel?"

"Why you gotta say it like that, yo?" she shot back. My sister probably idolized Cardi B, because that's how she spoke.

"Don't matter how the fuck I said it, what happened?"

She could tell I was growing impatient because she rolled her eyes and opened her mouth to speak. "He thinks I'm fucking some other nigga. Ain't no nigga up in here except for him. Then he gonna kick me out the house and refuse to open the door. Then he left out and went to Maryland, so I don't have n…. This that nigga calling me now." She damn near broke her screen to press the green button.

"Moon, you mad whack for this shit. No, you corny, nigga!" she yelled and started waving her long ass nails around. "Bet, you want me gone? I'm gone… we're over and yep, I was fucking one of the niggas on your team. His dick was bomb, better than your little shit," she continued to egg this nigga on.

With her mouth, it was a miracle that nobody socked her in her mouth already. "Where you want me to take you? Yo, where the fuck you want me to take you?" I broke up her little argument. It was too early and I didn't need to hear this right now.

My ass was supposed to be at the hospital being there for Thor. My nigga went and got the strip club shit moving quick too. He didn't speak to Michelle about it, but that's because he didn't want to stress her out being pregnant and all. The nigga had already had his realtor lease the place that he was supposed to use for the restaurant. If Mello was acting right, I would've put his ass in control of handling it, but he wanted to act like an entitled bitch, so I was gonna let him finish sulking.

"With you, nigga," she laughed. "He said it's over and I need to get out of his crib," she replied like that was my problem.

"You can't come stay at my crib. I got my daughter and girl at my condo," I told her. Felt bad for shorty, but she wasn't about to turn my crib upside down.

"Wow, you would think the little bit of family I do have would look out." She sucked her teeth. "You can drop me off to my girl, Swiss's, house, she lives in Brooklyn."

Everybody that knew me, knew I would do anything for my family. When she tossed the family card out, it had me feeling a way. I had a spare room that she could stay in, but I didn't want to cause issues with me and Kelsie. Guest usually didn't know when the fuck to leave, and baby Cardi here definitely didn't know when to make her exit.

"How long you need to stay with me?"

"Until I land me a baller to get me an apartment." She smiled at me.

"How about you stop chasing these niggas. You finished high school?" I questioned as I pulled away from the curb.

With her head in her cellphone, she replied. "Yep. Top of my class."

"So, why the fuck you chasing these niggas? You know it never ends good for the wife or the so-called ride or die. Sweetheart, these niggas are expecting you to really ride or die for them."

"And that's what I've been doing for my nigga. When he need me to bring work across the state line for him, that's what I'm doing," she sounded so fucking dumb.

"Wild dumb."

"Excuse you?"

"You heard what the fuck I said… you're dumb as fuck. Risking your life for a nigga that wouldn't even put money on your books if shit went left. You think he gonna risk his whole entire operation for an eighteen-year-old hot in the pants girl? I ought to beat your fresh ass with my belt." I flinched at her and she jumped, dropping her phone in process.

"You're not my father, so stop trying to act like him. I'm grown and been taking care of myself since I was thirteen years old." She flipped her hair and hit me in the face. I had to laugh because I guess this was what it was like having a little sister.

"Extra as fuck," I replied.

"Anyway, he's serious this time, so I need a place to stay."

"Did you really fuck his friend?"

"Hell yeah. He got better dick than Moon, so I don't know why he's tripping. But, when he asks me again, which I know he will, I'll tell him that I was just joking."

"If my daughter does half the shit you're doing, I'm going to jail."

"She won't. She has a daddy that loves her, I didn't have that."

"Neither did I. You see me out here wilding?"

"You were in the streets. So, I guess you were out here wilding too," her smart ass shot back.

"Your mama should have beat your ass."

"Too bad she was busy doing other things. I'm grown, Milli. You think of my age and think I'm one of these young girls that think about nails and niggas. Well, I do that too," she let out an annoying ass laugh. "That's beside the point. I've been through some shit, so I'm way more mature than the average eighteen-year-old."

"Living in my crib, you need to respect my woman, crib, and me."

"Done and Done... No, this nigga better not torch my shit," she gasped as she quickly started pecking away at her screen again. "I got too much designer shit for him to tear that up," she spoke to herself.

When we arrived back at my crib, Kendel couldn't stop from talking about it. She kept gasping at different shit that she had never saw. I was too annoyed to even answer half her questions. I showed her to the guest room and sat on the couch and closed my eyes for a second. The front door opened and closed and Kelsie came into view.

"Hey, baby, I just dropped Miracle off. Michelle had to be rushed into emergency surgery because the baby's cord is around his neck," she broke down and cried.

"Aww, come here, baby," I pulled her down into the couch with me. "God got Titan... Look at his name, he's a trooper," I told her and she wiped her tears.

"Thor told me to go back home. He didn't want anyone up there until Michelle was out of surgery and they got word that Titan was fine. I need to be by her side," she continued to weep.

"Babe, you getting yourself upset for no reason. If you could be there, Michelle would have had you there. She has to worry about the safety and life of Titan. She's not thinking of nothing else except her son, okay."

"This is the Mrs." Kendel walked out the back with a towel

wrapped around her body. Kelsie looked up and then looked at me. "Don't hit him yet, know what I'm sayin," Kendel laughed. "I'm his sister."

"I sure was about to beat the shit out of you, Milli," Kelsie laughed. "Hi, I'm Kelsie… Uh, what is she doing here?" Kelsie whispered to me as Kendel rummaged through our fridge.

"Her nigga kicked her out."

"When were you going to talk to me about this? I don't mind, but I feel like I should have been a part of the conversation, babe," she sighed.

"You should of and I'm sorry. It was some last-minute shit that was thrown onto me," I explained and she relaxed. "You know I would talk to you about anything that goes on in our lives."

Good news, son. They accepted the offer. Preparing on closing now. My mother's message came across my phone.

"We got the house," I told Kelsie and she smiled. Just that quick, her little attitude slipped away and she was all smiles and giggles.

"I'm so happy. That house was perfect for us."

We decided to go with the first house we saw. I mean, come on, it had an elevator, pool, and guest house. The shit was nice and I told my mother to negotiate some of the furniture into the deal too. The main reason that I wanted this house was for Miracle. She could go up and down the elevator when she needed to get from upstairs to downstairs. Plus, all she had to do is walk through the garage and we were in the house. No more long walks through hallways to get upstairs to the condo.

"Y'all bought a new house? Oh shit, you really out here securing the bag, huh?" Kendel ear hustled and came and sat on the couch with Miracle's Lunchable.

"That's my baby's Lunchable," Kelsie felt the need to tell her, like she probably didn't know. Obviously, she didn't give a damn because she was smacking on it like it was the last meal.

"Oh, my bad. I'll buy her another one when I go out tonight. Hell, I might buy me more, these are helping this drinking hunger."

"I already told you what it is, Kendel."

"Look, Moon wants me to come home. He apologized and I think I'm going to stay here for a few days to make him sweat, then bring my ass home."

Kelsie blew a sigh of relief. Shit, I did the same thing too. "Ight, bet. In the meantime, put some damn clothes on and stop walking around here like that."

"Okay, dad," she mumbled and walked to the back.

Kelsie laughed and leaned back on me. "We're going to be homeowners, you excited?"

"Hell yeah. I mean, I already own this condo, but to own something with you is what's up."

"My mom called me," Kelsie blurted. "She says she has to talk to me about something."

I didn't hate Kelsie's mom, but I didn't like her coming around. Last time she came to the crib, she had Kelsie so fucked up that she cried for days. The pain of a mother not wanting to spend time, or felt she was too busy to visit her child and grandchild was fucked up. It would be one thing if she had a demanding career and couldn't make the time, but to be too busy chasing dick, that you can't kick it for a week straight with your kid is a mother to me.

"Did she say what she wanted to talk about?"

"No, but she said it was important. I told her I didn't want to speak to her, and she told me that she had to get this off her chest."

"Babe, listen to what she has to say. You can always walk out if she talking bullshit."

She nodded. "I told her she can come by the house and we can talk. The last thing I want is for us to be in public acting a fool."

"Yeah, you know I'll take Toots to the mall or something to give y'all some space to talk. Don't need her seeing shit if it does go left."

"I don't plan on it going left. Soon as she starts, I'm going to show her the same door she walked into."

"Damn, you cold, babe."

"Don't have time for the bullshit. I really don't need her waltzing in here whenever she wants, then leaving. She makes no apologies and always has a new man that wants to show her the world. Obviously, these men are just looking for a quick fuck because she doesn't have a ring on her finger."

"It's her life, she gonna do what she wants."

"Sometimes, I wish that my aunt was my mother. The way she jumps up and does whatever Michelle needs is admirable. Like now, when I called her and told her, she hurried to the hospital with Bry."

"You know she'll be there for you too. She has been there for you like she does for Michelle. You need to let her into your life more and stop shutting her out. What about when Miracle got shot? You nor Michelle called and told her until Miracle was discharged out the hospital. I get why Michelle wasn't as close to her mother. Because she was with a fuck boy and was trying to hide it from her mother. Now, you, I don't know why you've hid or pulled back from her."

"How do I continue to get close to her when I know her daughter is getting her ass kicked? I love my aunt, I really do. It's just…. I couldn't bring myself to call her and tell her what was going on with Michelle. I didn't want to ruin my relationship with Michelle, and I didn't want to lose the trust I had in—"

"Babe, you didn't want to fuck over your relationship with Michelle, but shit could have ended differently for her… All that is the past. Stop pushing your aunt away, you know she loves and cares about you and Miracle."

"I know. I'll do better." She kissed me on the cheek and laid back. "I wish Thor would answer my messages."

"Kels, he's having his damn son. Calm your ass down, and go in the room and let me put a son inside you."

She winked then a frown came across her face. "Your sister is right down the hall."

"So? You acting like we can't put that lock on the door," I laughed and picked her thick ass up. She giggled as we ran down the hall.

Kendel was coming down the hall with the clothes she had on. I didn't understand the point of taking a shower, but I didn't bother to ask. "I'm going to meet up with my girls. I'll be back later tonight; can I have a key or shumin.'"

"Hell nah… you ain't getting a key to my crib. Call me and I'll have the doorman let you in," I told her and she sucked her teeth. "Stop sucking your teeth too!" I hollered behind her as she left out the door.

"Now, you sure you ready to pick up where we left off?" Kelsie giggled still in my arms.

"Oh, you know it. 'bout to break your back." I bit her ass and finished running down the hall to get knee deep in her guts.

Thor

Titan Maximus Percy was born and looked exactly like me. All Michelle did was carry him because he was all me, his daddy. For months, we spoke about having a nice and easy birth where I would hold her hand and encourage her to push. Then, I would look down right in time for him to come out, cut his cord, and carry him to Michelle after the staff cleaned him up. We both learned how shit could change in a blink of an eye. The doctor noticed the baby's heartbeat wasn't as strong. When it started dropping, he did a scan and discovered that Titan's cord was wrapped around his neck. They rushed Michelle into the operating room to perform an emergency C-section. I've never been so scared in my life, seeing them push my queen to the back while I had to wait. If it wasn't for Chelly, I was about to turn up in this hospital. She was the one who talked to me and calmed me down.

When I was let into the room, Michelle looked so scared. She was shaking and couldn't speak because she was so worried for Titan. Even me being there didn't soothe her some. Once they pulled Titan out and he cried for the first time, I felt like everything was right in the world. My boy had a set of lungs on his ass. He was chocolate as ever and was long as shit. He came out weighing nine pounds and eight ounces. I knew he was going to be big when everyone kept asking if we were expecting twins. The first person I ran to show pictures of him was Chelly. She cried as she hugged me. No lie, we stood in the middle of the waiting room for fifteen minutes just hugging. I've always felt at peace whenever she was around. Bry was there as well and was handing out chocolate cigars he found in the gift shop. After Michelle got out of surgery and was in recovery, I called everyone to come up and see my son.

"Babe, I really want some hot wings right now. I didn't eat anything all day except for those ice chips," Michelle complained as she breastfed our son.

"Nah, you not about to make my son's milk all spicy."

The nurse who was checking her vitals broke out in a huge laugh. "Although they do taste what you eat, I don't think he'll have some buffalo milk," she continued to laugh.

"Babe, I'll get you some barbeque wings, but I'm not getting you hot wings… I don't care what you say, Nurse."

The nurse held her hands up in surrender and giggled. "The new daddy has spoken," she smiled and left out of the room.

Soon as she closed the door, the door opened again and Kelsie flung herself inside the room. "Chelle, are you alright? I'm sorry I wasn't here, somebody told me not to come." She cut her eyes at me.

"Man, I was going through something. They were about to cut my woman up, and I couldn't think straight," I admitted.

Kelsie kept calling to see what hospital. Michelle switched which hospital she wanted to be at over a million times. When we did call and alert Kelsie on what was going on, I was speaking so fast and ended the call, so I never told her which hospital. Then, she started blowing my phone up, so I told her to head home until Michelle was out of surgery and Titan was here.

"I can forgive you now, Thor. Don't you ever play about my cousin." She pointed her little hand up at me.

"You got it."

Milli came strolling in behind her and dapped me up. "What's good, bruh? How's fatherhood?"

"Man, the shit is lovely," I replied. "Little man looking just like my fine ass." Shit, I took time to gloat at my masterpiece that Kelsie was now holding.

"He does look like him, Michelle. You were hating this man your entire pregnancy." Kelsie laughed.

"All I know is that I'm happy I didn't have to push him out of me. Nine pounds? Sheesh." Michelle dramatically tossed her head back onto the bed.

"My grandbaby is an angel. Kelsie, you washed your hands?" Chelly came into the room and took over right away.

I already knew she wasn't going home when we were discharged. Michelle was depending on her mother for everything. When Titan wouldn't latch to her breast, Michelle started panicking and Chelly got right to work on teaching her to get him to latch on. I never had a kid, so I could use all the help that we could get.

"Yes, I washed them before I picked him up, Auntie." Chelly hugged and kissed Kelsie. "Where's Toots?"

"With my mama. She picked her up from school," Milli answered.

"I don't know why Kelsie don't bring her over to the apartment.

Me and Bry have been bored over there waiting on Titan."

"Auntie, I don't try and toss her on everybody. You kn—"

"What I do know is that she's my great niece and I want to spend time with her." She cut Kelsie off. "Your mama called, and she's coming into town."

"I'm aware. You know what she wants to talk to me about?"

"I do, but I'll let her handle that. It's been a long time coming and I think she should have done this once you were old enough. That's neither here nor there, so I'll let her tell you."

Kelsie's mama was a hot mess, so I could only imagine what she was about to drop on her. Kelsie studied her aunt's face like she had the answer written on her face. She kissed Titan on the forehead and handed him to Milli, who was drying his hands on a paper towel.

"I can't believe you're a father, kid," Milli gushed as he held Titan. "He heavy as fuck too." He acted as if he was weighing him with his arms.

"For real, scariest shit of my life, but hearing him come out was the happiest." I smiled as I looked at Michelle. She was tired as fuck and was trying to hold on.

"Now, we need to plan this wedding."

"Mama, I don't want to think about planning a wedding. We still have to pack up the condo and move, then unpack. All we have in there is a kitchen table and bed. Lord, I don't even want to think about this." Michelle put her hands over her face.

"Babe, didn't I tell you that I was going to handle it? I got it, and it will get done without you having to lift a finger."

"That still leaves you to do everything while I'm recovering." She continued to worry.

"Baby girl, stop worrying so much. We'll handle and make sure everything gets done. Titan will have a nursery when he comes home, okay?" Chelly was able to get her to calm down.

"I don't want a big wedding, I changed my mind," she added.

"And how many times are you going to change your mind before you're satisfied?" Kelsie added.

"No, I'm serious. Just something with the people that matter. I don't want to stress myself to lose all this baby weight to stand in front of all our friends and family. It'll just stress me out more. I can't be all fat in front of all our family and friends."

"Well, damn. We ain't nobody special," Milli joked.

"You know what I mean," she giggled.

"We got enough time to deal with this, relax now," Chelly told her.

The nurse came in the room and took the baby back to the nursery so Michelle could get some sleep. I was amazed that she was still up and alert after having surgery. Kelsie and Milli stayed for a bit before they left so Michelle could rest. Chelly kissed me and Michelle and told me she would start packing things at the house with Bry. When I told her that she didn't have to, she swatted me and told me that she was going to help her kids. Shit warmed my heart when she mentioned me as one of her kids. It felt nice to have that kind of love from somebody. Once I turned the lights down, Michelle was knocked out and I laid out on the couch beside the bed. Today was a hell of a day, but we got through it and both my queen and prince were safe and sound.

Mello

"*Y*ou look nice," I complimented Patsy as she held the door open for me. "Look like you're getting ready for spring already."

"I'm so over this cold. Spring needs to come on so I can take Mella out," she laughed and walked into the kitchen. "Water, juice, coffee, tea, or beer?" She saw my face when she mentioned beer and laughed. "I'm just kidding."

"Oh ight, was about to fuck you up in here." I lightly punched her arm and she waved me away. "Thank you for letting me come through."

"No problem." She climbed up on the bar stool and started eating her fruit. "You okay? What's going on?" This is the thing that made me feel worse about what I did to her. Even after all that I've done to her, she still managed to ask me if I was good. If anything, I should have been asking her if she was the one that was good.

"Nah, I'm no—"

"Hold on one second," she told me as she grabbed her phone and went to the other room. I leaned back in the chair and waited for her to come back.

You suck at connect four, lol, Choc sent me a message. We had been playing a game via text message and she was whipping my ass. This thing with Choc was different. I didn't have to spend large amounts of money to impress her, or even act like something I wasn't to grab her attention. She was cool with coming over, watching a movie, and eating take out. Shit, she was the first person I had finished a Netflix movie with that didn't end in me bending her over the bed and fucking her brains out. Shit, I didn't say I didn't want to fuck the shit out of Choc. She was fine, smart, and funny as fuck. Then, she had this whole down to earth shit going for her too. A chick as pretty as she was, was sure to be stuck up, but she wasn't. She allowed me to speak about my problems and didn't judge me. Not that I didn't deserve to be judged, but it felt nice to have someone not constantly pushing their opinion or their disgust for your actions onto you.

Kenyetta's ass finally brought her ass back to New York. The first thing she did was come get KJ from me. KJ missed his mother, so I didn't mind. I had my little man with me for long enough and he was tired of my ass. She didn't say two words to me and didn't explain shit. When I called her to ask what was up with Kenzel, she told me not to worry about him, that he has a father. The shit was fucked up because I cared about that little boy; cared about him just as much as I cared for KJ. To be cut out his life like I never existed, was fucked up on Kenyetta's part. Even if he had a father.

"Okay, sorry. That was our accountant." She got back on the chair and placed her phone down.

"You ain't trying to drain me of all our money, huh?"

"Maybe…Just kidding. Me and Michelle was talking about opening a salon. I would run the business side, while she did the hair and hired the right people. I was seeing if something like that was even possible."

"Oh, shit. You trying to get back out there. Okay, I see you. What the accountant said?"

"Trying. He said that it was possible for me to invest some money into it. I'm just trying to do better and be something for Mella."

"You already are. Strongest woman that I know, besides Mama."

She blushed and looked away. After all of this, I still knew how to make her beautiful ass blush. "Thank you, Mel. What's going on with you?"

"I just want to kick it with you, and talk. We haven't talked in a minute, so I wanted to do that."

"You missing on your wife, huh?" she giggled.

"Just a little, but I see that we're better apart."

She dropped the piece of watermelon and stared at me for a second before she spoke. "Mello, you doing drugs or something?"

"Nah, nah. I just see how happy and upbeat you are, Pat. Looking back, I knew you were unhappy and I ignored it. I can compare now and then and see that I was the issue. Instead of ignoring you, as your husband, I should have fixed it... us. I should have fixed us."

Shocked was the understatement of the year. She didn't know what to say. Each time she kept prepping her mouth to speak, she would close her mouth. "Okay, I don't even know what to say. Like, I've envisioned this talk in my head a million times and what I would say, but I'm speechless."

"Pat, on the real. I sit in the crib by myself and think about why I fucked up. I was selfish and was too busy worried about what my niggas was doing. Now, when I need them to come out and chill, they're too busy with their girls laid up. Instead of being grateful that I had a wife that cared and loved me, I was too busy trying to run away from that."

"What made you realize that now?" She went into the fridge and grabbed two bottles of water, then checked the baby monitor. Mella was still sleeping peacefully.

"Sitting in the crib, then going to therapy, you realize a lot of shit. I had no reason approaching Kenyetta, let alone getting her pregnant, then moving her into a crib with a car, while paying for it on the low. You didn't deserve that shit from me, babe. All you wanted was for me to love you and stay home occasionally, and I was selfish. I didn't want to see that you were drinking more and more, but I did." Tears slid down my cheeks. "I saw that shit and the way it was breaking you down. Instead of helping you and making sure you were straight, I chose to run into Kenyetta's arms and get what I was missing at home. Thinking back, shit wasn't missing at home except me."

Patsy wiped another tear that fell down my cheek. When I looked up from the counter, she had tears coming down her eyes too. This woman still hurt when I hurt. After everything I put her through, she still felt pain when I was in pain.

"You hurt me to my core, Karmello. I didn't know how to feel, didn't think I could ever feel again. At that point, I felt like giving up. You were all I knew. My first in everything that I've ever done. To see those messages and hear those voicemails from you, the one person I thought had my back in this cold world, broke my heart. That day after therapy, I cried on my way home. As a woman, it made me question what she had that I didn't? What made you go into her raw while you had a wife at home? You loved her, Mello. People fall out of love and I get that, but why keep stringing me along if you loved another woman?"

At this point, we both had tears coming down our faces. Wasn't no excuse or reason I could give her that would make this better. "Pat, I don't know, she just made everything easier. It was easier to deal with her than to deal with the problem at home. As a man, I can stand here and tell you I was a coward and didn't know how to deal with it. I'm not your step-pops, so I couldn't just contribute to it. Mentally, I was thinking if I ignored it, you would straighten up and stop. I see that was the wrong way of going about it. I'm sorry, Patricia. Before, I think I was just saying it, but I'm truly sorry. I'm sick that I hurt you the way I did. Karma has gotten me and I'm sure she's not done with me. Our marriage is over and I now know that. I don't want to lose you as a friend."

"I asked myself plenty of times what did I do? What did I do to make you stay out all night, or go on business trips at the drop of a dime. I wasn't the perfect wife; please believe, I had my flaws, Mello. I do feel that I didn't deserve what you did to me."

"You didn't, and you were the perfect wife. I never went to bed without food, and you were always on top of shit. Hell, you took care of me better than my moms. Pat, you got a big heart and as much as it hurts for me to say this, Walt is lucky as fuck to have you," the words tasted like horse shit coming out my mouth.

Even though I was finally at a place where I could tell Patsy how I felt, and let her go and live her life, seeing her with another man would fuck with me, just like seeing me with another chick would still fuck with her.

"Me and Walt are friends, Mello," she replied and wiped the tears from her eyes. "We're really just friends."

"Tell that nigga to back up, he be all on your booty."

Patsy laughed and waved me off. "Yeah, whatever. Why you had to come over here and make me cry?" she sniffled and checked the monitor.

Mella was up, but she wasn't crying. Patsy went and got her out the bedroom and came back into the kitchen. "Come here, Daddy's princess." I held my arms out and grabbed my princess. Every time I held her, it seemed like she got bigger and bigger.

"She probably gonna need her diaper changed." Patsy left the living room again to get a diaper and wipe.

Where'd you go? Choc sent me a message.

With my daughter and wife. I'm not playing you in that game again.

Awe, she's a little cutie.

Thanks.

Why you saying thanks? I'm pretty sure she got it from her mama.

Oh word.

"Who is she?" Patsy's voice broke me from our text messages.

"Huh?"

"Mello, I know that look. Who is she?" she continued to press on for the answer she was looking for. "If you have a friend that's alright."

"Her name is Choc."

"Like her real name?"

"Yeah." I laughed. "Long story."

"How'd you meet her?" she continued to question. It didn't feel like she was being shady, it felt like regular talk I would have with Choc or something.

"She works in my building. Talked me into signing a lease with the hotel."

"Hmm, she has a job. That's a check. You like her?"

"Damn, you all in my business. You like homie?"

"Apparently not like he wants me to like him." She rolled her eyes.

"You were always picky as fuck... I remember when I scooped you." I pushed the bottle into Mella's mouth.

"You were one out of a million, so consider yourself lucky," she smirked. "It has nothing to do with him, I'm just not ready. I thought I was, but I realized that I like being alone."

"He know that?"

"Yeah and no. I mentioned us being just friends and he got an attitude. It was a whole mess because I took him to have dinner with my dad, and we got into it. Ugh, I'm getting a headache thinking about it."

"If he can't respect that you want to be friends, that tells you something."

"It does, and I'm upset. I thought he would be cool to be friends and hang with. Maybe get some bomb dick, since I have had non—"

If looks could have killed, Patsy would be pimp slapped and on the floor bleeding out. "Don't even play me like that."

"See, you engage in girl talk and then I got caught up."

"You know I can give you some dick... Friends do that," I smirked and she rolled her eyes. I knew she was thinking about it because of the way she bit down on her bottom lip.

"I can't fuck you because then you'll get all reattached again. I would hate for Choc to feel some way."

"Knock it off. Shit can't happen unless you want it to, right?" I put Mella over my shoulder and burped her.

"You got a point." She winked and got up from the table. "But, we're not about to cross that line today."

"Damn," I sucked my teeth. "You looking all types of right in those stretch pants." My tongue automatically licked my lips just staring at her.

She took Mella and kissed her on the lips before placing her on her little mamaRoo shit. Everything this little girl had was high tech. The damn stroller opened and folded with a push of a button.

While she was bent over, I came behind her and rubbed the side of her thigh. "You sure?"

"M...Mello, I'm very sure," she stammered as she walked back behind the kitchen counter. "You need to stop."

"Why you stuttering then?"

"Don't worry about what I'm doing," she laughed and walked back over to sit down. "Now that you got all of this off your chest, what else you need?"

"I wanna take KJ to Disney world and I want you to come with Mella."

"Like a family?"

"Damn, like a family? I thought we were family."

"My bad, we'll always be family. But, what about Kenyet—"

"Look, I don't give a fuck about how she feels. If you're not ready to be around KJ for a week, I respect that, ma. Just be upfront with me."

She debated with herself before she smiled. "For the kids," she smiled.

"Of course. I want KJ and Mella to be hella close."

"Closer than you and Mello?" Somehow, I knew this was going to come up and I wasn't ready to talk about it. "Mello, your brother loves you. You can't see that for some reason, but he does love you."

"I don't want to talk about it."

"Okay and I won't push you. Let me just say this one thing," she paused and sipped her water. "If it wasn't for your brother, that little girl that you love so much wouldn't be here and healthy. Your wife wouldn't be sitting here talking to you sober. That's all I'm going to say."

Why did she have to go and say those two things? Milli did come through a lot of the times I've needed him in my life. When it came to Patsy and Mella, he was there for my wife and daughter when I wasn't. While I was too busy trying to cover up the mess I had created, he was busy fixing it. Something in me wouldn't allow me to admit that aloud. Mello was the first person to say that Patsy was partying and getting fucked up. I knew she was drinking, but I never said it out loud. He was the first person to say something and make me acknowledge that my wife was going down a dark hole. It was hard for him to separate the father role from the brother role, and that's where our relationship became strained.

"I hear you."

"Do you though? That man is a damn good uncle and brother-in-law. He comes over or calls to check on Mella damn near every other day. He tried to stay out of our business because he knows it causes friction in y'all's relationship. Fix your relationship with your brother before it's too late."

"I definitely hear you, Pat. I'll figure this out, I promise," I promised her. If I didn't, she was going to make sure that I stuck to what I just promised her.

I chilled with Pat and Mella for a little bit and then left. It took a while to get to this place, but we were able to laugh again. When I thought of all the shit we went through, I never thought laughter and smiling would be possible.

"What's this?" She ran out the door and waved an envelope in her hand. "You left it on the counter."

"The signed papers," I told her and opened my car door. Her eyes got watery and she backed into the house, yet, still held the door ajar. "I'll call you tomorrow." I winked and got into the car.

When I pulled off, she was still staring out the door. Sometimes, it took guts to make a move that you would never normally make. I caused her enough pain, and the last thing I wanted, was to cause her more pain. If I couldn't have her as my wife, I damn sure wanted her as my friend. I would be foolish to believe that all the pain and hurt was gone with one deep conversation. It would take a while before she could put it in her past. The next dude she ended up with would probably have to work ten times harder to win her heart. It was cool with me, I wasn't in no rush for her to get another nigga. I could wait forever for that to happen.

Kelsie

"So, when were you going to tell me about this club, Shannon!" Michelle screamed as she fed Titan. I had requested some time off so I could help her out with the baby. My aunt was already on it, but Michelle still needed conversation with people, other than her mother.

"Michelle, stop yelling while you're holding my son," Thor told her calmly. This nigga Thor was like the real live DJ Khaled. Everything was about his son, and if it wasn't, he was about to make it about his son.

"Why am I just now finding out about it?" she continued like he hadn't said a damn thing. My aunt came out the room and took Titan to give him a bath.

"Y'all need to quit that fussing around my grandbaby." She scolded them and went into the next room.

Thor had a moving company packing their shit and moving it to the new place. So, he had booked a suite until everything was done. "You acting like I'm gonna be looking at them."

"You're not blind, Shannon," she continued.

"All I'm worried about is adding more commas to our account. All that other shit is irrelevant."

"When is it opening, Thor?" This was a question I needed to know.

"We doing a test run, nothing big. Me and Milli leased this place in the city and we're gonna do a few nights and see how it goes. If shit looks up, we'll buy the building."

"You just doing a test run with everything, huh? First, a restaurant and now, a strip club." Michelle snickered.

"Stop, Chelle," I told her. The way she was acting was ungrateful. I wasn't the happiest about the club, but I saw what Milli was doing. The more businesses he opened, the more he could step away from the streets.

"I'm tired." She rolled her eyes and got up from the couch. "I just find it real messed up that everyone knew before me. What about me? I'm the one sacrificing the most in this whole relationship, what about my career? You're running around being this businessman, while I sit back and just raise our son?"

Thor went to follow behind her, but she slammed the door. "I'm damned if I do, damned if I don't," he sighed and sat next to me on the couch.

"She found her voice and now I wish she would shut it up," I tried to lighten the mood. "Give her some time, Thor. She just had the baby and she isn't thinking clearly. If you thought our emotions were all over pregnant, man, they're worse once we give birth."

"We not doing this for the bitches, Kels. I'm trying to chase this bag so I don't have to be in the streets. I want to step away from this shit. I got a son and a fiancée now, that shit ain't it no more."

"Although I wasn't pleased, I see what you both are doing," I assured him. "She'll come around."

"Yeah. Tell her I'll be back later, I gotta go let the niggas in for the liquor."

"How'd you get a liquor license? Those things are hard to come by."

He chuckled and grabbed his coat. "I know a lot of people."

"Okay, don't tell me."

"Later," he said and headed out the door.

When I walked into the room, my aunt was all in Michelle's ass. "You need to stop acting like a spoiled brat. He may treat you like a queen, but don't lose your throne acting like a damn fool."

"A strip club, Mama. You know how many bitches are going to be on him?"

"It doesn't matter. He's not checking for none of them, and you're making a big fuss about it," Auntie continued to get in her ass. She actually beat me to it. "That man is worried about making more money for you and this little one. You're in a damn hotel suite that cost ten thousand a damn week, Michelle!" she hollered and startled Titan.

I took Titan from her and soothed him. Michelle was in tears as my aunt continued to yell at her. For the life of me, I didn't understand why she gave Thor such a hard time. With Tasheem, she allowed him to do whatever he wanted and never peeped a word. I was happy that she found her voice and refused to be walked over anymore, yet, she was using her voice on the wrong person. All Thor wanted to do was provide a life for him, her, and the baby. The strip club wasn't my favorite thing either, but I learned to allow Milli take lead and trust him. If he told me this was all business, then it was business.

"Why is she always taking his side?" Michelle wailed when my aunt left the bedroom. "Every time I complain about something, she gets on my case."

"Chelle, you've been a nightmare to live with while you've been pregnant. Every other week, Thor is on the couch or coming over to our condo. You're constantly on his case over the dumbest shit. That man loves the hell out of you, why are you making it so difficult?"

She wiped her tears. "Part of me doesn't want to believe that this will last forever. It's all too good to be true," she finally admitted. "How is this... All of this happening for me?"

"Because he knows what you deserve and you've been praying for this. God doesn't make any mistakes. There was no coincidence that night when we went out for Mello's birthday. Thor was sent into your life for a reason, not a season." I sat down and comforted her. "Look at this product of y'all love... Looks just like his daddy, but has his mama's nose," I smiled as I held Titan in my arms.

Michelle took Titan and kissed him on the cheeks and snuggled him. "I never loved something so much...This love is unexplainable." She continued to kiss and smell his little neck. The smell of a new baby was intoxicating.

"That's the love of a mother. I don't know what I would do without Miracle, and when I think about her not being with me, I get anxiety."

"Lordt, don't tell me that. I don't even want to think of me without him," she giggled and placed him down beside her. "Have you spoke to Milli about taking your birth control out?"

"Nope, and I'm not. We've been having sex like every day and night, so I know I'll be pregnant soon."

"Kels, I love you… you know that, right?" she started. I nodded my head yes, and she continued, "Are you doing this for y'all or just for Milli?"

"At first, I was thinking about him and only him… But, the more I think about a baby, I get so excited. When Mella was born, I was fighting baby fever hard, but I didn't want to speak on it, out of fear. Now, holding Titan, I want a little baby of my own…. Allow Miracle to be a big sister. For a while, it was just us, but now we're a family."

"Milli is crazy as hell, but he's a good father. Miracle doesn't want for anything and he knows how to handle her. You both would make a cute baby too… Maybe losing the baby was in God's plan, not you getting raped. I would never say that," she quickly added.

"No, I understand. If we had that baby, I don't think we would be together. We both were too consumed with playing games instead of building a relationship. Guess what?"

"What?"

"Milli's sister is staying at our condo for a few days."

"Sister?" she questioned.

"Yes, apparently, their father has an eighteen-year-old daughter. Girl, she's ratchet with a capital R."

"Wow… Does Kim know?"

"I don't think she does… I'm not saying anything either. Speaking of Kim, she ended up getting them to accept our offer on the house."

"The pictures you sent me were so beautiful. That elevator is perfect for Miracle and me."

"For you?"

"Yes, all those damn stairs in the picture. I'm gonna be winded going up those stairs," she joshed.

"I'm gonna be using it more than the stairs too. Especially, if I get pregnant," I giggled.

My aunt came back into the room with some food and set it on the bed. "I ordered some room service and a beer. You need your breast milk to come in more and beer helps," she informed Michelle.

"Thanks, Auntie." I grabbed the cheeseburger and French fries off the tray.

"You're welcome, Kels. We do need to have a talk little girl." She played with my hair like she used to when I was a kid. "I spoke to that man of yours."

"Okay…." I allowed my words to trail off because I didn't know what the hell Milli had opened his big mouth and said.

"Why do you feel the need to pull back from our relationship? I love you like a daughter, Kelsie. Hell, I was there and cut your cord when you were born. You don't need to distance yourself from me because I'm always going to be there for you, babe." She pulled me close to her and kissed me on the forehead.

"Auntie, I just feel like that's my mother's position. She should be the one that's there for me. I don't want to take you away from helping Michelle and being there for her. I know it sounds stupid."

"That's exactly how it sounds; stupid. I know what my sister is doing, and I know how it affects your relationship with her. Kelsie, I basically raised you when your mother was partying and hanging out when we lived in New York. You're my favorite niece and I love you and Miracle with my all my heart."

I smiled. "I love you too, Auntie." I hugged her.

"Aww, y'all so cute!" Michelle slugged the beer back and ate her food. "Now, tell her Mama," she coached my aunt.

Sighing, my aunt looked me into the eyes. "Your mother is in New York. She came in last night and she's been staying at my apartment."

"I thought she wasn't coming until next week or something?"

"She called me from the airport crying last night. She didn't have any money for the cab, so I sent Bry to go pick her up and brought her back to our place."

"Why didn't she call me?"

"I don't know, but I know you both need to sit down and talk, so I told her to come to your place tonight."

"Auntie? Tonight?"

"Yes, I'm going to bring Miracle over to my place for the night and you both can have that heart to heart."

"What is so important that she has to tell me?"

It was driving me crazy that she didn't want to tell me what was going on. My mother was never one for serious conversations, so I knew this had to be serious. Not to mention, she came into the city earlier than she had told me.

"You need to talk to her about that, babe."

"Thanks, Auntie," I said and hugged her.

***

Milli grabbed his wallet off the dresser and shoved it in his pocket. I watched as I laid naked in our bed. Sex had been something we did all the time now. Mostly, I was craving it and he never had a problem giving it to me. At first, I came in and was arguing with him about telling my aunt what I told him. When he explained that he was only trying to help and he didn't mean to betray my trust, I accepted his apology and it ended in us ripping our clothes off and having sex.

"You need to go shower because your mother will be here in a little while," Milli told me as he leaned over the bed and kissed me.

"I'm so tired. Why can't she come tomorrow," I whined and rolled around in the bed naked.

"Babe, stop because I'm 'bout to take my clothes off and go for round four." He gripped my ass and sat down on the bed.

"Leave me alone, I'm sore."

"Yeah, ight. When I get back home, I'm gonna break that ass in some more." He licked those thick and juicy lips at me.

Every time I stared at Milli too long, I wanted to rip my clothes off and have my way with him, wherever we were. The way he handled my body when we were in the bed would have some women jealous.

"Go to the club and make sure everything is alright. Y'all open soon, right?"

"Shit, we been working on this shit fast as fuck. I mean, it ain't where we want, the décor and shit, but we're just opening it how it is, and if we do decide to buy the building, we'll renovate."

"I'm happy that you both are doing something you guys wanted to do. What's going on with the restaurant and Thor?"

"Maggie still running it, but it's making money. He's bringing her to the strip club to make food there too… you know, since the restaurant is closed when the club opens."

"Long as she's not messing with him and Michelle anymore. She gonna need to work to pay for the condo because Thor's not paying for anything."

"He shouldn't. She's not his woman anymore, all those bags he securing is for his family."

"Yep. Let me go shower and make something quick." I kissed his lips and got up from the bed.

"I'm gonna head out… Kendel claim she coming back tonight, but she back with her nigga, so I doubt it." He slapped my ass and stood up.

"That girl is a mess, but alright," I giggled and went into the bathroom to shower.

After showering, calling my aunt to check on Miracle, and making a quick dinner, I set the table in the dining room. Last time, we ate outside and that ended up being a disaster, so I decided we should sit down inside at the table. My mother called me when she was ten minutes away in the cab and I told the doorman to let her inside.

"Hey, Mama, how are you?" I greeted her and gave her a hug.

Something about her seemed different to me. Maybe she was

skinnier, or something; I just couldn't put my finger on it. "Hey, baby! I just saw Miracle and she's something else," she laughed and came inside.

"That little girl keeps me on my feet. What was she over there doing?"

"She was over there reenacting the *Lemonade* album by Beyoncé… That's what took me so long to come over here, she had performance after performance."

"I miss her little self when she's not home. When she is home, her butt is a handful."

"I can tell," she added and we walked into the dining room.

While my mother got situated in the dining room, I grabbed the food I made. I made chicken cutlets, fried rice, and asparagus. I took a bottle of wine out the fridge and brought it into the dining room.

"You can pop this open, while I plate the food."

She grabbed the bottle and looked at the label. "Oh, you got the good wine. I had this on a yacht in the south of France."

My mother had been all over the world. Mainly because she found men that traveled and had money to travel. If her pussy worked, she would continue to travel. "Nice, I would love to go there."

"Baby, there's power in pussy," she cackled that annoying laugh.

I brought the plates to the table and sat down. For the life of me, I couldn't figure out what she wanted to talk about. Did I just bring it up? Or did I wait for her to bring it up? While she was talking, I wasn't paying no mind to what she was saying. In my head, I was trying to figure out what way should I approach the situation without seeming like I just wanted to find out what she was hiding, and kick her out.

"I can see your ass over there antsy, so I'm going to just start with what I need to speak to you about." She noticed me fidgeting with my food.

"You can't tell me something like that and not expect me to want to know."

She took a long gulp of wine and then placed her glass down. "I don't know how I'm going to tell you this, or how you're going to look at me after this."

"I'm sure I'll be able to look at you the same. Ma, not to be rude or kick you when you're down, but you haven't been there for me much. Growing up, I had to be independent because all you did was work and then hang out after work or on the weekends. You pawned me off to Auntie's house all the time, until I was old enough to stay in the house by myself. Then, when I got pregnant, you didn't support me because you felt I rushed things. Mama, you haven't been there for me emotionally since I was born. I never starved, always had food and a roof over my head, but you weren't there for me when I needed it. Then, you tell me you're moving with your boyfriend at the time, and don't give a shit where I would go. Thank God, Auntie took me in until she moved down there. Auntie deserved to move, she raised her daughter, retired, and could do that. So no, there's nothing else you can possibly do that will make me look at you differently."

All of what I had said were things that I've held in for years. I've always held what I felt in because, who am I kidding? My mother was never around long enough for me to tell her how I really felt. She was always gone or off with another man. Her friends, men, and partying was more important than spending an hour on the phone catching up on her daughter's life.

"Twenty-three years ago, I met a man at a bar. We had a good night and I ended up going back to his place. You were around two and a half at that time. That night before you had a fever that wouldn't break, I sat in the emergency room all night with you. Your aunt came and told me to go out… I never went out and she forced me to go ou—"

"Is this your way of blaming Auntie of starting your partying ways? 'Cause she was just giving her sister a break; you took it upon yourself to live this life."

She ignored everything I said and continued. "Anyway, I met this man and we had a good time. I went back to his place and of course, I slept with him. Your father was wherever and I just needed to feel wanted and needed, even if it was for the little bit of time." At this point, she wasn't making eye contact anymore and her eyes were glossy. "After that night, I thought we vibed and he would call. He didn't and I never saw him again. Three months later, I found out I was pregnant with your sister."

The sound of my knife and fork crashing onto my plate startled her and she stared up at me. "A sister?"

"I didn't know what to do when I found out. Abortion was out of the question because I didn't have the money. It wasn't like today, when you can use your insurance and get an abortion. You had to pay out of pocket and with a child, apartment, and bills, it wasn't something that

I could afford."

"What happened to her?" I whispered.

"I gave birth to her and gave her up for adoption. We had an open adoption, but it was too painful for me to keep updated on her. I had you to worry about, and as far as I was told, she was given to her a good family," she explained.

A little sister. All the times that I wished I had a sibling. Michelle was like a sister to me, but it was nothing like having a sister go through the same things you were going through. I'm pretty sure we would have been close because my mother put me through a lot of shit growing up. I wished I could remember something, anything from around that time. At two years old, I couldn't remember anything.

"Why are you telling me this now? I'm not understanding, Ma." I couldn't understand why she now decided to tell me. Why did she wait this long to tell me, or even tell me at all? It wasn't like I was snooping and found out information. Far as she was concerned, I was clueless and had not one clue.

"Our old next-door neighbor called me a few weeks ago. She told me a girl was asking questions about me and how she can get in contact with me. I didn't want this coming to you before I had the chance to explain this to you."

"Why didn't you keep her?"

Tears rolled down her face and she stared into my eyes. "Kelsie, you're a mother and before all of this came into your life, you saw how hard it was to raise one child. Imagine trying to work full time and take care of two children? I did what was best in the situation."

"What was best in the situation was to raise her, Mama. She's family."

My mother fumbled with something under the table and then slipped it onto the table and pushed it toward me. There was a beautiful, big eyed, chocolate baby girl wrapped in a hospital blanket. She had the thickest, but curliest hair I've only seen on one person's head, and that's Miracle.

"I'm not asking you to make sense of this. All I'm asking you to do is to take in what I told you and leave it alone."

"No, I refuse. What's her name?"

"I didn't name her, Kelsie."

"You know her name, Mama. What is her name?" I continued to push.

"Choc Aarons," she blurted and picked her fork back up. "Kelsie, don't go messing around and trying to know her."

"It's obvious she wants to know us. Why else would she go back to the old neighborhood and ask about you?"

"I don't want to know her, Kelsie. What will I tell her when she asks the same questions that you do? I raised you the best I could and now you have a man that takes care of you… My job is done."

"You never want to deal with things when it's too difficult for you. You didn't do your job because where were you when I was starving with Miracle? When I was raped in my own apartment? Where were you, Mama?"

She gathered up her purse and stood up. "Kelsie, what did you want from me? Your father left me to be a mother and father. Then, another man left me to do the same thing. So, I liked to have a good time, sue me. I know one thing, you better not contact that girl. Leave my past in the past and respect that!" she yelled and left the dining room.

The front door slammed a few seconds after that. I held the picture in my hands for a few minutes, before I went into the small corner where Milli had a computer up. I logged onto my Facebook page and searched her name. Everybody had a Facebook page, and if you didn't, you had some type of social media. With a name like Choc, she was the only name that popped up. She was so beautiful and chocolate. Her melanin was popping and coming right on through. Instead of friending her, I sent her a quick message on her Facebook.

Hey. I don't know how to say this. So, I'm just going to say it; we're sisters. You can call me at 718-876-3456.

Soon as I sent the message, I logged off and went and sat on the couch. I looked her up again on Facebook and strolled her timeline. She wasn't really on Facebook, so I was worried that she would never see my message. How could my mother do this and keep it to herself all these years? I had a little sister that I could have built a relationship with. Then, instead of trying to make it right, she didn't want to make it right. She wanted nothing to do with her daughter she handed off like a used car. It upset me that my mother was the way she was, but there was nothing I could do to change her. If her grandchild couldn't change her, and make her settle in one place, then there was nothing that I could physically to do.

Choc

Hey. I don't know how to say this. So, I'm just going to say it; we're sisters. You can call me at 718-876-3456.

My Facebook message just stared at me as I stared back at it. I had a sister? How did she find out about me? Did my birth mother tell her about me? A million questions floated through my mind as I thought about how she found me on Facebook. My heart was beating quicker and my breathing was shallow. It was as if this message took my breath away. All I wanted was to meet my birth mother. That was my whole goal when I moved to New York to find her. I prayed that she would love to have a relationship with me and build a bond that was taken from me when I was born. I promised myself I wouldn't judge her decision, and would make peace with the bitterness I felt, finding out I was given up for adoption. Seeing that I had an older sister, made me upset. What was so different about her than me? Was it because she was light skin and I was dark skin? A million questions popped into my mind, and yes, some of them were silly.

"What are you over there reading?" Mello asked through the camera. We were both lying in bed on FaceTime. I was in the middle of giving him my opinion, when the message popped up on the top of my screen. "Damn, you supposed to be helping me and shit, and you zoned out."

"Oh, my bad. I was reading an email," I lied. For some reason, I didn't want to bother Mello with this situation right now. "Tell me again."

"I'm torn if I should go meet up with my brother tonight. I know where he'll be, but I don't want all the fighting and shit like last time."

"Don't go if you still hold ill feelings toward him. From what you explained, your brother doesn't sound like he was being malicious toward you, Mello. Yeah, he sounds overbearing and maybe he's guilty of not letting you make decisions or letting you handle things. Yet, you didn't make it better when you cheated on your wife and decided to get this other woman pregnant. Yeah, you hurt your wife, but you hurt your family too. How do you think they felt not being able to witness those first with your son? Then, you have to take in account that your family and wife are super close. What happens when she finds another man, and he eventually becomes her husband? She'll be someone else's sister-in-law and daughter-in-law."

"Damn, you just broke shit down to me. I never thought of it like that."

"See, that's why you need me in your life," I giggled. "Just make it right, not for y'all, but for your mother. She doesn't want to see her two sons at each other's necks."

"You right. She got some surprise tomorrow at her Sunday dinner... I would invite you, but I think my wife is going to be there."

"No worries. I get it, and I don't want to cause any issues. You'll make it up to me," I told him and he laughed.

"Oh, word?"

"Yep."

"You never told me about that job, did you get it?"

"Yeah, I got it. I need the extra money, so that's good. Have you had a conversation with your baby mama?"

"Nah, but she told me she wanted to talk to me. Bitch could wait until I'm ready. How she gonna come and get my son, but don't answer none of my questions or shit?"

"Try and think of your son when talking to her. It's hard to have patience when it's someone who isn't your favorite person, but think of your son."

"Yeah, I'll try. She's so fucking annoying."

"Mello," I called out, he looked up. "Stop."

"Ight, I'll stop," he promised and stared into the camera. "You're so fucking beautiful."

"Oh, please. My hair is all over my head and I haven't slept in days."

"So, let me take you to the spa tomorrow. My moms' dinner isn't until later, so let me treat you to the spa."

"Only because I really need it, but I'm too poor."

"Choc." I looked up from messing with the blanket. "Stop," he mocked me.

"Yeah, whatever. I'll speak to you later on... good luck with speaking to your brother tonight," I wished him.

"Thank you."

Soon as we ended our video call, I typed in her number and stared at the number for a few. My body must have known that I was stalling and my finger hit the button on its own. I held the phone to my ear as I picked with my nails and waited for her to answer. Just as I was about to end the call, she picked up the phone.

"Hello?"

"Hi…Um, I mean hello. My name is Cho—"

"Choc? Hi! I was praying that you would get back to me," she sounded all too excited to hear from me. Did our mother die? Is that why she decided to reach out to me in the first place?

"Um, thanks, I guess."

"Look, I know this is probably weird and overwhelming too… can we meet? I live in the city, but I drive."

"I can meet in the city. My job is there anyway," I told her.

"Okay, so I'll text you where to meet and I'll see you in a few," she told me and we ended the call.

"Choc, this is what you've wanted… Mom would be happy, calm down," I had to calm myself. I quickly grabbed my purse, stuffed some important things inside, and then headed out. Since I had to take the train, I needed to leave right now.

It took me an hour to make it to the place that she picked. When I walked up, I felt like my ripped jeans, converse, and leather jacket were inappropriate. Still, I walked inside and asked for her. They led me to her table and she gasped when she laid eyes on me. Standing up, she walked slowly over to me and hugged me. I hugged her too and then we broke our embrace and took a seat.

"I'm just so shocked. You're a dark skin version of my daughter," she continued to stare at me.

"Am I really?"

"Yes, on your profile picture, you can't really see your face too well. Staring at you right now, I can see my daughter in you. It's so crazy."

"Wow."

"I found out about you the other night. My mother sat me down and told me about you, so I had no idea that you existed until a few nights ago," she revealed to me.

"So, our mother is alive?"

"Yes, too alive." She rolled her eyes. "She explained to me why she did what she did, and although I don't agree with it, that was her decision. A decision, I had nothing to do with because I was too young. However, I do want to have a relationship with you."

She didn't know that those words lit up my heart. All I wanted was to have some type of family. A big sister along with a niece was more than I asked for, but I was appreciative that I had one.

"I do want to get to know my mother."

She sighed and stared down at her hand. "She doesn't want to deal with answering to you. Maybe in the future, you both can sit down and have that conversation, but she's not ready."

"What is she not ready for? She dropped me off and didn't give a shit. Don't get it twisted, I was raised by a remarkable woman, but she died. All I wanted to do was get to know my birth mother and build a bond with her."

Kelsie reached out her hand and touched my hand. "I understand your hurt. Despite what you think, I didn't have the picture-perfect relationship you're looking for with our mother. I do want to have you in my life and be a part of me and my daughter's life."

When I came looking for my birth mother, I never thought that I would gain a big sister. "I always wanted a big sister," I smiled.

"Hey, I'm only two years older than you... I'm still young," she giggled.

"Is it just you and your daughter?"

She took a sip of her hot chocolate. "No, my cousin Michelle is like my sister and her mother is like my second mother. Then, it's my boyfriend, Milli, girl, that's another story, and my cousin's fiancé, Thor, and her son, Titan. Then, I have my best friend, Patsy, her daughter and her soon to be ex-husband, Mello."

"Mello?" I know I didn't hear her correct, did she just say Mello. The name Patsy had already struck me, but when she mentioned Mello, I was shocked. "As in Karmello?"

"Yeah, how do you know him? Please Lordt, don't tell me that you slept with him," she gasped and pleaded with her eyes.

"No. We're friends. He lives in the hotel I work at. I do like him though," I blushed. Mello was fucked up mentally, but he did have a good heart. He did a lot of wrong, but he was trying the best he could to clean it up.

"What the hell? It's really a small world. Patsy is my best friend, so just know, I'm going to tell her about you before you meet her."

"Oh, she knows about me. He tells me everything, we're really like best friends," I explained.

Whenever something happened with either one of us, we called or sent a message and told the other what went down. It was crazy how we had this bond in such a short period of time. If we never became something more than friends, I was satisfied knowing I had a friend in Mello.

"Seriously?" She stared at me shocked. "She never told me."

It was surreal sitting across from a piece of me. She was family and I thought I would never find a piece of me before I was given up for adoption. When I went by the last known address on my adoption papers, the lady told me she had moved away years ago. I begged her for a phone number, but she told me she didn't have a number for my birth mother.

"What made your mother just tell you?"

"Apparently, a friend from our old neighborhood called her and told her that you were asking questions and wanted to get in contact with her."

Something told me that the woman was lying. She was too much in a rush to slam the door into my face. "I asked the woman for her number and she said she didn't have one."

"All those women from our old neighborhood are shady as hell. They all sit on the benches and gossip like a bunch of birds. My mother's name is probably floating around that project and we haven't lived there in some years."

"Wow."

"So, tell me about you… Where did you grow up, what was your life like?" She was all too interested in me. She stared across the table and waited for me to speak.

"What you see is what you get with me. I love singing, cooking, and shopping. I work in a hotel here in the city, and my life was great growing up. My mother loved me and gave me the best she could."

"Were you guys close?"

"Super close, she was my best friend." I looked down at the table. "We did everything together and basically grew up together."

"I'm so jealous," she whispered and touched my hand.

"You're jealous? I'm jealous of you, you got to grow up with our mother."

She frowned. "Like I said, she may have kept me, but I didn't have the best childhood or parental guidance," she admitted.

"That sucks."

"Tell me about it. My mother has a lot of things she's probably still hiding. This was probably just one of her secrets."

We sat and talked about everything that could come to mind. She told me about her baby's father, and how he didn't care about or claim her daughter. Then, she told me about her daughter's disability and how she got with her current boyfriend. Before we knew it, it was dark and the restaurant was getting ready to close. I didn't want to leave, but we promised to meet back up and hang out again. She even offered to bring her cousin and daughter along so that I could meet them too. Sitting and talking with her felt natural, nothing felt forced or awkward. Making that call earlier, seemed like the best thing I had done in a long time.

Milli

Tonight was the club's opening. We really pushed through and pulled every contact we had to put this shit together. Niggas didn't do pop up strip clubs, but let us be the first to say, we did it first. Thor was the main person that worked around the clock and made sure everything was together. Everybody and their mama was wrapped around the corner waiting to get inside. There were just as many women as there were men. Since tonight was the first opening night, we decided to turn the tables and let men get in for free before eleven and make the ladies pay. We had a few ladies that felt like we were being sexist and refused to come in. Once they heard that music jumping and realized that our spot was the place to be, they changed their tune and paid the twenty dollars cover fee to get those ropes opened.

I was decked the fuck out with my silk Versace shirt with a few buttons opened, ripped distressed jeans, and a pair of Versace loafers. Shit, I even pulled my glasses out with the gold rimmed frames. If Kelsie was here, she would've said I was looking like a snack and probably would've tried to pull me to the back to fuck the shit out of me. Instead, my baby was home with our daughter watching movies. She wanted to come out to support, but I told her to stay home. There will be time for her to support when we fully open this shit up.

"The dressing rooms in the back are makeshift…. How the hell am I supposed to cover my body?" one stripper said and I looked at her confused.

"Ain't you about to hit the club half naked?"

"That's beside the point." She pointed her long multi-color nail in my face, then waved her neck in a circular motion.

"Man, get that funky ass finger out my face," I barked on her and she backed up. "Use the public bathroom, I don't know what the fuck to tell you."

She mumbled something and took her ass back to the back. Nobody had time to be arguing with her about dumb shit. In about ten minutes, her ass was about to be on stage in nothing but some dental floss anyway.

"Cousin!" I heard two voices and turned around. My eyes were deceiving me when I saw my two cousins walking up to me.

See, when Kelsie met me, she assumed that I only took my brother and moms out the hood. Nah, my cousins, Nancy and T'yanna, had their own shit popping off. All they needed was ten thousand dollars apiece and they opened a business and had money.

"Yo, when the fuck Nance get out here." I grabbed my cousin into a big bear hug. My cousin Nancy lived in Louisiana and we didn't get to see her that much. Her name rang bells down there with all the crawfish spots she had opened. You couldn't go down there without seeing big ass advertisements for 'Nance's Big Crawfish House.' And if her crawfish business wasn't enough, she had a five-star restaurant that had a six-month waiting list.

"Boy, I came down here to see what was up with T'yanna. She's been begging me to come visit… You know I'm done with New York."

"You moved down there and came up." I hugged her again.

"If it wasn't for you, cousin. You know I thank you every day for the shit you did for me." She hugged me once more.

"Eww, so y'all gonna act like it's not a big occasion to see me?" T'yanna popped her lips and rolled her eyes.

"Shut up, big head!" I said and pulled her in a bear hug too. "Y'all paid to get in?"

"Hell yeah, we gonna support like everyone else," she responded.

My cousin T'yanna was from Queens and didn't play games. Anytime I needed someone to knock a bitch head off, she would come running with the quickness. She ran a bunch of nail salons in Queens and one in Brooklyn. I didn't catch up with my cousin as much as I liked to, but when we linked, it was always a good ass time.

"Now, why T'yanna telling me about some old hoe trying to take your daughter?"

Once I signed the papers to adopt Miracle, my mama told our family like she was TMZ, so I wasn't surprised that they knew all my business. "Yeah, her fuck boy sperm donor's moms took us to court."

"This the same one that left her with him, and almost killed her?" Nance continued to question.

"Damn, y'all really need to stay off the phone with my mama."

"Listen, cousin, you know we're with the shits, so let us just knock the shit out of her one good time." T'yanna cracked her knuckles.

"Just tag me in," Nance added.

229

These two were hilarious and what made it funnier was that they were dead ass serious. "Chill y'all, we handled it."

"Still don't mean she can't be touched. Just so she knows not to try you or your wifey again," T'yanna continued. She wasn't trying to take no for an answer.

"Speaking of wifey, when we going to meet her?"

"Y'all coming to Mama's Sunday dinner, right?"

"Um, you know I didn't come all the way to New York not to come to one of her Sunday dinners. She called me personally and told me to come."

"So, y'all can meet her there… In the meantime, let my man put y'all up in VIP and everything on me all night," I told them as I kissed both of their foreheads. The security guard escorted them to their area and I went to check on the strippers.

"It's gonna be trouble, trouble, trouble," I said as I walked into the dressing room. They all laughed and looked to me to finish what I was going to say. "Ladies, tonight is important. If you want this to be something permanent, it depends on how hard you shake those asses. Have fun and let's get this money."

When I was walking from the back, I saw Mello coming toward me. If this nigga was going to start this shit, I wasn't in the mood right now. As he got closer, I tried to read his face and I couldn't.

"Can I talk to you for a second?"

Nodding my head, I took him all the way to the back where it was a room for an office. We didn't bother putting no desk or shit in here, because we didn't know if we would be buying the building.

"What's up? You good?"

"Yeah, I'm straight. I just wanted to come holla at you about what went down in Mom's office. Shit wasn't cool and I shouldn't have come at you like that."

"It's all love, Mel. I'm not sweating it," I told him.

"Nah, it's not cool. I was fucked up behind Patsy, and Kenyetta lying to me about Kenzel. Since I couldn't hit Kenyetta, I lunged at you and it was fucked up. All my problems are mine because I fucked up. You, Mama, or Patsy had nothing to do with my decision to fuck up and ruin my marriage. It was me who chose to fuck her and make KJ. Although, I don't regret my son, I wished I could go back and change shit, but I can't. All I can do is continue to move forward and try to be better than I was yesterday."

As I leaned on the wall, I watched my brother pour his heart out to me and I realized something different. He was different and something had changed. Here he was, taking responsibility for the shit that he had caused. He wasn't saying it was anybody else's fault except his own. It pained me to see my brother going down the path he had been going down for the past few months. Still, he had no one to blame except himself. Patsy didn't do anything to him, and I damn sure didn't anything to him, so I was confused about where his anger for me was coming from.

"Wow, kid. I'm proud."

"Huh?" He looked up from the floor and into my eyes.

"I'm proud that you're taking responsibility. All I wanted was for you to see the fault in your ways. I'm not trying to be Pops. All I want is for you to have the best, feel me? Remember, as much as you didn't want me taking care of you and raising you, I didn't either. I was forced to do it, but that didn't mean I was going to take it lightly. I love you, kid, and don't forget that shit." I walked over and grabbed him into a hug and patted his back. "And don't you keep my nephew away from me again."

"Don't keep my niece away from me then."

"Nigga, she always at Mama's crib, so quit playing." He chuckled and fixed his shirt. "On the real, we're all we got."

"Facts, love you, bro. And I never thanked you for saving Pat."

"Always, Pat will always be sis." We headed to the door and I turned around. "And your ass better stop popping those mollies too."

He laughed and punched me in the arm. "I been stopped when your ass threatened me over the phone."

"Come on, let's go to VIP with Nance and T'yanna."

"Nance in New York, word?"

"Yeah, she came through."

"Shit, I might need her and T'yanna to pay a visit to Kenyetta's crib." He rubbed his hands together as we walked down the hall back into the club.

"Nigga, you know they'll do the shit, so shut up."

"Yeah, you right." He chuckled as we continued up to the VIP area where T'yanna and Nance were.

After our cousins and Mello caught up, we popped some bottles and sat back while watching the women do their things. Low-key, I was feeling like something was wrong with me. The strip club used to be my second home, so when the women came on stage I used to sit back calm, but in my head, I was going crazy for their bodies and how they could do a split. Here I was, sitting back sipping my drink, and I wasn't even concerned with them. My mind was on Kelsie and what she and my daughter were doing right now. This family man shit was becoming more me by the day. The same shit that used to entertain me, didn't do the trick these days. I'd take sitting at home watching Moana over going to the club any day.

"Welcome this sensational beauty to the stage… Take those dollars out and show some love, y'all want *Sensations* to be here permanently, then order some bottles and get some ones," the DJ yelled over the mic and everyone went crazy.

The light dimmed and the stripper came on stage. I was leaned back thinking of my woman and what I was going to do to her. Thor didn't come out tonight because he was spending time with Michelle and Titan. He had put in so much work that I wasn't even mad that he wasn't here. I could handle this shit and we had some good help, so tonight was going to go off real smooth.

"Yo! What the fuck?" Mello barked and jumped out his seat. He jetted out the VIP area and me and my cousins were confused.

"I'll be back y'all," I told them and darted behind him. He was jetting through the crowd, knocking over shit on people's table. I apologized quickly to whoever's shit he knocked down and kept following behind him. When he made it to the stage, he went around the side and got up there, and snatched shorty down and dragged her off the stage.

"Mello!" the girl gasped and tried to cover herself.

Man, what the fuck was with these strippers and covering up their bodies? "Mel, what the fuck you doing?" I walked up on them.

"I know shorty," he briefly explained and turned his attention back to me. "Choc, you got a good ass job, and just got another one, fuck you stripping for?"

"I live in fucking New York City, Mello! Do you think that job pays for my two thousand dollar a month rent, or my monthly MetroCard every month? Not even including feeding myself and utilities. This is the second job I was talking about… I gotta do what I have to do," she cried into her hands.

Mello unbuttoned his shirt and put it around her body. "Nah, this ain't the way to do it." He told her and rushed her to the back.

Here Mello was trying to play captain save a hoe. I followed behind them and he was yelling at her about just asking him for money. "You think I wanted to ask you for money? We're friends, I don't need to add another bill to your life. You have kids to take care of."

"Yo, what the fuck changed?" He stared into her eyes. "Why you acting like this? This ain't like you." He held her shoulders as she pulled the shirt he gave her tighter around her body.

"I came all the way to New York City to build a relationship with my mother, and she wants nothing to do with me."

"How you know?"

"Because I met with my sister... You should know her, Kelsie," she sobbed and I started coughing.

"Yo, what?" Now it was my turn to talk.

Kelsie had been on cloud nine lately and here, I was thinking it was the good dick I was dropping off in her draws. Nah, she done met her blood sister and didn't tell me shit about it. When I asked her about what happened with dinner with her moms, she told me it was the usual and she didn't really wanna talk about it. I figured her mother was on her bullshit again and whenever Kelsie was ready that she would talk about it.

"She found me on Facebook and we had lunch. My mother wants nothing to do with me, and wants me to stay in the past where she left me. So, imagine how I feel when I'm paying these bills, not making decent money, and the reason I came out here doesn't want to even meet me."

"Can we leave out the back?" Mello asked.

"Yo, why the fuck is there always something with everybody. Every day, there's always something new popping the fuck up. Go ahead, but go to my crib because I'll be there later," I told Mello and he nodded his head.

"Bet, I still got the key," he told me and rushed her out the back.

I put my face into my hands and pulled my phone out my pocket. Kelsie's number was the last number I dialed, so I pressed her name and waited for her to answer. "Hey, baby, how's it going?"

"It's going good. Mello came and apologized and made shit right."

"Yay, I'm so happy you both are taking this step in making your relationship right. Your mother is going to be so happy."

"Uh huh."

"Baby?"

"Yeah."

"Why you sound like that?"

"Oh, some shit went down while we were chilling in VIP with my cousins."

"It did. What happened?"

"Mello's friend was stripping and he got mad."

"People have to do what they have to do, babe. He can't fault her for doing what she has to do." She continued like she was union chairwoman for strippers.

"I feel you. Then, I find out that the stripper is my girl's little sister."

The line grew quiet.

"Don't get quiet now, Kelsie."

"Babe, I didn't want to tell you right away. I was still processing it mentally. What do you mean she's a stripper?"

"A G-string, popping that ass stripper, Kelsie… What the hell else you thought I was talking about?" I yelled back. "They're on their way to the crib now."

"Okay," she whimpered. She knew she was wrong. "I'm sorry for not telling you, babe."

"Yeah, whatever. I'll handle you when I get back to the crib," I told her and ended the call. "Aye, get on stage," I told one girl who was coming out the bathroom.

"For real? I can go twice."

"Go before I change my mind." I told her and she rushed away and went to go see how everything else was going. These muthafuckas was about to give me gray hair in this bitch.

***

The club closed a little after three in the morning. Once we got everybody squared away with money, counted money, and deposited it into the bank, we closed up. We had a successful ass night and I called my nigga to let him know how we did. Niggas wanted to book private rooms and a whole bunch of shit. I was so happy about the turn out of the club that I almost forgot that shit that happened with Mello and shorty. Key word is ALMOST. I stuck my key into our door and opened it up. As I walked through the crib looking for Kelsie, I noticed all the lights were off. Cracking the door to Miracle's room, she was sleeping peacefully. Then, I went and peeked into the guest room and Mello was asleep in the chair, while Kelsie's newfound sister was lying in the bed.

Finally, I made it to my bedroom where Kelsie was sleeping like she wasn't a little liar. I went into the bathroom and filled up the cup I used to rinse my mouth out with and went back into the bedroom. Standing there, I debated if I should toss this cold ass water on her, but the devil on my shoulder won because I tossed it on her and she gasped so deep and loud, I was sure she woke the neighbors up.

"What the hell, Myshon... Why would you do that?" She panicked and touched her body then hair.

"My bad, I tripped when coming to sit down beside you."

"Why are you lying?" she questioned.

"Oh, you don't like to be lied to, huh?"

She got up off the bed and went into her closet. A few second later, she came out in dry clothes and was still drying her hair "Babe, I'm sorry. I lied and I can't take it back. Are you gonna continue to toss water in my face for the rest of my life?"

"Shit, I might."

"Milli, really?"

"Nah, I forgive you. Stop that lying shit though. Thought we talked about this."

"We did and I apologize. It was just too much to handle and I didn't feel like talking about it. We have to help my sister, babe. She can't strip and barely afford to pay her bills."

It was funny because I knew this was going to come up. "What you want me to do?"

"Can she move in the guest house of our new house? She'll have her own little place back there and she'll be close to me."

"Kels, how the fuck you know she wanna be close to you?"

"We just had a heart to heart and cried. I hate that she's hurting over my mother not wanting to get to know her. Pleaseeeee, babe." she begged and wrapped her arms around my neck.

"Fine. She can move into the guest house." Everything went through with the house and it was only a matter of days before we got the keys and could move in.

Kelsie jumped up and down and danced, then she came and kissed me on the lips. Giving my girls the world wasn't no sweat off my back. If helping someone else made her this happy, then I made the right choice by making her my girl.

Since going over to my father's house, I hadn't spoken to Walt. When I called, he would tell me he was swamped with work or kids. His kids were down to stay with him for a few weeks, so I respected that. Having just one child, I knew how hard it was to make time for yourself, more or less, your friends. I respected his space and told him to call me whenever he had time. Hell, I even told him that I missed him, which was true. Walt was an amazing friend and it felt weird not having him to talk to. We usually worked out together, but he even changed up his hours, so I couldn't even bump into him if I wanted. Why did men have to act like such women when things didn't go their way? I'm sure if I told him I was ready to be in a relationship with him, shit would have gone totally different.

Mello came over and got Mella for Kim's Sunday dinner. Of course I was always invited, but I started to distance myself from them a bit. Milli would always be my brother and Kim would always be like a second mother to me, but I needed to distance myself not only for me, but for Mello. How was either of us supposed to truly move on if I was always around. Not for one second, did I doubt that I would find another man. I would probably find me one that worshipped the ground I walked on. Until then, I was content with hanging with my friends, being a mother, and trying to slowly gain a friendship back in Mello. We could never be married again, it would never happen.

I understood that marriage was for better or worse, except it got way past worse for us. I commended those women that were able to stick it out and fix their marriage. It just wasn't in me to ever lay beside Mello again and act like I was happy. Every time I saw his son running through our home, it would remind me of how he betrayed my trust and shitted on our marriage. His apology meant everything to me, so that's why I'm able to put the best foot forward and work on our friendship. You know when you're done, when you want your husband to find another woman. As they said, stick a fork in me, I'm done. He'll always be a part of my life because we share a beautiful daughter together. If he ever needed me, I would always be there for him. Just because he hurt me, didn't mean I could turn my love and loyalty off for him. If anything, I was too loyal to a default.

I walked the few blocks down to Walt's townhouse. He could avoid me, but he couldn't hide. He didn't work today because it was Sunday and I was sure his kids were there. Still, I didn't give a fuck as I climbed the stairs and pressed his doorbell. It took a minute before someone came to the door, but when the door opened, Walt was standing there with this blank expression. He didn't even look surprised or happy to see me.

"Hey, can we talk?"

He stood there for a second before he replied to me, "Yeah, but we gotta wrap it up quick because I'm taking my kids to the movies."

Instead of pointing out how I didn't appreciate his tone, I decided to ignore it. He held the door open and I walked inside. Two kids were sitting on the couch watching TV and holding their iPads in their hands.

"Those are the twins?"

"Yeah."

Someone else came down the stairs and I stared at the girl, or woman. She had as much hips and thighs as I had, if not more. "Well, hello," I said to her. I didn't want to seem shady and this was a relative.

"Hi," she said with attitude and tossed herself on the opposite couch of the twins.

"That's my other daughter," he explained and went and grabbed a bottle of water. First, I thought it was for me, but he popped the top and drank the shit himself.

"When we both revealed part of our life, you didn't think to tell me that you had a daughter?"

He shrugged his shoulders nonchalantly and replied, "What for? We're friends. I don't have to tell my friends everything."

"You're so fucking emotional, man. What is so wrong with me having a good time, enjoying being single?"

"'Cause you're doing it on my heart. If you want to fuck around, go ahead. Do that shit on your own time. I got my kids, so you can bounce." He nodded toward the door.

"What is so wrong with me being single for a while? You got time to learn how to be alone, I didn't get to have that time," I sniffled. "I don't want to lose you as a friend, Walt."

"We're friends, friend." He walked over to his front door. I grabbed some tissue from the counter and wiped my eyes. As I was wiping my face, a tall, skinny, and blonde woman walked down the stairs.

"Sweetie, we have to reschedule dinner with my parents. My father just had to go to the Hamptons to see an old buddy of his," she spoke and didn't even notice that I was standing there.

It didn't take a genius to figure out that this was his ex-wife. "So, you went and got back with your wife," I laughed. "How pathetic."

"Excuse me? Who is this, Walty?" She walked over to him and put her arm around his waist.

"She's a friend."

"Why does she know about our marriage?" she continued to question him. "For your information, we realized that we ended our marriage without trying. We're working on repairing our relationship for us and our children."

"You know what, let me go," I laughed and walked toward the door. "I'm not mad that you're back with your ex. Everybody can't walk away and that's fine. I'm just hurt that you cut me off and felt like you couldn't come talk to me as your friend."

At this point, all of this was comical to me. Something inside of me told myself that he would get back with her. Walt was a good man and some would say he was a perfect man. Yet, he was a man that felt that he needed to be in a relationship. There were some women like that, that couldn't think straight if they weren't in a relationship. Walt was just like that. Although he said he couldn't stand his wife, sometimes, I felt like he did that to please me. Certain times, I would call him when he would visit his kids, and he would be whispering on the phone. If y'all are done, why do you need to whisper? Maybe he felt he could save his relationship and remarry the bitch, that was nice for him. For me, I deserved better and I was going to show my daughter never expect anything less from a nigga; always more.

My father had been calling my phone like every day. I didn't answer because I didn't want to speak to him. It was like he couldn't think for himself. With my mother, he allowed her to manipulate him and now, he's letting Erick do the same thing. All I was trying to do was have positivity in my life. I didn't need or want my father adding more drama into my life. He was there for me when I needed it, but it was time that I started to remove myself from his life. He had a new daughter that he had to focus on raising. I prayed that he did a better job than what he did with me. He had sent me a text message with the picture of the newborn. It was nice when he came and checked on me, but I had to realize that he would never come to my side. Instead of letting Erick say anything he wanted, he should have stepped up and told him to stop talking about things he knew nothing about. Instead, he sat back and let this man speak about me and my life like he had known me for years.

The one thing I did know was that, I deserved better. I deserved to be treated with respect and loved until they couldn't love me anymore. At first, I thought I would be able to move on and get into a relationship, then I thought about all the years I put in with Mello. Right now, it was time for me to be selfish and worry about myself. For once in my life, I didn't have to worry about my husband's needs, it was all about Patricia Gibbens. My time for love would come and when it did, I was going to make sure I rocked that man's life, but until then, I was cool with being single, doing me, and continuing to work hard every day on my sobriety.

***

I laid back on my bed with my phone in my hand. With Mella with her father, it was lonely around here. What did I do for fun before she came? I think that's a question that every mother asks herself when her child goes and spends time away from their mother. If I raided the fridge one more time, I was going to be forced to spend an extra hour in the gym this week. Growing up with a mother that was there physically, but not there mentally, I didn't think I could be a great mom. I just knew when Mella was born that I would suck as a mother because I didn't have someone to teach me what to do, how to be, and most important, how to love. When she came out and was placed in my arms, something in me sparked and I knew I would always be there for her. Yes, I would be that annoying parent that would cry the whole ride to drop her off at college. I'd also be that mom who would peek out the front window when she got her first kiss and cheer loudly for her. All in all, I wanted to be that mother that had a problem and realized that her daughter meant more to her than a bottle of gin.

My phone broke me from my little coming to Jesus moment. "Hello?"

"Hey, Pat, what are you doing?"

"Nothing lying in bed watching the wall… What are you doing?"

"Getting ready for Sunday dinner… you coming, right?"

The reason I didn't chose to go was because that was something I did when me and Mello were together. "No. Mella's gonna be there. Mello came and picked her up."

"Oh okay. Wish you were coming. I feel like I don't see much of you anymore."

"I know. You've been busy and I've been working out and taking care of Mella…. We'll catch up when the time is right for the both of us."

"So, my mom told me that I have a younger sister?"

If I had juice, I would have spit it all over my white comforter. "Your mom is pregnant?"

"No, she had her years ago. She's only a few years younger than me." She started, then she told me how everything went down.

"Wow, your mother really is the secrets queen. Did she bring her to meet you or something?"

"No, she told me not even to reach out to her."

"And you did, didn't you?"

"You know it. She's so cool, Pat. My mother is wrong for not wanting to meet her, she's the whole reason that she came to New York in the first place."

"Wow."

"Are you sitting down?"

"Girl, I just said I was laying down," I giggled.

"Oh yeah. Well, she knows Mello and they're friends."

"Ah, so she's the girl he was over here cheesing about."

"You know about her?"

"Not much, and I damn sure didn't know she was your sister. He didn't mention much about her, but I knew he had someone in his life."

"How do you feel about that?"

"I'm fine, girl. Mello is grown and can do whatever he pleases."

"You sure?"

"You said they're friends, Kels. I'm not worried about that. Girl, I don't need any more drama in my life."

"Okay. What's going on with you and Walt."

My eyes rolled so far into my head when she mentioned Walt. "He's back with his ex-wife. Oh, and get this, he has a sixteen-year-old daughter."

"What? Didn't she cheat on him?"

"Yep, but apparently, he doesn't care and they want to fix their marriage. That's fine with me, but why toss our friendship away like it doesn't mean anything?"

"Because it'll probably be too hard to just be friends with you. Doesn't make it right, but you know how men are."

"Yeah, well, we will never be friends. He acted like a jerk and like we were never friends at one point. It's whatever, I'm not losing sleep over it. I don't need a fuck boy as a friend."

"Damn, Walt, I had hope for you," she laughed. "He'll come around and you guys will talk."

"I'm not holding my breath," I yawned. "Bring me some food from Kim's please," I told her. She promised she would bring me some food and we ended the call. I turned over and closed my eyes to catch a quick nap before standing around the house doing nothing.

As far as Mello and his new friend; I didn't mind. As long as he continued to be a good father to our daughter, I didn't mind who he dated as long as they did the same thing. Why was I going to be salty? This woman didn't do anything to me, so I wasn't going to throw shade at her. Especially since she was Kelsie's sister. She was damn near family. It was crazy how small this world was. At the end of the day, long as Mella is good, then I'm good.

Michelle

$\mathcal{K}$im invited us over for Sunday dinner, so I was going to go. I hadn't got myself into a kitchen and living in the hotel, I just needed to get out of the suite for a bit. Thor was going to check on the restaurant and the club, so I told him to drop me off at Kim's house. After meeting my new cousin through FaceTime, I was ready to finally see her and give her a huge hug. I would say I couldn't believe my aunt would hide a secret like that, then again, I could believe it. She was known for doing shit like this and hiding it. Just as quick as she came into town, one of her boyfriends was whisking her back off again. My mother had faith that she would stick around long enough to see my baby, but she didn't. If she barely saw her grandchild, she didn't give a damn about seeing my child.

"Babe, can we just get married next year?" I blurted.

It had been something that was on my mind for a while. We were still settling into being new parents and Thor had both the restaurant and strip club to worry about. We didn't need to be worried about getting married right now. I was content with where we were and I didn't need us to rush and not enjoy the experience.

"You sure, baby?" He looked from the street over to me. "It's no sweat, we can hire someone that can do the work for us."

"I want to be involved in my wedding. I don't want to just hand the task off to other people, babe. If that means I need to wait, then I'm fine with that," I told him.

"We'll do what you want… What's been on your mental lately? You and Pat been talking a lot and then you end the call when I come into the room, what's up?"

Patsy and I had been talking and brainstorming about opening a salon. Raequan wants me on the west coast and I can't be there right now. With Titan here, it would be too much for us as a family. The more she talked to me about it, the more I was ready to make this dream a reality. Thor had businesses that were thriving and I just wanted to have one that allowed me to continue with my career. The months I've been pregnant all my clients had been begging me to do their hair.

"I want to open a salon, Shannon."

"So, let's do it," he said without breaking a sweat. He was all down for it like I had asked him for something simple.

"Seriously?"

"Yes. I know that's what is going to make you happy."

I smiled as I leaned back in my seat. "I appreciate you, babe."

"Oh, now you appreciate me? You lucky you ain't been wilding with those hormones lately," he joked.

"I feel like I'm getting my body back. Not physically, but mentally. I don't feel like a maniac anymore."

I can admit and say that I was crazy during my whole pregnancy and then for a few weeks after I had Titan. Now, that I had control over my body, the house was much more peaceful. Thor could tell because he was in the bed every night with me.

"Good, 'cause I missed my babe. You were being crazy as fuck and making me feel like I was losing my mind."

"I'm sorry, babe. Your son made me crazy. Blame his bad butt." I looked in the back and Titan was sleeping peacefully.

"You ready to have my daughter now?"

"What?"

"Yeah, I'm ready for a baby girl, we need to knock them out now."

"Shannon, you're drinking that good stuff if you think I'm about to have another baby." I nudged him.

He was dead serious and I almost passed out. We didn't need another baby when we had a newborn. I barely got two hours sleep at night, and he thought I was about to do this pregnant thing again?

"In a year or two. Let me get the salon off the ground and you get your little strip club together."

"Yo, you always tossing shade at the strip club."

"Because those hoes are nasty."

He laughed as we pulled up to Kim's house. After helping me into the house and greeting everyone, he kissed me and headed to the club. Kim was in the kitchen cooking, so I joined her and helped her with what she needed, while I waited for everyone to arrive. Kelsie sent me a text and said she was five minutes away.

"So, how's mommy hood?" Kim asked.

"Tiring…. Why didn't anybody tell me this? I know people say they're tired all the time, but this is another level."

"Child, try having a newborn and a one-year old? Mello was such a cry baby that I couldn't put him down four minutes before he would start crying again. Milli thought he was too grown and was trying to use the bathroom at just a year old."

"Thor wants another baby, but I'm not ready."

"If you leave it up to Thor, you'll have five damn kids by the time you're thirty. Girl, get on some birth control if you're not ready. I love my boys, but if I knew what I know, I wouldn't have had them back to back."

"You did so well with raising them though," I complimented.

"Yeah and nearly drove myself mad in the process. It's one thing if you want to make Thor happy, but you need to think of your happiness. The happiness of a woman affects the whole house, Michelle," Kim warned me.

Another baby wasn't even a thought right now. I appreciated the advice, yet, I wasn't thinking of no babies. "I hear you, Kim."

Kim washed her hands and then went over to Titan's car seat. "Let me see this little chocolate button." She picked him up. "Thor's ass ain't been over here for more than five minutes. I told both of y'all I need to see my grandbaby more."

"You can come over to the hotel whenever you need."

"Why are you both in a hotel? I have more than enough room here," she offered.

"Kim, we have a new baby and don't want to get on nobody's nerves. Plus, the house is almost done and we'll move in by next month."

"Well, you both need to stop acting like my home ain't no good and come on. I have two bedrooms upstairs that aren't being used. Miracle and KJ sleep with me when they come over, and Kenzel ain't in the picture anymore."

"I meant to ask, what happened with that?"

"Kenyetta doesn't let him see him anymore. His real daddy is back in his life so Mello can't be in the picture. She supposed to drop KJ over here today."

"Wow, he raised him since he was born. It's not right what he did to Pat, but he is a good father to those boys."

"Truthfully, I think that's what has him out of sorts lately." She sighed. "My baby boy can't seem to get it right."

"He's not a baby anymore, Kim." I put my hand on her shoulder. "Mello is a grown man that has to find his own path, on his own."

"Watch when I tell you that when Titan gets older. Your ass gonna be ready to knock me clear on the floor."

"I bet I will. That little boy is one thing I don't play about."

Titan is my world. Never did I think that I could feel love the way I loved my baby boy. Almost losing him during birth nearly scared me. Every night, I woke up to check and see if he was alright. The doctors assured us that it wouldn't cause any long-term issues with him, but I just had to be sure.

"We're here, Glamma!" Miracle yelled through the house. All we heard was her foot stomps on the wooden floors until she found us in the kitchen. "Glamma, you giving all my kisses to stinky Titan?" She stood there with her hand on her little hips.

"Oh no, I'm not. I have enough to give my princess." She bent down and kissed Miracle on the cheek. "I made some mac and cheese for my big princess."

"Hey, Ma." Milli walked into the house with Kelsie. "Damn, it smells good as hell in here." He started lifting up pot lids and stuff.

"Mama, she shitted and I'm gonna throw up." Mello came in behind them holding Mella in his arms. Mella was making spit bubbles with a smile on her face.

Kim stopped sniffing Titan's neck and stared at her two boys. "What in the hell? Y'all not ripping each other's heads off?"

"We're good, Ma. Don't make it more than what it is," Milli told her.

She took his advice and smiled. "I know one thing, y'all need to stop having sex. I'm gonna run out of room and arms for all these babies. Take my chocolate drop so I can change little miss Mella. How's Patsy?"

"Everything is good, Mama," Mello smiled. "She said she was going to catch up on some shows and relax."

"I just miss that girl coming over for Sunday dinner," Kim sighed.

"We all do, but she's doing her," Milli reminded her. "She gotta have her time away from Mella, all that girl do is take care of her."

"Who is this?" Kim ignored what Milli said and stared right at Choc.

"My new cousin… Come here and give me a hug." I went to her

and wrapped my arm around her. "Excuse the leaking boob and baby, girl."

"No, you're fine... nice to meet you in person, cousin." She hugged me tightly.

"This is my sister, Kim," Kelsie started then told her everything that went on.

"Oh God... Nice to meet you." Kim hugged her. "Call me Kim, and my house is everybody's damn house apparently," she laughed.

"Thank you... nice to meet you too, Kim."

"Alright, everybody in the dining room because the food is done... let me change this diaper and I'll bring the food out."

"What's this surprise?" Milli questioned.

"Don't worry about it, you'll find out soon enough," she smiled and then headed upstairs to change Mella's diaper.

The doorbell rang, so I went and answered the door. Kenyetta was standing there with KJ standing beside her. "Chelly, Chelly!" KJ hugged my legs and then ran into the house before I could even say anything to him. "Daddy! Daddy!"

"He's so rude," I laughed and Kenyetta didn't bat an eyelash. "I'll have Mello call you," I said and started to close the door.

This hoe had the nerve to side swipe me and walk into the house like she was invited. "Mello, I need to talk to you," she smacked her lips.

Mello came out the kitchen confused. "Oh, now you got time to talk? What about when I've been asking to talk."

"Look, I don't have time to go back and forth. I'm moving back to Atlanta."

"The fuck you not!" Mello barked.

She waved her hand in his face and smirked. "Obviously, someone else saw fit to put a ring on my finger. My husband wants me in Atlanta, so that's where I'll be."

"Who stopping you? Go to Atlanta," he told her.

"I'm taking my son with me. We can arrange for you to come see or get him every other month, but KJ needs to be with me."

"I'll keep you in court so much, that your nigga will have no choice but to divorce your ass. Didn't he just get out of jail? A nigga like that wouldn't want to step foot back in a court house."

"Mello, I'm with someone else, get over it."

"My problem isn't with you being with someone else, my problem is with you trying to take my son away from me. I have no choice but to deal with it when it comes to Kenzel, but I'll be damn if my son will be taken back to Atlanta."

"He lived there before, so what's the difference? You didn't have a problem when you were hiding him from your wife. Now that everything is all out in the open, you're cool with him being here…. Get the hell outta here," she chuckled.

Mello stepped closer to her and I stepped in slightly. I knew he would never put his hands on a woman, but the way Kenyetta was acting, I wanted to punch her in the head my damn self.

"You don't want to worry about if your new husband might be murked. I mean, I would hate for you to be a widow and your marriage just st—"

"Chill, son." Milli came out the kitchen just in time. "If you move that's your business, but we just went through a custody battle and guess who won? We'll bring up all the petty shit you've done and how you lied about your baby's father. I mean, if you want to go through that, then let's get it."

"Y'all don't scare me," Kenyetta laughed.

"Well, maybe I do." Kim came down the stairs. "I've been patient and some may even say nice. My son messed up and he's paying for it. I can finally start to see the change in him, so you doing this is now interfering with my family. As you know, I don't play when it comes to any of these people under my roof, excluding you. You'll leave KJ here if you move back and we'll give you visits. If not, then we'll go to court, but I'll make sure to make your life a living hell until the judge gives his verdict."

Kenyetta almost backed into me trying to get away from Kim. "You can't take my baby from me."

"No one is trying to take your baby away from you. You're trying to take a man's son away from him."

"I'm tired of you all jumping in when I need to make decisions with him." She turned and walked out the door.

Kim slapped Mello in the head. "You picked such a bum bitch," she sighed and went into the kitchen.

We were all seated at the table catching up on everyone's life. Kim had the plates passing around and I couldn't help but to wish that Thor was here. I knew he wanted to make sure that business was running, so

I couldn't be mad.

"Mama, you kept us in suspense long enough. What's the surp—"

Just as Milli was about to ask, the doorbell interrupted him. Kim wiped her hands on her pants and looked back at all of us with a nervous smile. I don't think I've ever seen her nervous since I met her.

"Hush," she said and left the dining room.

"What the hell is so secret?" Mello smacked on cornbread.

"Shit, she better bring Obama in this bitch with all this shushing she doing," Milli countered.

"Word."

Kim walked in holding a hand. A man followed and I didn't know who he was. Milli dropped his fork and stared at the man like he knew him. "Pops, when the fuck you get out? Mama, this the nigga you been fucking with?"

"Watch your damn mouth," Kim scolded.

"I'm being mind fucked," Mello laughed. "How could you, Mama? That nigga left us to starve and you take him back."

"First thing, how the fuck you get out of jail? Last I heard, you had a hefty sentence." Milli just had to know.

"On a technicality," Kim answered. "I'm not asking you to support my decision, but I am asking you to respect it."

"Man, it's no use fucking fighting her on it. She can have an opinion on everyone's life, but nobody can give theirs." Milli stood up.

"What are you talking about, Myshon?" Kim challenged. They both were headstrong and weren't about to let the other get the last word in.

"Did he tell you about our sister? She's eighteen years old and running around here wilding the fuck out. Bet he didn't mention that shit to you."

"I know all about Kendel. Who do you think argued and tried to fight her mother when she was pregnant with her. I'm not living in the past, Myshon. I want to be happy and your father has been making me happy."

"Until when? When he must run the streets again? You had to work all your life like the Color Purple to take care of us... While he did what, Mama? Ran the streets carefree."

"I wasn't the best father. There's shit that I regret and I'll continue to live my life regretting it. Y'all and y'all's sister needed me and I wasn't there. I was too busy worried with the streets that I didn't care about your mother. She's a good woman and has always been. All I want to do is spend that time making it up to her, and getting to know my grandbabies."

"Glamma?" Miracle called.

"Yes, baby?"

"If that's my grandpa, he has to be there like Daddy. Daddy doesn't miss anything with me," Miracle smiled and ate her food.

"Miracle, grown folk's business," Kelsie reminded her.

"Sorry, Glamma."

"Ma, if this is what you want then who am I to tell you not to get back with him." Mello stood up and tossed his napkin in his plate.

"Choc, come on," he said.

"When this happen?" Kim felt the need to ask. "You're not even divorced and you're already with someone else."

"We're friends," Choc spoke up.

"I'm out too," Milli said and grabbed his plate and left the kitchen. "Babe, go get foil 'cause we bringing this food home too."

"Well, my grandbabies are staying with me."

"No the hell they aren't. I'm taking KJ and Mella to the movies," Mello called from the front room.

"Great. I want to do something for myself and everyone has a problem. For years, I've lived for you both and never brought a man around you guys. I've been happy these past few months. You hear? Happy. Go ahead and walk out, but know this. If none of you reach out in two days, you can forget all about me. I'm tired of fixing y'all problems and helping y'all and you all can't support me."

Kelsie got up and kissed Kim on the cheek. "I'll call you in the morning, Kim." She told her as she walked into the kitchen with the foil.

"Thank you, baby," Kim called behind her.

I told Thor what went down and he told me he was on his way to get me and Titan. Today had been a full day and all I wanted to do was lay in bed with my two boys.

Kelsie

"Damn, Kelsie, piss faster," Milli rushed me as I peed on the pregnancy test. I knew the minute I threw up when I smelled food that I was pregnant. It was funny how our bodies reacted the same way once we've already had a baby. Soon as I started feeling like that, I told Milli. With Miracle, I found out I was pregnant alone and I didn't want a repeat of that. When I told him, he went and bought every test they had in the store.

"Okay, here put the top on and sit it on the tub," I instructed and he did as I was told.

"You don't shake this shit or nothing?"

"No, babe, just relax."

I had just told him to relax, but I couldn't even relax. We both were pacing our bathroom quietly. The past few months had been crazy, but good. Milli and Mello were talking to their mother, but they refused to talk about anything that had to do with their dad. Kim and I spoke and she broke down and told me how she loved their father and never stopped. One visit to get closure, turned into something more. She fought with her decision to allow him back into her life until she couldn't anymore. From what I witnessed, she was happy whenever she spoke to him. Maybe they needed the years they spent away from each other. My life was far from perfect, so I couldn't tell Kim how to live hers. She was grown and knew what she wanted and was going to do what she wanted to do.

"Pregnant! You're fucking pregnant!" Milli yelled and jumped up and down. He picked me up and spun me around our bathroom while kissing me. "Baby, we're having a baby!" he screamed into my ear.

My heart was beating so fast that I could hear it in my ears. I was pregnant. It took me a while to finally understand and smile. We were going to have a baby together. This time, we would be on the same page. At first, I was scared shitless about having another baby. I felt like I would be forgetting all about Miracle. Maybe she might feel left out, but I had to remember what type of parents both Milli and I were. We would never allow Miracle to feel left out. Plus, she was too spoiled and loud to be forgotten.

"We gotta get ready for Michelle and Thor's engagement party." Milli kissed me on the lips and grabbed my ass. "We going to tell everyone there?"

I giggled and kissed him back. "Only if you want to."

Tonight, was Michelle's surprise engagement party. Patsy had put her dislike aside for Maggie and planned the party in the restaurant. Just because she didn't want to have her wedding until next year, didn't mean that we couldn't throw her a party. She had no clue that Patsy had planned this entire thing. Although I was ready to tell everyone that we were expecting, I was nervous for Patsy to meet Choc. Choc and Mello were still friends, but I didn't know how she would react. When I spoke to Pat, she told me she was fine and wasn't thinking about Mello's relationships. If it didn't have anything to do with her daughter, she was fine with it. I just didn't want any issues tonight. Tonight was all about Michelle and Thor's love, so everyone needed to check their issues and support Michelle and Thor.

"Damn, I'm about to be a father again. Bae, I'm fucking excited," Milli said as he placed me back down onto the floor. "Damn, man," he sniffled and wiped his eyes.

"Is Myshon crying?" I joked.

"Shit, you and Miracle the only ones that can bring it out of me," he laughed and hugged me.

I wiped his tears and stared into those eyes I loved so much. "Babe, I just appreciate everything that you've done for us. You came into our lives and always showed love and cared. It's been awhile since someone showed us the love you show us. You stepped in and took control of Miracle's life like you helped me make her. I love you so much for that, babe."

"We in this shit forever, ma. I wanna give you a ring one day, but let's move into our crib and have this baby first." He kissed me on the lips.

In the future, I saw myself marrying Milli and living my happily ever after with him. I wasn't looking for a ring because I was pregnant with his child and we were moving into our first home together. When he was ready, then that's when I was ready. Right now, all I was focused on was trying to be an amazing mom to two children and an even better girlfriend to Milli. When the ring came, then that's when I would take my place as Mrs. Gibbens. While Patsy was ready to step out of the Gibben's name, I was ready and prepared to take the name and wear it with pride. Kim didn't have to step in and become like a mother to me. That woman taught me so much stuff that I almost wanted to cry just thinking about it. When she talked about Miracle, I could tell she loved her genuinely and would never hurt her. Last week, we spoke about her will and she told me that she added Miracle to it when she added Mella, Titan, and KJ.

"I just feel so complete, yo," Milli said as he walked in and out our closet, putting his clothes for the night on our bed. "Like, I thank the Big Man upstairs. He's been looking out for me since I was a kid and now, he's blessing me with my biggest blessings; y'all."

I kissed him on the cheek and went to apply my makeup. "You're our blessing too."

We continued to talk about baby names and things we would do when the baby was born. Last time I was pregnant, we didn't even do that. It was all about stress and the fate of our relationship. This time around, I had a feeling that everything was going to run smoothly between all of us. Kim was going to pull her hair out because she already had three grandchildren. I love that she included Titan as her grandson. She had always stepped into the role as acting like Thor's second mother, but now that his mother is gone, she really stepped into the role. All I wanted was for all of us to get along and be happy. Milli and Mello didn't like their father being around, but doesn't he deserve a second chance? Everyone deserves a second chance and yes, it's up to the person to give it to them. In Patsy's case, she didn't give Mello a second chance, but Kim was giving their dad a second chance.

"Babe, can you stop walking so fast," I called behind him as he handled business on the phone.

"My bad." He stopped and waited for me to catch up. It wasn't easy trying to maneuver down this hallway with six-inch stilettos on. "You looking fine as fuck, babe." He winked at me and then ended the call.

"You're not looking too bad yourself," I smirked.

Milli had the valet bring the car from the garage. I knew tonight was special because he never used them. He claimed they were overpriced and his quarters were gone last time he allowed them to park his car. This time, it wasn't one of Milli's cars. It was an all-white Audi.

"Babe, that's not ours." He lowered some so I could whisper in his ear. Tonight, wasn't the time for them to fuck up and cause Milli to lose his shit.

"You're right, it's yours," he told me and handed me the keys. Stuck in place, I turned from the car to Milli with a shocked expression on my face. "You been patient and never asked for a car… instead, you drove my whips and never asked for anything. Matter fact, you never ask for anything so that's why I wanna give you everything."

My make-up was gorgeous and I worked so hard on it for an hour, but those tears didn't give a damn about my make-up. Tears poured down my face as I did the most ugliest cry in front of all these people in front our building. Milli pulled me to the side, while laughing and moved my hands from my face.

"Why you crying, ma?"

"Pa, nobody has ever done something like this for me. I wasn't expecting this and then you go and surprise me with a car." This time, I sobbed into his shirt.

"What did I tell you? I want to give you and our princess the world. You never ask me for shit and you work so hard. Every time you get paid, you try to pay a bill and get mad when I tell you no. Other chicks in your situation wouldn't even be worried about working, and damn sure wouldn't be trying to spend their money on bills. We been through a lot of shit and some of that caused frowns on both of our parts. For now, all I'm trying to see is smiles on all our faces."

Reaching up, I cupped his face in my hands and gave him one of the biggest kisses I've ever given him. "And for that, I thank and love you so much."

"Alright, now drive us to the party and stop all the crying." He handed me the keys once again.

Miracle was already there and kept calling me from her Glamma's phone. "Okay," I smiled.

If you would have asked me if I would be moving into a huge house, driving my own Audi, and having my own office, while perusing a real estate career, I would have laughed in your face and told you to stop drinking. Since meeting Milli in the club, my life had taken many turns. From almost losing my daughter, almost losing one of my best friends to drinking, and trying to be there for my cousin, while she found the strength to finally be done with an abusive relationship. Then, there was my mother. We would probably never have the relationship I've always dreamed of. She would never stop her ways and settle down and be a grandparent to her grandchildren. I had to learn that she was the one missing out. One thing I was grateful for was that she told me about my sister.

I promised her that I would never leave her side and as long as she had me, she would be good. It pained me that she had to strip just to pay her bills. Choc had been a blessing to many of us because she was truly helping Mello through his tough time. They weren't together, but they were good friends. Time would only tell if she decided to take it further with him. My only wish was that he wouldn't hurt her the way he hurt Patsy. I prayed that he grew and saw his ways were damaging to the people he loves.

"Damn, who the hell did Pat invite."

"I don't know, but it looks jumping." I smiled as we drove past all the people out front drinking or smoking a cigarette.

There was parking out back for us, so I parked the car and we made our way inside through the backdoor. When I walked in, Michelle had this beautiful white gown on, her hair was done, and she was holding Titan, who was in a matching outfit to his daddy. We arrived late, so we missed everyone surprising her.

"Thor, now why you make Titan wear a linen suit?" Milli laughed and we all broke into laughter.

"Stop fronting, my shit is official."

"Yeah, if you were fifty on the beaches of Jamaica with your wife," I added.

"Fuck all of y'all," he said and grabbed his son. "Come on, nigga. There's mad food and shit. Your brother just showed up with Choc." Thor nodded toward the front, and he and Milli left us alone.

"I'm pregnant, Chelle." This news was eating me alive and I couldn't hold it in. Milli knew, but that wasn't enough, I had to tell my favorite cousin in the whole world too.

She squealed and jumped up and down. "Ahhh! Does Milli know?"

"Yeah, we took a test together. He cried, Chelle."

She hugged me tightly and kissed me on the cheek. "I'm so happy for the both of you. Y'all really deserve these blessings that's coming your way."

"Thank you. Apparently, the Big Man upstairs is listening to little ol' me down here."

"Of course. We serve an awesome God." She did the church finger and then hugged me again.

"I'm out there playing party planner and promoter, what y'all doing back here?" Patsy came to the back. All that baby weight was gone, as she rocked a white romper and a pair of gold glitter heels.

"Akaee," I screamed and hugged my friend. We hadn't spent much time together lately, but we all were dealing with things in our lives.

"Girl, you know I came to make a few niggas drool." She twirled and lost her footing.

"See, that's what you get for being fresh," Michelle laughed.

"Anyway, why y'all back here whispering and stuff?"

"Kelsie's pregnant," Michelle spilled the beans.

Patsy hugged me tightly and then rubbed my flat ass stomach, like it was poking out or something.

"I'm so happy for you and Milli. Does Kim know yet?"

"Not yet, we're gonna tell everyone together."

"Yas, look at all of us coming through with the life moves." Patsy smiled. "Well, since we're spilling the beans and shit, let me just say, me and Mello are going to Disney with the kids."

"Seriously? Y'all getting back together?" Michelle questioned.

"Hell no, we're trying to be friends and I think it's going well. He invited me to Disney a few weeks ago and he sent me the tickets last night. I even told him to invite Choc, she seems cool."

"Wow, that takes a strong woman, Pat. Y'all are going to have so much fun there."

"Yeah, I'm done hating him. Hating him is like me drinking poison and expecting him to die. My life is beautiful, and I'm blessed with an even more beautiful daughter, so I need to move on and start to figure out what makes me happy."

"Good for you, Pat. A man is going to come along with a big ass dick, watch," I added and both she and Michelle turned and stared at me for a second.

"Since she been getting dicked down on a regular, that's all she talks about," Pat pointed out.

"You ain't lying," Michelle co-signed.

We all went to the front and greeted everybody. There was so much food and people. Some people I didn't know, but they swore they knew me because I was with Milli. Once everything died down, people started to leave and it was just all of us. We all sat down at one table and

Thor stood up. He held his drink up in the air and stared at each of us.

"Man, this past year has been hard. I lost my mother and then welcomed a son. I proposed to my beautiful fiancée and fall in love with her more and more every day. Me and my brothers grew apart, but came back together like nothing ever happened. All my nieces and nephews are healthy. Me and my brothers decided to all go in and start this new business venture, so I'm grateful for that. I want to thank Pat for taking the time out and thinking of us. We appreciate everything that you do, and you're always family. Start bringing your ass around more," he said and went over to hug her.

"Love you, bro." She hugged him tight.

Milli got up and hit his knife on his red plastic cup like only he would. "Piggy backing off what Thor said, y'all need to add another niece or nephew to the list, because I'm pregnant."

"What?" Kim gasped.

"I'm pregnant, Kim. Your son is just an asshole." I stood up.

Kim rushed over to me and hugged me tightly. "Y'all are trying to make gray hair pop all over my head with all these babies. But, I love all of these babies," she smiled.

"And Daddy's getting me a dog," Miracle felt the need to announce. Everyone laughed except me, because when the hell did this happen.

"Yes, I told princess she can have a dog," Milli confirmed.

The baby news would probably hit Miracle when she started to see my stomach get bigger, and when the baby was actually born. Right now, all she was thinking about was getting a dog.

"To family. We may not always get along, but we're always there for each other."

"Family," we all yelled.

EPILOGUE

Milli

*T*hese past few months have been something short of amazing. Kelsie's pregnancy was going well and she was now officially five months pregnant with another little girl. All these girls around me was going to drive me crazy. I only had Miracle's dog, who was a boy, but imagine walking him and having to call him Prince Poo-poo Pants. We moved into the house and had someone come out and decorate and pick the pieces out. Kelsie was overwhelmed with how big the house was, so spending bread to make sure our crib was together didn't matter to me. My baby passed her real estate exam and was now a licensed real estate agent. Pregnant and all, she still got up every morning and went to work. If you asked me, I wanted her to stay in bed and get fat with my baby girl she was carrying. Kelsie's relationship with her mother wasn't fixed. Her mother was upset because she reached out to Choc. I told her moms not to call while she's carrying my seed. The last thing Kelsie needed was her bullshit and the stress of that.

We allowed Marina to come over and visit with Miracle. She came over twice and then the third time she complained that she didn't feel welcomed or comfortable. Shit, I don't know how, when we were both nice to her. If it was up to me, I would have allowed my cousins to run up on her ass when she was on her way home from work. Her ass took us back to court and this judge told her that if she didn't feel comfortable, then we could meet at a state approved children's center. Ever since then, she hadn't reached out or came for a visit. Kelsie felt bad and reached out to her so they could do dinner with Miracle and she told her that we brainwashed Miracle. Miracle still loved Marina and was happy when she came around. She was a child and couldn't help that she spoke of my mother a lot. My mother spent a lot of time with Miracle. Kelsie said she would continue to keep trying with Marina for Miracle's sake, but I told her she needed to leave it alone. Marina knew where we lived and if she wanted to visit, she could come ring the bell.

Mello, Thor, and I decided to all partner on the strip club. We bought the building and have been making moves to get it renovated to our liking. We were going to open it in time for Mello's birthday. This nigga wanted to bring in his birthday right in our club, and Thor and I didn't have no problem taking the ten bands he offered to put down on the place. Shit, we had to invest in ourselves, right? When I wasn't working on the club, I was helping my moms with this apartment building she finally told us she bought. My pops was doing most of the construction work, since he worked in that field before we were even born. My mother told me, in a year, the building would be worth more than she bought it for, so I trusted her. Both Mello and I had always trusted our mother's judgement, so we allowed her to make purchases with our money. In the end, if it was going to continue to make us rich, I didn't have a problem with it.

My mom and dad were still going strong. He kept a smile on her face and that's all I could ask. We went and had a drink together once or twice. That's where I told him that I would shoot him in the head if he did my mother wrong again. As for a grandfather, the nigga was awesome. He was always taking Miracle and KJ somewhere. Last weekend, he took them to the zoo and Miracle talked about it the entire week. So, when it came to my pops, I had no complaints. I just wished my moms would have kept it real and told us that she was back with him. At the end of the day, it's her life, so I couldn't be mad at her. What I did was my choice, and she had her own choices she made.

Patsy and Mello were better off as friends than married. They had a few good years before their shit ended horribly, but now they were friends and that seemed to work better for everybody. They went to Disney World and had a good time. The pictures they sent us, you could tell they all were genuinely happy. Choc went along too and it's crazy because she and Mello had made their relationship official. They started their relationship before going to Disney, so I just knew the trip was about to be ruined. Nah, Patsy and Choc were cool and there were no problems. Hell, Patsy even threatened Mello about not hurting Choc. There divorce was finalized and Patsy came off like a fat cat, but only 'cause Mello felt like she deserved it all. When it came to Pat's father, she didn't speak to him or reach out to him. She felt like he didn't care about her and would always choose his now huswife (Her words) over her.

Kenyetta ended up staying in New York. Her so called husband didn't move with her, so she made trips to Atlanta twice a month so Kenzel could spend time with his father. Mello didn't care because that meant more time with his son. Kenyetta may have been married, but she was still missing Mello because she called him when she was in New York to fuck her at least twice a week. Mello could finally see Kenzel, but he still wasn't allowed to take him when he took KJ. It was best that he didn't, since Kenyetta was going to keep being petty when it came to him. I told him as hard as it is, he needed to focus on KJ.

As for Patsy and Michelle, they were opening their own salon in a few short months. Once Michelle told Thor what she wanted, he shelled the money out to make her dream into a reality. Once she got her feelings in control, Michelle stepped into her role as a mother quick. Titan was the apple of both, her and Thor's, eyes. That little boy was going to be spoiled when he got older. They finally moved into their new place and put their condo on the market. Michelle offered to allow Choc to live there, but Kelsie wasn't having it and she moved into our guesthouse. My apartment went on the market and you'll never guess who bought it? Mello's ass. I made his ass pay top dollar for being a dick head to me. He was making his own changes to make it his. It had enough rooms for both, Mella and KJ.

As for my sister, she was still around. She called me when she needed me, and sent me a message to let me know she was good. I didn't expect that this girl was going to drive me crazy. I wanted her ass to go to school and sit her ass down somewhere, but she wouldn't. To her, the streets were golden and she wanted to run them. I warned her that there were only two places you went when it came to the streets; the grave or prison. She knew the consequences and she still ran them, so she had to deal with them.

"Babe, the phone is for you," Kelsie called from upstairs. "Take it in your office," she told me.

I walked to the office and took a seat. Today, I planned to chill and relax, I didn't want to do no work. For once, both my baby and I was home together. I fixed the maternity pictures we took as a family and picked up the phone.

"Yo, who this?"

"It's Kendel," she sniffled into the phone.

"What now, Kendel? I only hear from your ass when you need me," I vented.

"They shot him, Milli. They shot, Moon!" she screamed and sobbed into the phone. I sighed because this was what came with the streets. She belongs to the game.

It's been real, y'all. Bless up!

THE END

SERIOUSLY!

MAKE SURE TO CONNECT WITH ME VIA SOCIAL MEDIA:

http://www.facebook.com/JahquelJ

http://www.instagram.com/_Jahquel

http://www.twitter.com/Author_Jahquel

Be sure to join my reader's group on Facebook

www.Facebook.com/Jahquel's we reading or nah?

JAHQUEL J.

"Using Reality To Tell Her Story!"

Looking for a publishing home?

Royalty Publishing House, Where the Royals reside, is accepting submissions for writers in the urban fiction genre. If you're interested, submit the first 3-4 chapters with your synopsis to submissions@royaltypublishinghouse.com.

Check out our website for more information:

www.royaltypublishinghouse.com.

Text ROYALTY to 42828 to join our mailing list!

To submit a manuscript for our review, email us at
submissions@royaltypublishinghouse.com

Text RPHCHRISTIAN to 22828 for our
CHRISTIAN ROMANCE novels!

Text RPHROMANCE to 22828 for our
INTERRACIAL ROMANCE novels!

Get LiT!

Download the LiT eReader app today and enjoy exclusive content, free books, and more

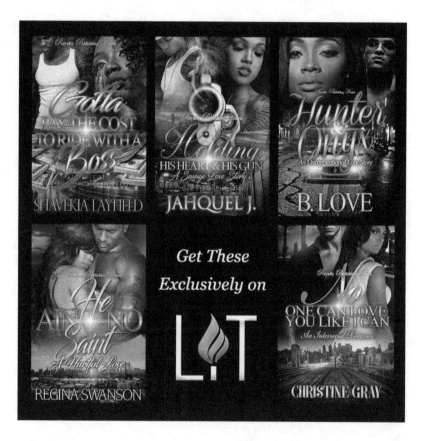

Do You Like CELEBRITY GOSSIP?

Check Out QUEEN DYNASTY!
Visit Our Site: www.thequeendynasty.com

CPSIA information can be obtained
at www.ICGtesting.com
Printed in the USA
LVHW08s1746210918
590922LV00010B/552/P